Vampire with Benefits

SUPERNATURAL
SELECTION

E.J. Russell

Cover art: L.C. Chase https://lcchase.com
Editors: Carole-Ann Galloway, Kelly Miller, Rachel Haimowitz

ISBN: 978-1-947033-76-4

Second edition
March 2024

Contact information:
ejr@ejrussell.com

Vampire with Benefits

SUPERNATURAL
SELECTION

E.J. Russell

Dedicated to everyone who never quite fit in.

M4 100YO VWB

(Man for 100-year-old
vampire with benefits.)

*Extreme nightlife.
Drinks and dinner. ;-)
No garlic.*

Supernatural
Selection

Chapter One

I thought being a vampire would be more fun.

Casimir Moreau stalked down the sidewalks in Portland's Pearl District, hipsters to the right of him, hipsters to the left, the early-autumn darkness illuminated by streetlamps and the spill of light from restaurants and storefronts. *Where's the danger? Where's the thrill? Where's the terror?* Well, perhaps terror wasn't exactly what he wanted. A terrified host was very inconvenient. Half of them pissed themselves, which ruined the scent of their blood. The other half—well, the other half tried to be Jackie Chan. And failed.

He had a feeling that if he flashed a bit of fang to the passersby, nobody would bat an eye. *Because this is Portland, and vampires are nearly as hip as brewpubs.* Really, it was disheartening.

Before he'd taken that last irrevocable step from mediocre silent film actor to creature of the night, he'd imagined a freewheeling eternal life, flitting between candlelit parties with women dressed in sparkling gowns and men in the delicious formality of white tie and tails. A veritable smorgasbord from whom he could choose his sexual partners and blood hosts at will. The reality had been somewhat different.

Who knew that bastard Will Hays with his infernal Production Code and threadbare Midwestern morality would ruin everything?

His silk scarf fluttered in the chilly November breeze, and he tucked the ends under his cashmere overcoat. Not that he needed either the scarf or the coat—it would take far more extreme temperatures to make him uncomfortable—but fashion was one of the ways vampires blended in. To wear a tank top and shorts in November would have drawn attention, *the* unforgivable sin, not just for vampires but for any member of the supernatural community. Not that Cas would venture to wear a tank top and shorts—the flash of his paper-white skin would probably blind everyone within a mile, given the impossibility of him ever getting a tan.

A burst of laughter from a nearby clot of revelers made him snarl, startling the couple pushing their toddler in a stroller. He smoothed his expression to bland, to match his clothes and his grooming and his existence. It wasn't their fault he was on his way to get married to somebody he'd never even met. It wasn't their fault he'd made his last drastic miscalculation.

It wasn't their fault he was dead.

No, that's all on me. On me and that fucking bastard Henryk Skalding. If he hadn't been convinced Henryk was plotting to undermine him with the vampire council again, if he hadn't been so determined to expose Henryk in the most flamboyant way, stupidly failing to recognize the trap Henryk had set for *him,* he wouldn't have gotten slapped with a sanction. *Rules and regulations. The Secrecy Pact. Threat to our very existence.*

Blah blah blah.

In Cas's opinion, humans could use a little excitement in their lives. In fact, that was the only thing he and Henryk agreed on —that vampire society was far too stodgy and paranoid. Had the council browsed the shelves of the romance section in Powell's lately? Had they watched Netflix? Had they caught any of those dreadful movies with the wooden-faced actors? Vampires were *fashionable.* Trendy. Imagine the celebrity, the influence, the *fun* they could have if they revealed that they were real.

They could correct some of those egregious lies about vampire nature too.

But the council was too blind to see the advantages. And they certainly didn't appreciate Cas's attempts to rattle their chains a bit, to free them from their restrictive lifestyle.

Although even Cas had to admit that his last caper had gone too far. He swallowed convulsively. *I thought it was just another prank in our ongoing feud. If I had known what Henryk was really up to, I'd never have done it.*

So now, since pointing fingers was not Cas's way, he was about to be married. Permanently. To a supe of the council's choosing. *For your own good, and the good of the race.*

Whatever.

He strode past a falafel restaurant and into the lobby of the building that housed Supernatural Selection, the supe matchmaking agency the council had contracted to execute Cas's sentence. The place was run by a witches' collective, and as far as Cas was concerned, that damned it right off the bat. Vampires and witches had *never* gotten along.

On the other hand, vampires didn't get along with many supes in general. All the dueling power trips and influence one-upmanship? It wasn't pretty.

He mounted the stairs and entered the lobby. The lighting was low, well within the most soothing spectrum for vampires, although the other occupant of the room—some kind of big, bearded supe in denim and flannel—was squinting at his magazine, brows bunched in annoyance. Cas was tempted to turn the lights out completely. He'd have no trouble in the dark —vampire sight was optimized for low light conditions—but the other guy would. It might be amusing for a few minutes to see the guy flail about.

Amusing, yes. But bad. Making the distinction between *funny* and *poor fucking choice* had been Cas's problem since before he was Turned. In fact, it was *why* he was Turned. If he hadn't thought it'd be a lark, he'd never have gone with his sire that night when the fellow had stepped out from behind Rudolph Valentino's crypt, all smoldering eyes and windblown hair, like some kind of Gothic romance cover model. Not that there *were* Gothic romance cover models at the time.

Cas supposed being a vampire had its advantages, although at the moment he was too cross to think of any. *Too bad time-surfing isn't a real thing. I'd surf back to that cemetery and tell my sire to go fuck himself on the nearest weeping angel.*

The reception desk was unoccupied, although it sported a *Be Back Momentarily* sign. If Cas was still breathing, he'd have sighed. Technically, he could—his lungs functioned, otherwise he wouldn't be able to talk. But the management of breath was a conscious choice now—one it had taken him a good three years post-Turn to figure out.

He sat in one of the earth-toned chairs and folded his hands in his lap. He hadn't brought anything to read, and the other occupant of the room was monopolizing the only material other than Supernatural Selection brochures. Cas tapped his index fingers together, wishing for his phone. Kristof Czardos, the leader of the vampire council, had confiscated it.

Confiscated his damned phone, as if he were a recalcitrant high school student. Cas scowled, tapping his foot in opposition to his fingers. Kristof had shown up at Cas's house five minutes after sundown—and Cas would give a lot to know how the man moved so damned fast. True, he was the oldest vampire on the planet, but still.

Cas had barely woken up, and was lying in bed, scrolling through his various dating apps, when Kristof was suddenly *there*. He'd plucked the phone out of Cas's hands and handed it to one of his honor guards—a couple of hulking brutes who'd probably been Vikings when they were alive. Or possibly Neanderthals.

"Casimir. You have not presented yourself at Supernatural Selection to sign your mating contract."

Cas blinked up at him. "I've got time. The party isn't until . . . until . . ." He peered at the calendar above his neglected desk. "Shit. Is *that* the date?"

"Yes. Your reception is tomorrow night; however, this presupposes that the wedding will have already taken place. Don't you think it would have been polite to at least *speak* to your prospective mate before the ceremony?"

Cas sat up, brushing his hair out of his eyes. He didn't have to look up too far—Kristof wasn't especially tall. Five six or so, but then average heights in the twelfth century had been smaller. Who knew? Maybe he'd towered over his enemies back then.

Now he intimidated them by sheer force of will.

Besides, Cas wasn't a giant himself, not like the honor guards. Five ten, and *that* had been tall back in his living days.

"I don't see the point. It's not as if I got to choose her. Him. Them." He squinted at Kristof. "I forget. Did you tell me their name?" Maybe he should have read the wedding invitation. Presumably his prospective spouse would have been listed—in flowing Old World copperplate, no less.

"Your contracted spouse is Quentin Bertrand-Harrington, an incubus of a highly respected and influential dynastic 'cubi family."

An incubus. Huh. "I thought they dined on the life energies of their hosts." He gestured to himself. "Not a lot of life energy going on here."

Kristof's lips flattened just a hair. "Your energies will be sufficient for him, as his blood will be sufficient for you. The council has no wish for you to *suffer*, Casimir, you or Mr. Bertrand-Harrington."

"No," Cas muttered. "Just to force us both into a permanent marriage. What if we hate each other?"

"Supernatural Selection guarantees any match of their making will be perfect."

"'Perfect'? According to whom? Why should I trust a bunch of witches to tell me who's perfect for me? And why would the council trust the spell to solve its little"—Cas pointed to himself

—"*personnel* problem? Since when do you relinquish that much control?"

"Perhaps I should clarify." His gaze flickered away from Cas. "The match is guaranteed perfect within the parameters set by the client: commitment type, relationship longevity, social and emotional compatibility. The spell matrices are quite sophisticated. We presented our requirements—"

"*Your* requirements?" *What about* my *requirements not to have a live-in watchdog of your choosing?* "Then why don't *you* marry him?"

Kristof's eyelids drooped a fraction in his version of annoyance. "You are the youngest of us, Casimir, and your First Life was unlike ours. You experienced an unreasonable degree of freedom, the consequences of your actions handled by your studios, your wild and extravagant behavior rewarded by greater fame. That is why we've chosen a mate for you who is well versed in etiquette, who is confident in society."

"So you think I have no manners?" Cas sounded sulky even to himself.

"It's not your fault. Your sire should have provided better guidance, but he was foolish and irresponsible. His reckless arrogance is ultimately why the council condemned him to greet the sun." Something like real sorrow flickered across Kristof's pale face. The emotions swirling in Cas's belly when he remembered his sire weren't as straightforward—anger, regret, annoyance? It hardly mattered anymore. The man was twice dead, and had been for over half a century. "This is for your benefit as well as ours, Casimir. Trust me. You will be perfectly compatible."

"Does this Supernatural Selection place guarantee love too?"

"Of course not. Nobody can do that. But that is hardly apropos for a vampire anyway. It is not as if we have a heart to engage, after all."

Oh sure. He *gets to make jokes, but whenever I try, I get my ass sanctioned.* Unless . . . maybe it wasn't a joke. Cas hadn't felt the least twinge of fondness for anyone since his sire had met the sun—and that hadn't been affection so much as the bond between sire and fledgling.

"Fine. I'll go tonight." He held out his hand. "Could I have my phone back?"

Kristof regarded him for an extremely long and awkward moment. "Not yet. I will return it to you at the reception tomorrow. Perhaps that will provide the incentive that even the threat of the sun has not." He twitched one eyebrow. "You young people. So attached to your gadgets."

Another fucking joke. Cas was almost one hundred and sixteen, but he'd only been a vampire for ninety-two years, making him one of the two youngest vampires on the planet. And since vampire status was tied directly to age, he'd always be on the bottom of the hierarchical ladder.

Kristof had whisked off with his troglodytes—probably to practice his stand-up routine on some other hapless captive audience—leaving Cas to brood in relative peace.

I might not be a comedian, but I've got passive aggression down to a science. So Cas dawdled through his grooming routine, taking at least forty-five minutes to select the right suit for marrying a stranger—*wool; charcoal with a subtle herringbone; pearl-gray shirt with French cuffs.* He didn't bother with a tie, because he was just that kind of rebel.

Finally, though, he'd run out of things to do to his hair, his clothes, or his shoes, and since he'd already watched everything decent that Netflix had to offer, he'd left his house before he could be crushed by sheer boredom.

Now he was slumped in Supernatural Selection's oh-so-comfy chair, his legs stretched out in front of him, which meant that his formal Converse were directly in the other guy's sightline.

The guy glanced at Cas, irritation written all over his broad face. *Who knew that a beard could actually look irritated?* In the absence of any other entertainment—damn Kristof and his "incentives" anyway—Cas studied the guy. Not that studying him was a particular hardship, "stud" being the operative part of the word. *Good lord. Under that all that flannel, he must have biceps bigger than Francis X. Bushman's.*

He couldn't be human, not in this place. He was as big as a Sidhe warrior, but with those whiskers, he obviously wasn't fae. They were all beardless. Too ruddy to be a vampire. Cas sniffed surreptitiously. He didn't have the telltale sulfur-and-sewer reek of poisonous shifter blood. What *was* he?

The guy sighed and laid his magazine in his lap. "May I help you?"

Cas offered his best no-fanged grin—which he could do without thinking now, although it had been a struggle to master in the early years of his undeath. "Just curious about you. Magazine interesting, is it?"

"It is to me. I doubt you'd like it much."

"Oh, I don't know. My . . . tastes are quite eclectic." This time he let his fangs creep into his grin.

Bearded Guy snorted. "Vampire. Figures."

"What's that supposed to mean?"

"You all have issues with personal boundaries."

"Oh nice. Why not clue me in on your nature so I can make a few snap judgments too?"

He cracked his magazine open and masked his face with it. "Not my problem." Cas saw that the magazine was something called *Journal of Light Construction.* And just because it annoyed him that Bearded Guy was right about it not interesting him, Cas sat up, crossed his legs, and threw down.

"You can't be a shifter. You don't stink."

Bearded Guy didn't look up. "Thanks for that." He turned a page. "Happens you're wrong, though. Beaver shifter."

"*Beaver?*" Cas laughed, probably forcing it a little too long. "Can you seriously say that with a straight face? Or without other people making sex jokes?"

He glared at Cas over the top of the magazine. "This is Oregon. Only assholes make rude beaver jokes here." He lifted an eyebrow. "Well, assholes and Ducks."

"Ducks." Cas rolled his eyes. "Oh please. Don't tell me you're a beaver shifter who became an actual Beaver."

"Yep. OSU College of Engineering."

"Hence your fascinating reading material."

"It's important to keep up with current construction trends. Do *you* keep up with anything? What *do* vampires do with their time anyway?"

"Ah, that would be telling. So, did you enliven any of your frat parties by shifting into the avatar of your alma mater?"

The magazine crinkled in Bearded Guy's grip. "Inactive. Not that it's any of your business."

"Inactive? You're a shifter who can't shift, and you're giving *me* grief? If you ask me, you're not even a supe. In fact . . ." Cas leaned forward, raking Bearded Guy with his patented hungry look. "I doubt you'd even qualify as refreshments. Come on." He licked his lips. "I dare you to prove me wrong."

Chapter Two

Rusty knew he shouldn't rise to the bait. Vampires were notorious pot-stirrers, which made a certain amount of sense considering they were so much longer-lived than most supes that they must get really freaking bored—and this irritatingly pretty one didn't even have a phone to occupy himself with.

Rusty had *feelings* about being some entitled bloodsucker's Candy Crush equivalent. Besides, the guy had hit him right in his tender spot—he couldn't shift, and he was so much bigger than any other beaver shifter in history that even his own clan chief had speculated that the mutation in Rusty's blood meant he didn't belong in the community. And when he'd found out that Fletcher felt the same, that Rusty wasn't fit to marry . . . Well, that was why he'd registered with Supernatural Selection in the first place.

I'm an adult. I own my own business. I belong to the Chamber of Commerce, for Pete's sake! But none of that translated to respect in the eyes of his clan mates.

Or in the eyes of random vampires, apparently. *Even if the eyes in question are an unfairly gorgeous gray, hell if I'm putting up with the attitude.*

Rusty closed the construction journal and folded his hands on top of it. "I hear your council chief can't drink blood. Does that mean he's not a vampire anymore?"

The vampire glared at him, which probably would have terrified a human. Another supe? Not so much. And shifters were immune for another reason—shifter blood was poisonous to vampires, so they posed zero threat except for the annoyance factor.

"I wouldn't let him hear you say that. And how do you know about it anyway? That's privileged information."

Rusty shrugged. "Rumors." Then he grinned. "But I guess they're true. Good to know." He picked up the journal and opened it at random, pretending to be fascinated by the page, even though it was nothing but an ad for a cordless drill that he wouldn't be caught dead purchasing.

Vampire dude huffed and flounced around in his chair for a minute, then stood up. "Fuck this. I'll come back later when it's not so *crowded.*"

"Suit yourself." Rusty flipped the page. *Oh good. An ad for tile grout. Thrilling.* "You might want to pick up a magazine of your own before you return. So you won't be tempted to insult anyone else."

Rusty caught a glimpse of the flare of that ridiculously dramatic duster as the vampire fled. *Good riddance, although I gotta admit, the guy's got style.* He chuckled to himself, but as he tried to get into an article, his belly started to knot. *What the hell am I doing? I'm not the guy that picks fights. I'm supposed to be the stable one.*

Stable? Ha! That was a laugh and a half. Ever since Fletcher, his best friend from when they were kits and his boyfriend once they'd hit puberty, had announced his engagement to a woman from a beaver clan up in Coeur d'Alene, Rusty had been as stable as a three-legged sawhorse.

Fletcher had claimed it was politics, not personal, because of course he had. That had been his excuse during their entire relationship, the reason he wouldn't come near Rusty at clan gatherings, the reason he'd kept a double arm's length away whenever his father showed up unexpectedly, the reason he'd never shown the least affection to Rusty in public.

But getting engaged to somebody else? Fuck *yeah*, that was personal.

Rusty had signed up for Supernatural Selection the next day —after acting out in an extremely unstable way. Yeah, the memory of his little (okay, *big*) meltdown still made him squirm uneasily in his chair. But he'd fix that. Just like he'd fix his stupid broken heart with a match with someone who knew all about his Inactive status and didn't care.

So what if Rusty didn't believe in love anymore? Love wasn't the point here. Acceptance. Companionship. Self-worth. That was the ticket. He and Ted, his guaranteed perfect match, would have a good life. A productive life. A useful life.

He dug out his phone and pulled up the Supernatural Selection messaging app. The texts from Ted were sweet and somehow innocent. Nothing earth-shattering. No deep philosophical conversations. Just a couple of pictures of the sunrise over a lake, the beach at sunset, a self-deprecating comment with an eye-roll emoji about how much he was eating leading up to hibernation season.

Maybe Rusty would never be in love with Ted the way he'd been in love with Fletcher, but he could definitely see himself becoming fond of him. Ted was handsome in a mountain-man kind of way. Taller than Rusty by a couple of inches. *What will it be like not to be the biggest guy in the room?* That alone would be a novelty, even if Rusty didn't find Ted all that physically attractive since he'd been conditioned to appreciate smaller men. *Men like Mr. Random Vampire, perhaps?*

He snorted. *Not likely. Although, those eyes . . . Wonder what he looked like when he was alive?* Rusty shook off the pointless thought and typed out a quick *Hey. How you doing?* text to Ted, but for some reason, it didn't go through. He frowned at the phone, poking at the Send button a couple more times. Nothing, even though he had perfect connectivity in here. The witches wouldn't stand for anything less.

"Mr. Johnson?"

Rusty jerked, nearly dropping his phone.

The dark-haired man standing next to the reception desk, a file folder clutched to his chest, smiled apologetically. "I'm sorry. I didn't mean to startle you."

"Nah. It's okay."

The man held out his hand. "I'm Zeke."

Rusty shook with him. "Call me Rusty, please."

"Of course." Zeke glanced around the lobby, his brows puckering over his wire-framed glasses. Rusty caught the glint of a vision spell in the low light. "Where is ... That is, I understood Mr. Moreau was here as well?" His voice rose on the last word, asking a question even if it was phrased as a statement.

"Vampire? Reddish-blond hair? Gray eyes?" Zeke nodded. "Yeah, he was here for a while. Said he'd be back later."

"Oh dear. I had hoped to explain this to you both at once, but —" Zeke glanced behind him, at a shimmering golden pillar of light that had drifted into the room and hovered at his elbow.

Wow. They've got an angel interface. Why the heck would they need an AI unless— "You're a demon."

Zeke's eyes widened, and he swallowed convulsively with another glance over his shoulder. "Yes. Is that a . . . a problem?"

"Oh hey. Didn't mean to freak you out. It's not a problem for me. I was just surprised. You don't see many demons in the Upper World. You must be on that new Sheol work-release program, right?"

"Um . . . yes. However, we have some rather important things to discuss, and my status is—" the AI flared orange "— immaterial. If you could follow me to the conference room upstairs?"

"Sure." Rusty brandished his phone. "But did you know your messaging app is on the fritz? I tried to text Ted just now, and it didn't go through."

"Yes. Well. That is one of the things we need to discuss. Upstairs?"

"Right."

Rusty tucked his phone into his pocket and followed Zeke and his golden shadow up the stairs to a slate-floored conference room. The walls were painted ombré, fading from orange to deep violet, like a sunset. *Trust witches to keep the nature theme going, even in a room with no freaking windows.*

Zeke gestured to a chair at the long conference table. "Please have a seat."

Rusty chose a spot that faced the door, expecting Zeke to sit at the head of the table, but instead, he sat across from him, the AI taking up a position at the head, directly on top of the chair. *Hunh. Wonder if the angel can actually sit or if it just likes to hover menacingly.* Kinda weird that the angel was creepier than the demon—who was actually kind of cute with his curly dark hair and big dark eyes.

"So." Zeke flipped open the file folder and spread several sheets of paper out in front of him, not glancing at Rusty. "Thank you for coming in tonight. I know you hadn't planned to finalize your contract until next week."

"Yeah. Got a thing I have to do first." Rusty wanted to get past the welcome reception for Fletcher's fiancée first. No point in subjecting Ted to that kind of drama—especially since Rusty intended to medicate himself for the event with large amounts of high-end scotch at Fletcher's father's expense. The wedding, though—he fully intended to attend that with his new husband as his plus-one.

"Well. Yes. You see, there's been a . . . a complication."

"Complication?"

"Yes. Earlier today . . ." Zeke darted a glance at the AI, and ice pooled in Rusty's belly.

The blocked message. The special meeting. "Did something happen to Ted?" *Gaia, no. Not to that sunny, guileless guy.* "Please tell me he's all right."

Zeke's eyes popped wide, and he extended a hand across the table, although it was too big for him to reach Rusty's arm. "No, no. He's fine. He's in perfect health. It's just—"

"Thank Gaia." Rusty ran a hand over his face. "You had me worried."

"The thing is, though . . ." Zeke took a deep breath. "He's married to somebody else."

Rusty stared at him for a full thirty seconds, his jaw sagging.

Then he stood up and punched the wall right in the fucking sunset.

Chapter
Three

How could Cas have been stupid enough to let slip the truth about Kristof's condition? This was exactly why he was such a fucking terrible vampire—which the council never let him forget. *Too volatile. No control. Immature, impulsive, and thoughtless.*

Too bad he'd just proved them right.

He stalked down the street toward his Jag, but at the cheep of the security disengaging and the flash of headlights, he stopped dead—*Yeah, yeah, juvenile joke, but it never gets old.* As much as he relished the idea of screaming down I-5 in the dark and wind, he still had to sign his fucking marriage contract tonight.

And if I'm about to be shackled to some incubus, I want one last chance to choose my own partner, damn it.

He locked the car again, caressing the hood and imagining it purring under his hand like the big cat it was named for. *That's one thing I don't miss about my living days. The Jag beats the Model T six ways from Sunday.*

If he'd had his phone, he could have used one of the hookup apps to find somebody nearby, although the one thing he wanted—to be topped—would never happen. Something about vampire *mesmer* made every receptive partner . . . well . . . receptive. *Maybe the incubus will be different.* He was a sex demon, right? Surely he'd be an expert at fucking. Besides, from what Cas had heard, 'cubi had their own version of *mesmer* —'cubi thrall. Maybe thrall would trump *mesmer*.

He huffed a laugh, imagining their first sexual encounter as one big game of Rock-Paper-Scissors. Shoving his hands in his trouser pockets, he scanned the streets for a likely spot for a little action. The Pearl District was a little too upscale for the kind of rough he was hoping for, but there was a shifter bar in Old Town that might do the trick.

His enhanced vampire speed ate up the sidewalk until he realized people were staring at him. He forced himself to slow down, wondering whether that big shifter asshole would tell anyone that Cas had let slip Kristof's blood aversion. His face burned, and he tried to calm himself. Wasting the heat from his last feeding on something as stupid as a blush was just pathetic.

Would 'cubi blood have the same heat as human blood? Would 'cubi *essence* be the same, call to him the way the humans had enticed every vampire in the history of their kind? He'd never known a vampire to feed on 'cubi before—not that there would have been much opportunity. There weren't very many 'cubi outside Sheol. In fact, the 'cubi might be the smallest supe population outside of vampires.

But then, 'cubi could reproduce. Make little 'cubi/human hybrids that would grow and learn and make their own little hybrids someday. All living supes could do that—shifters, druids, fae—although the method was a little weird for the high fae. Life begetting life. But vampires? The only way for them to "reproduce" was to make a fledgling. In other words, death begetting death. But the druids who'd helped evacuate the vampires after WWI had insisted on a fledgling moratorium as a condition of their aid—some nonsense about balance and natural assimilation. Cas's own technically illegal Turn in 1926 had nearly broken the pact and stranded a lot of vampires in Europe, which had gotten his sire slapped down. Hard.

Which was also why he'd gotten in such deep shit with the council when they'd found out about the brand-spanking-new fledgling right here in Oregon, where their most recalcitrant citizen—*that would be* moi—was staging his latest rebellion. *Like sire, like fledgling.* At least that was the council's attitude, the reason they'd found it so easy to pin the crime on Cas. Well, that and the fact the man had been in Cas's house the night of his Turn.

Cas pushed open the massive oak door of the Bullpen and stalked over to the bar. Yeah, he'd hooked up with the guy that night, but he hadn't Turned him. He'd never do something like that. But the council had presented him with the evidence and asked him to explain himself.

He probably shouldn't have refused to answer on principle. That had sealed his fate right then. But what would have been the point of declaring he wasn't guilty? Nobody would have believed him. They'd tried him in their minds before they'd ever hauled him in.

He took the only empty seat at the bar, next to a lanky bespectacled man with dark hair that had apparently been styled with an egg-beater. The guy was sporting tortoiseshell glasses and a plaid shirt and tie—really? What kind of pathetic fashion victim wore ties with plaid? Hipsters were incomprehensible.

The bartender set a cocktail napkin on the counter in front of him. "What can I get you?"

Bourbon. Neat. That's what Cas craved, more even than his next taste of blood. But his sire had left a few pertinent details out of his rosy picture of vampire existence. If he'd told Cas, *You'll never be able to smell or taste anything except human blood again. Not coffee. Not bacon. Not booze.* Would Cas have agreed to their bargain? Ah, well. No point in belaboring it now. "Perrier Lime."

Not that he could taste the lime, but it looked less sketchy than ordering a glass of water straight up.

As the bartender set Cas's drink on the bar, his nerdy neighbor jostled him with an elbow while pulling out a phone. "Sorry." He offered a grin that might have caught Cas's attention if he hadn't just spotted a *much* bigger fish across the room.

Mal Kendrick. Cas licked his lips and took a swig of his Perrier. He'd heard about Mal's exploits in the club scene. Who hadn't? The hunky fae had cut a wide swath through the club boys in no fewer than six cities. *He can cut a swath through me anytime he wants.*

Cas studied Mal's ass, hugged lovingly by his leather pants. *That ass would be illegal in seven states because of the riot it would cause in the streets.* But it wasn't Mal's ass Cas was interested in tonight—it was the . . . package . . . on the front of his body, which, now that Mal had turned slightly, was outlined in stunning profile.

This is it. My chance to be topped. Why hadn't he ever considered that before? Fae *glamourie* was supposed to be right up there with vampire *mesmer* and 'cubi thrall. *There's the third in my Rock-Paper-Scissors scenario.*

Well, here was his chance to test it out. Would *mesmer* win out over *glamourie,* or would *glamourie* throw down *mesmer* and make it beg? *The second one. Please oh please.* Cas hadn't been topped since that night with Billy Haines at the Cocoanut Grove in 1924, and he was more than ready.

Just then, Mal glanced his way. Cas gave him his best come-hither look from under his bangs and—*there.* The wicked grin he got in return was a check he had every intention of cashing tonight.

"Now that's what I'm talking about," he murmured, probably a bit too loudly because his nerdy neighbor looked up from his phone and turned to him.

"Pardon?"

"Nothing you need to worry about. Just one very, *very* fine fae."

"Have you . . . um . . . gone out with him before?"

"'Gone out'? Mal Kendrick doesn't 'go out' with anybody." Cas smiled slyly, with just a hint of fang to see Nerdy Guy flinch. He didn't. *Weird.* "Mal goes *in,* if you get my drift, and the back rooms here are his temples."

"Have you even met him?" Nerdy Guy was peering at Cas through those thick glasses, his head tilted to one side like a big gawky bird. *Why do I feel like a worm all of a sudden?* "Because I'm not certain—"

"Look. Everyone knows Mal's reputation. Ask anybody. Ask that guy he was hitting on over there."

Nerdy Guy glanced at the spot where Mal had been standing —although he'd made it partway to Cas before he got stopped by some other cockblocking asshole. "I don't think he was hitting on him. That's his—"

"You must be new around here if you don't know Mal Kendrick's reputation. Trust me. My pants will hit the bathroom floor faster than this glass hits the bar, and he'll be pounding my ass like a sledgehammer. Guaranteed."

"I think your data might need a refresh. From what *I* know —"

"Did you see the look he gave me? Trust me. He's a sure thing." Cas leaned against the bar on one elbow, arranging his body in its most elegant curve. There was an advantage to his slender physique where Mal was concerned. Everybody knew he only did twinks.

Nerdy Guy was still looming next to him, blocking Mal's access to Cas, and from the stench, a mob of shifters had boiled in behind them, so he couldn't sidestep and meet Mal halfway.

Finally Nerdy Guy moved, but only to stand up straight— shit, he was almost as tall as Mal—and face the incoming fae. Was he planning to warn Mal of Cas's evil intentions? Cas scowled at the shifter gang behind him, who'd started singing some kind of college fight song. *Great. Frat boy shifters.* He sniffed experimentally. *Frat boy werewolves.* One harassed-looking guy, who was probably their RA since he seemed a little older, was trying to contain them, without much luck.

When he glanced back at his quarry, Mal had stopped in front of Nerdy Guy. *Good. Maybe Nerdy Guy will listen when* Mal *asks him to move.*

"Hey." Mal's deep voice, with its buried laughter, sent a shiver from Cas's scalp to his balls. *Here it comes. Any second he'll ask the guy to move aside.* Cas lifted a finger to get the bartender's attention and pointed to Mal and himself. Might as well get the obligatory drinks started and out of the way so they could get to the evening's main event.

But Mal didn't ask the guy to move. Instead, he gripped the back of the nerd's neck and hauled him in for a kiss.

What the fuck?

Cas turned to flee, but he was blocked in by a wall of shifters, their overwhelming new-alpha reek as solid a barrier as their barely contained physicality. He hunched over the bar, which now held another Perrier Lime and a Double Mountain IRA, which must be Mal's drink of choice. *Damn efficient bartenders.*

The kiss next door finally broke, and Mal said, "Sorry. I didn't see you over here before Hamish cornered me."

"No worries. I just got here myself. Faculty meeting ran long."

Mal moved in closer, inside anybody's idea of personal space. "I think I liked it better when you were on sabbatical. I didn't have to share you with anybody then."

Nerdy Guy chuckled. "Just the druid council, the neighborhood association, the wetlands board, and my research."

A druid? Cas sneaked a sidelong glance in time to catch Mal's hooded glare. "Now that you mention it, there are way too many people who want a piece of you. What am I going to do about that?"

Holy shit. Not only did Nerdy Guy know Mal, but apparently they had some kind of relationship. Shame burned through Cas like sunlight. *Why didn't I hear that little rumor? I need to get out of here.* But the werewolf pack had grown, and he couldn't see a way to get through without retching.

Cas edged as far away as he could with the harassed RA hemming him in on the other side as Nerdy Guy brushed a wayward lock of dark hair off Mal's ridiculously noble forehead. "'Do'? Grin and bear it?"

"Nah. Not my style." Mal glanced down at his feet and then peered up through his lashes. "You know me by now, Bryce. You know I'm not the most romantic bloke. I'm supposed to get down on one knee to do this, but I think somebody spilled their pint down there." He set a little box on the bar and nudged it toward Nerdy Guy—whose name was apparently Bryce. The expression on his face was so tender that Cas wanted to look away, but he couldn't. The answering smile from Bryce nearly set the bar ablaze.

Not just a relationship. A fucking *relationship.* Shit, Cas had boasted about getting fucked by Mal Kendrick to his thrice-damned fiancé. *Just stake me now.*

Bryce cupped Mal's jaw with one big hand. "As I recall, the first gift I ever gave you was a paintball tagger, so we won't argue on who's the least romantic. But if you're asking what I think you're asking—"

"Let's do it up right, love. Consort ceremony in Faerie. Wedding here in your bloody wetlands."

"Now *that* sounds perfect." Bryce leaned in for a kiss that went on for over ninety seconds—Cas counted. Then he pulled back and murmured in Mal's ear. Nobody else could have caught it, not with the werewolves playing some kind of loud drinking game that involved howling to the tune of the *Gilligan's Island* theme song, but Cas had vampire hearing. "You can get on your knees later."

And *that* kiss was still going on when Cas shoved his way through the partying werewolves, stench be damned, and stumbled out of the bar.

Rusty's hand ached like a son of a bitch. *Serves you right. Haven't you had enough throw-downs with walls lately to come in better armed?* Zeke had offered to get one of the on-call witches to come in and work a healing spell on it—for a price, of course —but Rusty figured he needed the pain to remind him not to be such a damned fool.

But that didn't mean he wanted to endure it without a little self-medication, so he headed into Old Town. Ordinarily he'd avoid the Bullpen. Too many of the patrons were there for a turn in the underground fight pits to settle a score, or work off aggression that hadn't bled off from their last shift, or just because their animal nature was belligerent.

Apparently all Rusty needed to take out his aggression was some convenient Sheetrock. *Damn it.* His equilibrium had gone down the toilet when Fletcher had sprung the news of his engagement on him.

He turned the corner, the Bullpen in sight halfway down the block, but as he passed the adjacent alley, he heard something that froze him in his tracks.

"Gimme your wallet."

"Really? I am *so* not in the mood for this."

Rusty recognized that voice, with its faded French accent and snooty tone. The vampire. What had Zeke said his name was? Moreau? Yeah. Something-or-other Moreau.

Rusty reversed course and peered into the alley. Yep. It was Moreau all right, facing down some punk in a grimy Trailblazers hoodie, whose foot-long knife blade glinted in the moonlight. *Just great.*

Two things could happen—either the attacker would knife Moreau and Moreau would retaliate and rip his throat out, or the attacker *wouldn't* knife Moreau and Moreau would rip his throat out. Either way, the Secrecy Pact was about to get exploded. *Guess it's time for me to do something marginally intelligent and useful today.*

The idiot attacker's attention was focused on Moreau, so Rusty sprinted down the alley—he might be big, but he wasn't slow—and grabbed the guy's wrist.

"Drop it."

Moreau snarled at him. "What the fuck are you doing here? Go away!"

The attacker jerked his arm, trying to break Rusty's grip. "Yeah. Go away."

"Not likely." Rusty dug his fingers into the pressure point inside the attacker's wrist until he cried out and dropped the knife to the pavement with a dull *clang*. Rusty released him, shoving him toward the street. "Now get out of here."

"My knife—"

"Is now my knife. Gaia preserve me, are *all* criminals this stupid?" Rusty shoved him again. "Go!"

The idiot finally got a clue and stumbled out of the alley. Rusty picked up the knife with a sigh. He probably should have called the police. Who knew whether the guy would try his tricks on somebody else tonight. But the safety of the supe community was the main issue right now. *Even if they hardly consider me part of them anymore.*

Moreau brushed irritably at the sleeve of his duster. "He couldn't have hurt me. Not with that pathetic pig-sticker. What's the blade made out of? Tin?"

"It ain't carbon steel." Rusty put the knife under his boot and snapped the blade, then shoved the pieces into a nearby overflowing dumpster. "I wasn't worried about *you*, Moreau."

"Oh, thank you for that."

"Don't be a douche. You go all Vlad the Impaler on him, and there goes the Secrecy Pact and your ass is grass."

"My ass, as you so eloquently put it, is already grass when it comes to the council. But he wouldn't have remembered it anyway. That's one of the things *mesmer* is good for."

"You were gonna suck him? Out here?"

Moreau wrinkled his nose. "Ewww. I can think of few hosts less appetizing, unless it's that mob of drunken werewolves in the bar at the moment. Besides, we never drink from a host who isn't willing. It's rude."

"So vampire etiquette is a thing?"

He rolled his eyes, which were surprisingly light. Rusty had noticed they were a very pretty gray back at Supernatural Selection. "You have no idea."

"Well, I guess it's a good thing you're nice to your victims before you kill them. Classy."

"For your information, we don't kill our blood hosts. We haven't in forever."

"'Forever'? That's not what I've heard."

"Okay, maybe not forever. But certainly since I was Turned. I've never killed a host in my life."

Rusty smirked at him. "Don't you mean 'in your death'?"

Moreau gave Rusty a look sharper than the mugger's knife. "You're not as funny as you think you are."

"And you're not as tough as you think you are. Listen, Moreau—"

"How do you know my name? Is mind-reading a skill you pick up as an inactive shifter?"

Rusty shook his head. "You really are a piece of work. The Supernatural Selection counselor told me. But I can't remember your first name. Sorry."

Moreau sniffed. "It's Casimir, if you must know. But Mr. Moreau will do nicely, Mr. . . . ?"

"Johnson. Rusty Johnson."

"Charmed, I'm sure." He shrugged, settling his coat on his shoulders. "Since you're not there to annoy me, Mr. Johnson, I might as well go back to Supernatural Selection and get married."

"Yeah, well, don't count on it."

"Why?" Casimir's eyebrows quirked up. "Have I suddenly turned lucky? Has the vampire council granted me a reprieve? Did the building explode? Or perhaps get overrun by a convenient plague of locusts?"

"Sorry to disappoint you. The building's still there. But your fiancé isn't."

"The incubus? What, did all demons suddenly get extradited to Sheol?"

"No. He got himself married. To *my* fiancé."

Casimir stared at him for a moment, his mouth dropping open to reveal his fang tips. *Oh Gaia. He's not going to have some kind of vampire meltdown, is he?*

Rusty patted him awkwardly, Casimir's shoulder trembling under his hand. *Is he about to cry? Can vampires cry?* "I know it's a shock."

But instead of crying, Casimir threw back his head and laughed like a fucking lunatic.

For an instant, Rusty panicked. What did you do with a hysterical vampire? But when Casimir's laughter went on and on and *on*, panic faded. *Who cares what you do with a hysterical vampire?*

"You know what? Laugh it up. Do whatever. I never figured a vampire would give a hyena shifter a run for their money in the annoying laughter department." Those bozos were the worst practical jokers in the whole supe world, and they didn't think anyone was funny except for themselves.

But then Casimir started to wheeze and clutched Rusty's arm, folding over on himself.

"Hey hey hey. Calm down. Breathe."

"C-c-can't. Have to . . . th-th-think . . ."

Ah, shit. One of the only pieces of vampire lore that Rusty knew floated up in his brain: They didn't have autonomic responses anymore. Those vanished when they Turned, since they controlled systems that the vampires didn't need.

So how the hell did you handle a hyperventilating vampire?

The things they don't teach you in school.

There was a dilapidated crate sitting next to the dumpster. Rusty hooked it with the toe of his boot and pulled it into the middle of the alley. "Here. Sit down." He eased Casimir onto the broken slats, helping him lower his head between his knees, the fabric of his coat soft under Rusty's callused palm.

"Take it easy. Breathe. Or maybe don't. Whatever vampires are supposed to do." Rusty winced. *Way to be competent.* Casimir's back was taut under his hand, so Rusty rubbed it in slow circles. "Don't rush. Take your time. Shhh."

After a minute or so, Casimir shuddered and then stilled. As in *completely* stilled. No movement at all, which sent Rusty's heart rate into the panic zone. *Shit. Was he dead?* He grimaced, giving himself a mental facepalm. *Of course he's dead, you idiot. He's a fucking vampire.*

Then Casimir's back expanded slightly. "If you don't mind removing that plus-sized paw off of me, I'd like to sit up now."

Rusty snatched his hand away. "Right. Sorry." Guess it was too much to expect gratitude, but then, Rusty was used to being taken for granted.

Casimir sat up, blinking like a kit just out of the water. Rusty braced himself for another blast of attitude. But instead, Casimir smiled. And it was extraordinarily sweet—no fangs at all. "Thank you. I haven't lost control like that since the first days after my Turn."

Rusty rubbed the back of his neck. "You're welcome. Would you have . . . you know . . ."

"Disintegrated? No." He screwed up his face. "Well, probably not."

Rusty goggled. "Disintegrate? Is that what happens to vampires when they . . . you know?"

"Hit Second Death? Yes. Dust to dust, you know. Saves enormously on cleanup, let me tell you, not to mention heading off awkward questions by the police about the provenance of a corpse of someone last seen three hundred years ago on a different continent."

Rusty blinked. "Huh. Good point."

Casimir glanced down at the crate. "What in blazes am I sitting on?"

"Uh . . . broken crate."

Casimir stood up, holding his coattails aside to brush off the seat of his pants. "No wonder I've got splinters in my ass."

Rusty peered at said ass—which was very nice—in the dim light. "You want me to check for you?"

Casimir fluttered his eyelashes. "Want to get your hands on my ass, do you?"

Rusty backed away, heat washing up his throat. "Gaia, but you're a piece of work."

"Yes, I believe that's been said before." He grinned wryly. "I'm sorry. It's a knee-jerk reaction by now to be . . . well . . . a jerk."

"Yeah." Rusty knew all about knee-jerk reactions—and their consequences. "Listen, you want to grab a drink?"

Casimir grinned, fangs flashing white in the moonlight—unless they glowed on their own, which wouldn't surprise Rusty in the least. What he didn't know about vampires would fill the Willamette. "Careful. That means something completely different to a vampire."

"Yeah, well—" he pointed to himself "—shifter, so you can't chomp on me unless you want to get poisoned, and I'm sure not gonna watch you bite some other guy. I meant in a bar. Alcohol. Lots of it." He held up his hand, which was throbbing in time with his heartbeat. "This hasn't been the best day."

"Tell me about it." Casimir's shoulders drooped. "But I can't drink. Nothing but water anyway."

"Really? Why? Does that poison you too, like shifter blood?"

"Perhaps I should say there's no point in me drinking anything but water and"—he tilted an eyebrow—"the usual vampire beverage of choice. I can't taste liquor, I can't smell it, and it doesn't affect me. Why waste the money only to torture myself with what *isn't*?"

"Damn." Rusty tugged on the hem of his jacket. "How do you feel about keeping me company while I imbibe a little anesthetic?"

"I suppose I could manage that." Casimir glanced behind him at the Bullpen. "Not there, though. I may have burned my bridges a bit. Besides, there's some kind of werewolf twenty-oner party going on in there."

"Hells no. Let's head back to the Pearl and try one of the hipster bars. They're used to an eclectic clientele."

"Well, nobody's more eclectic than us. Lead on."

Chapter Four

Cas glared at Rusty in the low light of the bar. They'd been lucky enough to find a relatively unpopulated place where their vastly different wardrobe choices didn't cause comment. They'd even scored a corner booth. Rusty had been surprisingly civil to him, considering Cas hadn't really exerted himself to be charming—he saved all his charm for his blood hosts, where it was necessary.

But Rusty was on his third double bourbon, staring at the glass between his gigantic paws as if it held the secrets to the multiverse. It wasn't the lack of attention that Cas objected to. It was the bourbon—mid-shelf, for crying out loud. It was a crime against nature.

Of course, if any of the tragically hip twentysomethings dotting the bar knew what Cas and Rusty really were, they'd consider *them* a crime against nature. Well, Cas, maybe. Rusty, despite his shifter heritage, could almost be human.

But the bourbon. Gods above and below, but Cas missed bourbon. He missed being able to drink the way Rusty was now, as if one more glass, one more sip, could make the bullshit go away.

It never did, of course. Go away, that was. You still had to face it when morning dawned with its attendant hangover.

Not that Cas ever saw the dawn anymore. Or hangovers either. He wasn't sure which he missed more. Not the hangover per se, but the ability to have one.

He took a slug of his Perrier as Rusty finished off his double and signaled for another.

"Far be it from me to interrupt someone who's obviously courting alcohol poisoning, but don't you think you ought to slow down a little?"

Rusty peered at him, his eyes red-rimmed. "I will. Eventually."

Cas tilted his head, considering the big Inactive. He was certainly attractive in a rough trade sort of way. Wavy medium-brown hair, although his beard was red. Brown eyes. Roman nose. Broad cheekbones. And of course, the massive shoulders and prodigious chest. *Powerful. Strong. Probably masterful too.* He'd be a natural as an extra in *Game of Thrones*, or in a Viking reenactment, pillaging his way through a medieval village. *He could pillage me. Hold me down and—* Augh! No! Shifter, remember?

"Is Rusty really your name?"

He snorted, accepting his new drink from the server. "No."

"What *is* your real name?"

"Rather not say." He took a sip of his bourbon. "'S stupid."

"You're talking to someone named Casimir. Let's not get into name-judging."

Rusty glared at his bourbon. "No."

"Come on."

"Don't wanna."

"Pleeeaaase?" Cas batted his eyelashes, walking his fingers across the table to flick Rusty's arm.

A growl rumbled in Rusty's chest before he sighed, huge and deep. "Elmer," he muttered.

"El-Elmer." Cas suppressed his laugh because he'd promised. "I can see why you prefer Rusty. Is it because of your beard?"

"My—" He pawed his beard as if he'd forgotten it was there. "Oh. No. When I was a kit, my mom said my laughter sounded like a rusty hinge."

"You know," Cas said, leaning back and laying his arm across the top of the bench seat, "I never understood nicknames. I mean, if you're going to call somebody something, why not just start out that way? What's the point of the instant alias?"

"I was named after my grandfather. I'm actually Elmer Douglas Johnson the Third. But Granddad was still alive then, and my father, Elmer the second, was called Doug, so they had to come up with something that would make it possible to know who to call for dinner."

"That's another thing I never understood. How unbelievably arrogant to name a child after yourself. Isn't its existence enough of a tribute? Besides, it gives the progenitor an unreasonable notion of ownership." Rather like the ownership of vampire sires over their fledglings. All in all, Cas was rather relieved that his own sire had met Second Death in 1948. Not that he'd wished for the fellow's demise precisely, but he far preferred having no fetters on his independence—the council's ridiculous micromanagement notwithstanding.

"My *progenitor* had no trouble disavowing all knowledge of me once I turned out to be Inactive. He probably would have changed my name officially to something else then, except my mom wouldn't let him." He swirled his bourbon into an amber vortex. "Last thing he wanted was to have everyone know his namesake was defective." He held out his arms, like he was putting himself on display. "And I'm a little hard to miss, especially in the middle of a clan gathering. Nobody comes up higher than my shin."

Cas raised his eyebrows. "Granted you're quite a tall specimen, but I didn't realize beaver shifters were so short. Or are all clan gatherings conducted in shifted form?"

Rusty frowned at him. "What are you talking about?"

"You said nobody comes up higher than your shin."

"Not shin." Rusty set his glass down and focused on Cas's face with apparent difficulty. "*Chin,*" he said, with exaggerated enunciation.

Cas chuckled. "Okay. That makes more sense. Although the notion of you in the middle of a roomful of beavers is quite the picture."

"They wouldn't. That'd be stupid. They couldn't talk then, and that's all they want to do. Talk talk talk. Talk about making an impression on the Idaho clan with the rehearsal dinner. Talk about the wedding. Talk about the reception. Talk talk talk."

"You said that."

"Yeah, well, so do they. Talk talk—"

"Talk. I'd think you'd be happy about them discussing your wedding."

"Not *my* wedding. Fletcher's. My . . . my boyfriend."

Cas froze with his Perrier halfway to his mouth. "Wait a minute. If you have a boyfriend—"

"Had. Until last month. Guess that makes him my ex-boyfriend, huh?"

"You broke up with him last *month*? And he's marrying somebody else?"

Rusty nodded morosely. "He's the clan chief's son. Has to keep the line going, so he can name some poor kit Fletcher Bradford Dawson the umpteenth."

"You're joking. They've kept that dreadful name going for that many generations?"

"Nah. It'd just be Junior. Fletcher's the fucking first. At everything."

"Was he the first at you?"

Rusty scowled, and for a minute, Cas thought he'd deny what was obvious to anyone even as drunk as Rusty—and Cas was unfortunately sober, as always. But then he sighed, cradling his glass. "Yeah. First boyfriend. First sex. First lo— Never mind."

"So I take it that you're not desperately in love with your Supernatural Selection match."

Rusty gave him a slightly off-kilter *get-real-dude* look. "Hard to be in love with a guy I've never met."

"Really? You've never met your fiancé either?" Cas held up his fist for a bump, but when Rusty held up his, with its rather grimy and spotted gauze . . . "Never mind."

"He seems like a nice guy though. And the agency guarantees a perfect match."

"In that case, why didn't he go through with the wedding?" For that matter, why had Cas's incubus bailed on him too?

Rusty squinted up at the lights. "There's something . . . Oh. It's only temporary. There was some kind of clerical error that caused a spell snafu, but Ted and your guy are going through some ritual at the full moon to get divorced, so everything'll be back on track. Assuming they don't leave us at the altar again. Third time's the charm, right?" He squinted at his drink. "Or is it bad things always come in threes? People who come up with shit like that should make up their fucking minds."

A pit opened in Cas's belly. "Wait. So we're not off the hook? We'll still have to go through with it?"

"Sure. Why wouldn't we? I mean that's why we were there, right? They emailed me a reminder for my calendar. You probably got one too. Check your phone."

"I can't. The council chief *confiscated* it."

"Why not get another one?"

"For one day? Too much of a pain in the ass to set up. Besides . . ." Cas sniffed. "It's the *principle* of the thing."

"Oh. Principles. Right Those're important. I guess." Rusty's sigh caught on a faint hiccup. "You know, I really wanted to have a husband and a new home by the time of the wedding." He glanced sidelong at Cas. "Don't want to keep living down there and have to face them every day."

Cas drummed his fingers on the table. The full moon was only a couple of weeks away. Would that be enough time for his alleged fledgling to regain consciousness and exonerate him? That was the only way for Cas to avoid getting shackled for life to somebody not of his own choosing.

Besides, the reception in honor of his own marriage was tomorrow night, with all the vampire glitterati in attendance. The top flight of the council would look down their ancient, supercilious, perfectly preserved noses to verify that Cas was suitably hobbled, and if he didn't show up married, they could vote on an alternative—and possibly more permanent and even less palatable—punishment for him.

Granted, his mating was intended to be permanent, but he'd still exist. The other alternatives Kristof had threatened him with were rather more . . . terminal.

Rusty hunched over his bourbon, staring morosely into the (very reduced) depths. "I shouldn't have put it off. Ted wanted to tie the knot a week ago, but there was a job I had to finish." He snorted. "Yeah, and *that* turned out so well."

"I put it off too, although not for the same reason. The difference is you seem to want to get married. I don't."

"You don't? Why not? Don't you want somebody to spend your life with?"

"My life, your life, *every* supe's life, provided we're not fucking idiots, will last longer than any relationship possibly could."

"You don't believe in love, then?"

"Oh I believe in love. I just believe it's finite. Enjoy it while it's green and lovely, but don't be afraid to move on when it turns zombie on you." He poked the melting ice in his glass with the cocktail straw. "It's the permanence that they're forcing on me that's the problem. I mean, I could face a temporary relationship with *anyone*. I could even stand *you* as long as I had an end in sight. A very imminent end."

Rusty chortled into his glass. "That'd make our councils shit a whole pallet of bricks."

Cas stared at him, a smile tugging at his lips as a wonderful, terrible, audacious idea bloomed in his mind. "They would. And damn it, why shouldn't they?"

Rusty blinked at him. "Why shouldn't they what?"

"Shit bricks. Because, my fine inactive beaver, you and I are getting married."

Chapter Five

Rusty goggled at Casimir for what felt like ten minutes but was probably only a few seconds. He hoped. The way the room was getting blurry around the edges, it was hard to tell.

Casimir raised one of those elegant caramel-colored eyebrows. "Catching flies are we?"

Rusty snapped his jaw shut. He raised his glass, stared at the inch of bourbon still remaining, and set it back down with a thump. He signaled the server. "Um . . . water? And maybe a bathtub of coffee?"

To his credit, the server didn't bat an eye. "We're fresh out of bathtubs. Will a carafe of each do?"

Rusty nodded, and when the guy sped off, he turned to Casimir, leaning over the table to hiss, "That's insane."

"Why?"

"Because— Because—"

"You know, I've never cared for that justification. It's so . . . unspecific." He grinned, and Rusty wasn't sure if it was the light or his own inebriated state, but he could swear Casimir's fangs glinted with those stupid FX sparkles. "Although I admit that I've used that lack of specificity to my advantage in the past."

"You mean you're a scam artist."

"I mean I'm a vampire—"

"Shhh!" Rusty glanced around wildly. "We're not in the Bullpen anymore."

"So? How likely is it anybody here would take that literally?"

Rusty scowled, hunching his shoulders as if that could make him any less conspicuous. "You don't know. They could. It's Portland. People expect the weird."

"They expect a guy in a kilt and Darth Vader helmet, playing flaming bagpipes while riding a unicycle weird. They don't expect undead creatures of the night and beaver shifters weird."

"Still. Keep it down."

"I could point out that *you're* the one whose voice is carrying. Do you have any idea how audible stage whispers can be? That's why they're called stage whispers." He took a delicate sip of his Perrier. "As I was saying, I'm a—" he bared his teeth "—you-know-what who used to be paid for pretending to be everything from a cattle rustler to a gigolo to Cardinal Richelieu."

"Why would you— Oh. You were an actor."

"Yes. In silent films. Before the studios caved in to the pressure of the tedious morals of the bourgeoisie and temperance unions. I even—" he leaned forward "—appeared naked in one or two."

An image of what Casimir must look like naked—pale and slender and lithe—had Rusty downing his remaining bourbon, because *damn*. "They, uh, allowed that then? But—but—"

"Hollywood was a strange and glorious place until it became so relentlessly middle class. When you consider it, movies made vampires of us all. There we were, capering about onscreen, undead and unchanging forever. Or at least until the film disintegrated." He toyed with his glass, casting a coy glance at Rusty from under his lashes. "However, I should qualify that while the scenes were shot with me naked, the film itself was doctored with flames in strategic locations. Primitive special effects, but they served."

"Wow."

"Yes, indeed. Wow. So you know I've got the chops to pull off this particular role."

"You might, but I don't. I'm just a construction engineer who builds houses for a living." *And sometimes destroys them.*

"Oh come on, *Elmer.*"

Rusty scowled, leaning back as the server delivered his coffee and water. He put the scowl on hold for a second to smile at the server. "Thanks." Once the guy left table-side, though, he let it descend full-force. "Don't call me that. Nobody calls me Elmer."

"Then stop acting like an Elmer. Come on. What have you got to lose?"

"Uh—my life?"

"Seriously? You're a shifter. I can't feed off you. You're twice as big as I am—"

"You're exaggerating."

"Hardly. And I'm not a killer, so I'm not likely to turn rogue and come at you with a machete. You're perfectly safe."

Rusty downed half a glass of water and refilled it from the carafe. "Now I know you're lying. You're a vampire. You've got to have killed *somebody* sometime."

"Now who's being indiscreet?"

Rusty winced, sneaking a glance at the nearby tables. Damn it. He shouldn't drink so much in public. Or anywhere. Especially when he was in the company of confusing vampires. The combination was clearly lethal to his common sense. *That's gotta be why this conversation feels more intimate—and dangerous—than any I ever had with Fletcher.* "Sorry."

Casimir waved his apology away. "Just act normal. As if we're discussing Kurosawa or Fellini."

"Yeah, I really look like a guy who'd be discussing foreign films."

Casimir glared at him—and wow, the guy could really *glare.* "Why are you so obsessed with appearances? That's rather biased, don't you think? Outward appearances have so little to do with preferences and aptitudes."

"Are you kidding? Everybody makes assumptions based on appearance. Right now, if you asked anybody in this place which one of us swings a hammer all day and which one of us does . . . whatever vampires do all night, I doubt any one of them would get it wrong."

"Perhaps not. But we're veering off the subject."

Rusty's brows bunched together. "What was the subject again?"

"Marriage." Casimir grinned again. "Ours."

"No. Just no."

"Why not? You want a husband to flaunt in front of Fletcher and your stodgy clan—"

"You don't know my clan is stodgy."

"Darling, if they're busy judging you for your shortcomings instead of your abilities, then they're stodgier than Calvin Coolidge." Casimir brandished his glass of Perrier as if it were a flute of Dom Pérignon. "You want to show Fletcher the First that he's Fletcher . . . if not the Last, then definitely Fletcher the Past. And I need to be married before tomorrow."

"Why?"

"Let's say that if I'm not, there could be unfortunate consequences." Rusty's alarm must have shown on his face because Casimir patted his arm. "Not to you. To me."

"Can't you just tell them that the agency made a mistake?"

"If I tell them that, then they'll come up with another real candidate for me and I'll be just as trapped— That is, no. It wouldn't be appropriate. Besides . . ." His grin was positively wicked and, for some insane reason, went straight to Rusty's dick. "I rather want the council to shit those bricks."

"But if you marry me—" Rusty couldn't believe he was actually considering this "—you'll be just as trapped, so what's the difference? And what happens in a couple weeks when our real matches are free again?"

"We won't *actually* be married." From the exasperation that flickered across Casimir's face, Rusty could swear that he'd intended to add *you idiot*—or perhaps something less complimentary—to that statement. "We'll just be pretending."

Rusty lifted the creamer pot to doctor his coffee, but thought better of it and took it black. Bitter and strong, it still didn't make this idea sound any less crazy. *Maybe I should have stuck to bourbon.* Although the way his head was spinning, he wasn't entirely sure he hadn't.

Even struggling through his mental haze, though, he was pretty sure there was a flaw in Casimir's logic. If he could just aim his brain at it for a second he could— *Ah.* "But the contracts at Supernatural Selection are magically registered. If we just tell people we're married but we're really not, they'll be able to find out by checking the registry. Won't they?"

Casimir flopped against the booth back. "Drat. You're right. And my council chief is exactly the sort to check."

"Yeah. Fletcher probably would too." He'd never believe Rusty could have moved on, not so quickly. *Or at all.* When Rusty thought about it, Fletcher didn't have that high an opinion of him. Or rather, his opinion of himself was a heck of a lot higher.

Casimir snapped his fingers. "I've got it." He topped off Rusty's water and pushed it toward him. "Drink. You'll need to be unimpaired for this next bit or Supernatural Selection won't let you sign the contract."

The hair on Rusty's neck lifted. "Contract? What contract? We're not signing a contract."

"Oh yes, we are. Just not the one everyone—including you— expected. According to my chief, Supernatural Selection's guarantee is perfect within client-defined parameters. Their parameters happened to include handing me a life sentence, but *our* parameters are very different."

Gaia, I wish my head were clearer. "What, uh, are our parameters?"

Casimir's eyes glinted in the low bar lighting. "I believe we've covered that. A partner to get us through the next two weeks. And of course"—Casimir waved one pale, elegant hand —"the accompanying brick-shitting."

Rusty choked on his water. "We can't *tell* them about the brick-sh—"

"Not in so many words, of course." Casimir passed Rusty a napkin. "We'll simply get them to draw up a contract for us that ends on the day our real matches are free again. That way, you'll be able to marry this guy who's truly perfect for you—who is he anyway?"

"Bear shifter." Rusty blotted water out of his beard. "He lives in the Coast Range." Far away from Fletcher and the clan. *But at least there's a lake there.*

"You'll be able to marry your bear shifter and flit off to your castle in the Coast Range. And I—"

"It's hardly a castle. More like a cabin."

"Hush. I'm waxing eloquent here." Casimir pressed his wrist against his forehead and closed his eyes. "And I will be able to —" He opened his eyes, blinking several times. "Well, never mind that."

"Oh no." Rusty took a gulp of his coffee, and it burned all the way to his belly—all the better to shock him out of making a really stupid decision. "If I'm gonna agree to this crazy scheme, I need to know what you're getting out of it. Otherwise, you could throw me under the bus anytime. I mean, I don't really know you, do I?"

Casimir nodded graciously. "A point. But my situation is rather . . . complicated."

"You think because I work construction that I can't do complicated? Have you ever translated blueprints to working drawings?"

"My dear beaver, I—"

"Beaver?" A guy from the group of twentysomethings at the next table scooted his chair back until it hit the edge of Casimir and Rusty's booth, slopping Rusty's overfull water onto the table. "Awesome, man. We're all Beavs too!" He gestured to his orange OSU hoodie. "And we won today! Were you at the game?"

Rusty shook his head. *So much for people not paying attention.* "Not this time. I graduated a while ago anyway. But go Beavs, right?"

"Absolutely!" He offered a high five, which Rusty returned with the hand he hadn't punched the wall with, then scooted back to join his friends.

When Rusty turned back to Casimir, the vampire was smirking. "I can't believe you went to OSU. I mean seriously?"

"All—" Rusty scowled, slanting a glance at the noisy OSU table, and mouthed, *beaver shifters.* "—on the West Coast go to OSU. It's tradition."

"Sounds more like lack of imagination to me. Shall we?" Casimir started to slide out of the booth.

"Not so fast, bucko. You haven't told me about this complicated situation of yours." Rusty crossed his arms and leaned back, the water and coffee doing a reasonable job of clearing his head. "Let's hear it. Either you give me the whole story, or I'm leaving right now."

Chapter
Six

For a moment, Cas was tempted to sigh. But that would take too much effort, and this evening had already been far too trying. "Fine." There was no earthly way he was admitting the whole story to Rusty. For one thing, it was vampire business, and Cas was already in deep enough shit for verifying Kristof's weakness.

For another, Cas made it a point of honor never to reveal any more than necessary to anyone. He'd learned that his first days in Hollywood, where *everybody* had something to hide or was running away from something. Where *everybody* hid their real selves behind personas that the studios manufactured and the fan-centric press ate up like chocolate and cream.

But that determined jaw discernible under Rusty's close-trimmed beard, the glint in his (slightly bloodshot) eyes, hinted at a stubbornness that Cas really didn't want to challenge right now. Although if time hadn't been running out on his best chance to sidestep his unwanted fate, Cas would *definitely* be tempted to test Rusty's *masterful* limits.

He ran his finger around the rim of his glass. "The council thinks I'm rather a loose cannon."

Rusty snorted and downed another half glass of water. "That's an understatement."

Control. Control. You need him, so don't get pissed off and lose this chance. "There have been . . . incidents in the past. They believe a carefully chosen"—*by them*—"mate will rein in my risky behavior. Smooth my rough edges. Provide stability."

Rusty jerked, his eyes widening. "'Stability,' huh? Think it'll work?"

"It has to." Cas pushed his empty glass away. "It's my last chance. If I fail . . ." He shrugged.

"If you fail, then what?"

"Then I greet the sun."

Rusty's jaw sagged. "They'd do that? Kill—" He glanced at the college kids at the next table, but they seemed occupied by a large plate of nachos. He leaned forward. "*Kill* you?" he whispered.

"My dear beaver, they wouldn't hesitate." This time Cas did sigh. "Not if they thought it would keep them safe. Keep the supe community safe." He smiled wryly. "*I* may never have killed anybody, but the same cannot be said of them."

"Wait. I thought you were shitting me before. You mean you've *really* never—" Rusty jabbed his neck with two fingers, then drew them across his throat. *Subtle.* "Never?"

"No." Cas chuckled. "Yet another reason why—according to the old guard anyway, who are all about *our common heritage*—I make such a fucking terrible vampire."

"Hey, you're not so bad," said the fellow in the orange hoodie, who was leaning over his chair arm. *Shit. I don't need an audience for this discussion.* "I mean the coat and the scarf are a little too, I don't know, modern? Try a cape. Or some glitter. That's what we do whenever we do vamp cosplay."

Cas smiled tightly, his lips firmly pressed together. "Thank you. I'll take that under advisement."

"No problem." The kid beamed. "Anything for a fellow Beav. Or friend of a Beav." He scowled. "Unless you're a Duck."

Cas pretended horror. "Bite your tongue."

The kid laughed. "Yeah, my buddy here—" He punched Rusty's biceps, his eyes going wide before he shook out his hand with a wince. "He'd never hang with a Duck. Not on game day. Hey." He scooted closer. "You guys want to join us? We just ordered another pitcher and some sliders. You're welcome to share."

"Thanks, pal." Rusty stood up and patted the kid's shoulder. "We appreciate the offer, but we can't stay." He extended his hand to Cas. "We're on our way to get married."

Dumbfounded, Cas let Rusty draw him to his feet and lead him across the bar to accompanying hoots and cheers from his college fan club. Once they were on the street, Cas stopped dead —*still never got old*—halting Rusty's juggernaut progress.

"Just a blooming minute, Elmer. What made you change your mind?"

Rusty scratched his ear, one side of his face squinched up. "You said they'd kill you. I'm not down with that. I don't care who you are or whether you're telling the truth about never offing a host. Executing you because you *might* be a threat to them? Ending you because you're not *stable*? No. If I didn't stop something like that, I couldn't look at myself in the mirror."

Cas regarded the enormous man in front of him with something like awe. "You really are an incredibly decent person, aren't you?"

"Not that it's ever done me any good. Come on." He held out his hand. "Might as well put on a good show for the demon."

"Demon?" Cas took Rusty's hand, stumbling a bit at its warmth. *Oh.*

Rusty glanced down at their clasped fingers, as if surprised that he'd offered and Cas had accepted.

Cas let go at once, falling into step next to Rusty a safer distance away. "Sorry. You were saying. Um, demon?"

"Oh, that's right. You left before he showed up. The counselor at Supernatural Selection is a demon on the Sheol work-release program. He's got an AI observer hovering at his shoulder like it's ready to smite him at the least infraction." He shrugged. "If neither of us throw a hissy fit about our prospective husbands marrying each other instead of us, it'll probably take some heat off him." He winced. "Although I already sort of threw a hissy fit anyway. Maybe this'll help make up for it."

Their hipster bar was only a few blocks from Supernatural Selection, and the two of them walked the rest of the way in silence. Cas glanced sidelong at Rusty from time to time. He wasn't frowning exactly. But he looked . . . serious.

This is not a frivolous guy. Cas doubted Rusty had ever danced the night away in underground speakeasies with lethally handsome men in impeccable evening dress or women with rouged knees and daringly bobbed hair. But then it had been nearly a century since Cas had done so either. And really, had it *ever* been a good idea?

Had all his more deplorable actions (at least deplorable from the council's perspective) been attempts to recapture that life, those feelings? He'd blamed his sire for robbing him of those days and nights, when the reality of life in Hollywood was all the excitement and risk anybody could want. But really, even if he'd lived his life out as a mortal man, those days would have been lost to him with the Great Depression, the Hays Code, and World War II. What was he still fighting for?

He glanced at Rusty's profile again—so intense and determined and honorable. *Is it time for me to fight for something else? Something bigger? Something better?*

Perhaps Kristof was right after all. It was time for him to grow up.

When they got to Supernatural Selection, Rusty put one ginormous hand on Cas's shoulder. "Are you sure this is a good idea?"

Cas raised an eyebrow. "Did the walk in the cold wind sober you up?"

"I was plenty sober before we left the bar." *Riiight.* "But think about it. What's gonna happen the day after the full moon when my clan and your council find out the truth, because hello? We'll be married to other people."

Cas flicked his fingers as if brushing away an insect. "*Pfft*. They'll be so happy—your clan that you're not mated to a vampire, and mine that I'm not shackled to a shifter—that all will be forgiven." By that time, Cas had every hope that his sentence would be commuted anyway.

Rusty frowned at his battered hand. "You have more faith in forgiveness than I do."

"Well, I know it's far easier to obtain than permission." *Unless we're talking about creating a vampire fledgling. Then either one will get you dead.* "And there's no point in worrying about it now. Right now, we have more immediate problems to resolve."

For a moment, Rusty looked as if he wanted to argue, his broad forehead creasing and his chest rising with an enormous breath. But then his shoulders sagged and he expelled the breath in a sigh, although his worried frown didn't entirely disappear. "Yeah. You're right. I guess."

"Then shall we?" Cas opened the door and let Rusty precede him into the building and up the stairs.

When they entered the lobby on the second floor, an opaque pillar of shimmering light was hovering behind the unmanned reception desk.

Rusty leaned down, his lips a breath from Cas's ear. "AI," he whispered. "I think it's kind of a douche." The pillar flared orange.

"I think it can hear you, big guy."

Rusty's cheeks flushed redder than his beard, but before there were any further throw-downs with the angelic host, a man almost exactly Cas's size hurried in from a door in the back, his dark curly hair rumpled and his eyes more than a little wild behind wire-framed glasses.

"I'm so sorry I wasn't here to— Mr. Johnson!" He stumbled to a halt next to the AI. "I, ah, didn't expect to see you again so, um, soon."

Rusty rubbed the back of his neck with his uninjured hand. "Yeah. Me neither. Listen, I'm sorry about your wall. Won't happen again, I promise."

"Of course. Don't worry about it. The maintenance and repair spells are already at work."

"Great. So this is Casimir Moreau. Casimir, Zeke Oz."

Zeke's mouth rounded in an O, and his gaze flicked from Rusty to Cas.

Cas held out his hand. "A pleasure."

Zeke jerked himself out of his apparent trance. When he gripped Cas's hand, Cas nearly jerked his hand away because Zeke's palm was fiery hot against Cas's cooler flesh. *Holy shit. Are all demons so . . . incendiary?* No wonder the AI was hovering like a . . . well . . . like an avenging angel.

Cas donned his best charming non-fanged smile. "I'm sorry I ran out earlier before we had a chance to chat." He slid his hand around Rusty's arm. "Rusty here filled me in on the problem though."

Zeke's Sheol-pale skin flushed in rather unbecoming red blotches. "I'm really sorry about that. I don't know how the names got switched on the contracts. I checked them myself thrice, as required, and they were perfect every time. The Supernatural Selection global matching spell *guarantees* it. But somehow—"

"Never mind that. We're not here to complain or reprimand you." He added his second hand to Rusty's arm and leaned his head against that massive—and rather comfortable, when it came down to it—shoulder, and gazed up at Rusty, fluttering his eyelashes. Rusty stared at Cas like he'd sprouted several additional heads, so Cas pinched his arm surreptitiously. "We're here to get married."

"M-m-married?" More blotches bloomed on Zeke's skin—and really, how did someone who ran that hot have such pale skin in the first place? Since Sheol had no sunlight, it probably was just as difficult for demons to get a tan as it was for vampires. Although apparently they could escape from Sheol under the right conditions. Could they walk in the sunlight? "But—"

"Yes, yes. We know that our *true* perfect matches will be released from their current unfortunate arrangement by the full moon. We want to enter a *temporary* contract. I believe you offer those?"

"Yes. Of course. But—"

"Then sign us up."

The AI drifted closer to Zeke. Was its pulsing indicative of laughter or suppressed rage? Hard to tell when the asshole hid its face inside a pillar of freaking light. Zeke edged away from it and gestured to the same door he'd rushed out of.

"In that case, if you could come into my office? There are a few formalities, and we should discuss the details of your contract." He glanced over his shoulder at them as they followed him into a cramped and cluttered office. "Although I must tell you that it might be impossible to grant your request."

Cas settled into one of the two guest chairs in front of Zeke's desk as Rusty tried to somehow compress his bulk into the second one. The chairs were obviously sized for supes not of such mythic proportions. "Why might it be impossible?"

"Well, because of the spell, of course. It controls the manual contracts—those requested by the parties involved—as well as the automatic ones. Our house witches will only officiate ceremonies that are in compliance. In fact, our systems will outright reject any application without a predictably successful union, even before the match-guarantee spell is invoked. Obviously you aren't *perfect* matches. We know that already because the spell *was* invoked and your real perfect match—"

"Let's set that aside for the moment, shall we? Because as I understand it, your clients are allowed to define what constitutes perfect for them within certain parameters. Isn't that correct?"

"Yeeessss."

"So who's to say there's only one perfect match per person if different criteria apply?"

"Well." He glanced at the AI again. "Nobody, I suppose."

"What if your client's parameters specify more than one person at a time? What if they prefer serial monogamy? What if their preferences shift—" Cas shot a glance at Rusty "—so significantly after the spell-casting that *perfect* no longer applies?"

Zeke's eyes darted between Cas and Rusty. "Um . . ."

Since Rusty seemed to have turned to noncommunicative stone, Cas leaned forward. "Look, Zeke. May I call you Zeke? Our requirements—our *parameters*—are really quite simple. Don't you think you could at least *try* to accommodate our wishes?"

"Yes. Of course." Zeke swallowed convulsively, Adam's apple bobbing, and clutched his computer mouse. After a few spasmodic clicks, he lifted his gaze, although he didn't meet either Cas's or Rusty's eyes. "The AI is recording. If you could verify for the record that you, Casimir Moreau, and you, Elmer, aka Rusty, Johnson wish to enter into a temporary mating contract from this date to end on midnight the night of the next full moon?"

"I, Casimir Moreau, so verify."

Zeke waited expectantly, his fingers poised over his keyboard. Cas glanced up at Rusty, who was staring at the front of Zeke's desk, and really, second-rate maple veneer was *not* that interesting. Cas nudged Rusty's knee with his own.

Rusty's head jerked up, and he blinked several times as if he were just surfacing from an unexpected dunk in the water. "What? Oh. Yeah. I, Rusty Johnson, so verify."

"Thank you." Zeke's fingers flew over the keyboard, and he peered at the screen. "That's something, anyway."

"What?"

"The program didn't prevent me from entering your names." More red blotches. "I kind of expected it to reject the whole application for incompatibility."

Cas spread his hands. "You see? You never know until you try."

"Now, just a few more questions. Some boxes to tick, if you will." He smiled tentatively, obviously trying to get back into his usual patter for hopeful supe lonely-hearts. "Cohabiting? Yes, no, or partial?"

"Yes," Cas said just as Rusty said, "No."

Cas gritted his teeth. "Let's say partial, shall we?"

"A-a-all right." Zeke clicked his mouse. "Name changes?"

"No," Cas said, and Rusty shook his head as well. Apparently he'd decided to retreat into muteness again. "Not for such a short time."

"I understand. I had to ask, though. Following protocol is crucial in such an atypical case."

"Of course. Please continue."

"Consummation? Yes, no—"

"Forget the consummation clause," Rusty growled, finally roused out of his stupor. "That's not what this arrangement is about."

Zeke licked his lips, glancing sidelong at the AI. "I should perhaps mention that the contracts Mr. Farnsworth and Mr. Bertrand-Harrington—that is, your original matches—signed, um, in blood, included the consummation clause. So in order to terminate their contract—"

"They have to fuck. So what? They're technically married to each other. It's not like they're cheating on us." Although from the bleak look on Rusty's face, that was what he thought. *Farnsworth was just one more person who picked somebody else instead of him.* Didn't matter that it was the result of a clerical error. Rusty still got left at the blooming altar.

Zeke's gaze darted between Cas and Rusty. "I can't really *forget* it. The program requires a non-null response."

"What were those choices again?" Cas asked.

"Yes, no, or, um, optional."

Cas patted Rusty's arm. "We'll take optional, then, don't you think, darling? So much less . . . confining."

"Suit yourself," Rusty growled.

He didn't object. Which put a number of highly inappropriate ideas into Cas's head, considering the whole *never shall the flesh of vampire and shifter meet* thing. Although now that he thought of it, it was *blood*, not flesh, that was inimical. *Hmmm . . .*

Cas scooted his chair closer to Rusty's so he could lean against him, the heat thrown off by his big body oddly comforting and—dare he say arousing? He was like a mega-human. Human-plus. Although from what he'd said—and from the way Cas had reacted to him and jeered at him, Rusty probably felt more like shifter-minus.

Well. It's all in the perspective, isn't it?

I shouldn't have drunk all that bourbon.

Rusty stared at the gold band on his left hand, placed there by Casimir at the end of their very abbreviated ceremony conducted by an extremely disapproving witch. He hadn't even thought of rings, but Zeke had bustled into the altar chamber with two velvet-lined boxes in his arms and displayed the contents.

"The rings are part of the service if you don't have your own. Only fourteen carat, but for an additional fee you can upgrade to eighteen carat. Or even platinum."

Rusty had reached for the standard job as Casimir said, "We'll take the platinum."

They'd compromised on the eighteen-carat model. Casimir had tried to pay for the upsell charge himself, but Rusty was at least sober enough to insist on paying his half. Although apparently *insane* enough to get married to a vampire he'd only known for three hours and hadn't liked that much for at least half that time. *Although if I'd seen those eyes in a living man . . .*

Zeke escorted them downstairs from the altar room to the lobby. "Congratulations to you both. I have commemorative versions of your marriage contract for you here. Suitable for framing. If you—"

"Right." Rusty took the parchment, decorated with gold curlicues and looping calligraphy, and folded it in half, then in half again before tucking it into the inside pocket of his jacket.

At Zeke's gasp, Casimir took Rusty's arm. "That's my husband. So sentimental. Shall we go, darling?"

From the heat in Rusty's cheeks and forehead, he probably looked like an emergency flare. "Sure. Thanks, Zeke. We'll see you in a couple of weeks."

"Of course. Thank you for using Supernatural Selection, where your perfect match is . . . um . . . well. Good-bye."

Rusty fled the lobby, only slowing down on the stairs when Casimir stopped, his iron grip on Rusty's arm not letting him continue. *Jeez, vampires are stronger than they look.*

"Listen, *darling*, we both agreed to this, so you might at least *pretend* that you can stand to be with me. Otherwise, remember that little blood test they administered before the ceremony? When it comes back with your undoubtedly elevated alcohol level, I'm likely to be charged with coercion."

"You wouldn't. I'd never go back on a deal."

"Then smile. How about that for a start?"

Instead, Rusty scowled and trundled on down the stairs. "Do you know how annoying it is when people tell you to smile?"

"Oddly, yes. And I warn them that my smile is not for the faint of heart." Casimir clattered down behind him, his fancy-ass shoes beating sharper against the marble stairs than Rusty's work boots. "Then when I give in to their continued blandishments, and they almost faint, I have the satisfaction of saying 'I told you so.'"

Rusty slowed in the middle of the lobby. "Do you always talk like you've got a thesaurus and a dictionary of clichés in your back pocket?"

"What can I tell you? I cut my eye teeth—" Casimir flashed his fangs "—on press junkets in the twenties. Purple prose is mother's milk to me."

Rusty's stomach heaved at the mention of milk. *I really shouldn't have drunk all that bourbon.* Although a tiny voice in the back of his mind whispered that his nausea might have more to do with his impulsive marriage than with overimbibing.

Casimir hurried closer, placing a hand on Rusty's arm. "Are you all right? You look a little green around the gills."

"Beavers don't have gills."

Casimir's eyebrows made little peaks on his forehead when he lifted them. *Gaia, that's ridiculously cute.* "I was drawing from my cliché dictionary there, not speaking literally. Except for the green."

"I'll be fine. I'll roll down the windows on the truck on my way back to Eugene. The fresh air will take care of it."

Casimir's gray eyes took on a steely glint. "If you think I'll allow my new husband to get behind the wheel after consuming half a bottle of bourbon, you're seriously deluded."

Rusty's uneasy stomach gave a little skip—but not in a bad way. *He cares what happens to me.* Who outside his mother had ever bothered to do anything more than frown at a risky choice? Not that he made many of those. *I'm the stable one. The boring one.* "Thanks, but—"

"You dying in a fiery crash on our wedding night would be an ironic cliché of such epic proportions, neither one of us could ever live it down. Besides, if that should happen, I'd have no one with whom to prove my compliance to the vampire council tomorrow night."

His stomach returned to its original programming. *Right. This isn't about me. It's about our bargain. About sticking it to the vampire council. To Fletcher. About saving Casimir's life and my self-respect.*

Plus, he was still unsteady on his feet, and although he wasn't sure the bourbon was the sole cause, it was definitely a component. And yeah, shifters were sturdy and could heal quicker than most, but fire could do in any supe except a demon. Besides, nobody had ever figured out exactly how far off the genome inactive shifters had strayed.

Better safe than sorry. He wasn't in a happy place in his life right now, but that didn't mean he wanted that life to end. "You're right. I'll check into a hotel and—"

"Hotel nothing. You'll stay at my place." Casimir grinned. "Didn't we just check that 'partial cohabitation' box?"

"Uh . . . yeah."

Casimir laughed, and Rusty tensed. Was he about to hyperventilate again? But he kept the hilarity contained. Mostly. His grin was still wide when he tucked his hand in Rusty's arm.

"Now I know what a deer caught in headlights would *sound* like if it could talk." He tugged on Rusty's arm, leading him onto the street. "Come on. My car is just over there, and my house is in the West Hills. And don't worry. Despite that *other* box that we, shall we say, equivocated on? I have no designs on your virtue *or* your blood. You're safer with me than on the highway."

Chapter Seven

The next morning, by the time Rusty had banged his shin on at least seven different pieces of furniture in Casimir's pitch-dark, deathly quiet living room (how many stupid little tables did one guy need anyway?), discovered that vampire kitchens didn't include a coffee maker (or coffee, for that matter), and that their refrigerators apparently were used to store nothing but cold air, he wasn't so sure that hitting the highway last night wouldn't have been preferable.

For me, anyway. But Casimir had obviously been right about Rusty's impaired decision-making. Otherwise he wouldn't have married a guy for less than a month with the intent to marry a different one immediately afterward, all while probably still hung up on his first love.

I didn't need a drink last night. I needed an intervention.

He finally groped his way to the front door, unwilling to turn on lights that might disturb Casimir's rest. Although ... could vampires be disturbed in the daytime? There was so much he didn't know about them, since shifters and vampires were usually two non-intersecting circles in the supe Venn diagram.

He crept outside, blinking in the overcast morning. *You know that house had to be dark when the standard Portland gray weather seems like midday in the Mojave.* Casimir's midcentury modern house had a high fence enclosing a neat lawn with native plants in naturalized borders. One side of it was a rock garden with an ornamental bridge over a river of gray-blue pebbles, raked into stylized whorls.

Hunh. A Zen vampire. Go figure.

Rusty eased open the gate—no creaks. Whatever else Casimir might have, he had a kick-ass landscape maintenance service. Once on the sidewalk, Rusty headed to the corner and checked the street signs to get his bearings. The hike into downtown where he'd parked his truck in an overnight lot helped clear his head, and by the time he was on the road—after stopping by Peet's for a large coffee—he felt almost human . . . er . . . shifter. But the wink of gold on his left hand kept catching his eye.

Married. Gaia give me strength. Maybe he should think of this as practice for his real wedding. Ted deserved a husband who wasn't still mooning over his ex-boyfriend or borderline psycho because said ex-boyfriend had thrown him over for a political match.

He pulled into the driveway of his little bungalow in south Eugene, studying the broad windows in the living room, the double row of dormers in the upstairs bedroom, the kitchen and dining room doors where he'd chosen glass instead of wood to let in more light. *No cohabiting for Casimir here.* He'd burn up before breakfast. If they were intending to be married for more than a dozen days, it would be a problem. But since it was short-term? Any cohabiting would have to happen at his place.

Rusty sighed and climbed out of his truck, tossing his empty coffee cup in the recycling bin on the way to the front door. He stuck his key in the dead bolt, but when he tried to turn it, he discovered that it was already disengaged. *What the fuck?* He *always* locked up when he left the house. Sure, this was a nice neighborhood, but the house was a little isolated, nestled amid trees on its two-acre plot, and he wasn't *stupid*.

He opened the door cautiously, alert for any sounds, any items out of place, sniffing for an intruder's scent. But what he smelled was—

"There you are."

Fletcher. And coffee.

Rusty frowned and stepped inside, pushing the door closed behind him. "Fletcher. What are you doing here?" *And why didn't I ask him to give his key back?*

Fletcher lounged in the kitchen doorway. Long torso, barrel chest, short-ish legs, the same general shape as all male beaver shifters—except Rusty. He slurped out of Rusty's favorite OSU mug. "I swung by the lake house this morning."

Rusty's hands suddenly felt as cold as Casimir's. "You did?" Of course he did. And Rusty noticed that he didn't say *our lake house* anymore, as he had until last month. "Why?"

"Why?" He strode forward and set the mug on Rusty's grandmother's antique sideboard, slopping coffee onto the embroidered linen runner. "Oh, I don't know. Maybe because Sylvie is arriving in two days and I wanted to make sure the house is ready to show her."

"Oh."

"Yeah. 'Oh.' What the fuck, Rusty? The bedroom is a disaster area. It looks like someone took a sledgehammer to the walls."

Probably because someone did. "It's on my schedule for tomorrow."

"Tomorrow?" Fletcher scowled, crossing his arms and lifting his chin—he had to tilt his head back since Rusty was nearly a foot taller than he was. In the old days, Rusty would have sat down to make it easier for them to see eye to eye. *Not today.* "No way will the mud be dry on the Sheetrock in time for Sylvie's tour."

"I'd feel worse about that, Fletcher, if you'd bothered to tell me this tour was happening—and when."

"It shouldn't matter. The house was supposed to be done two weeks ago."

Rusty didn't say anything. He just stared at Fletcher, not smiling, not frowning, willing him to remember the not-so-tiny detail that had caused Rusty to blow off a construction deadline for the first time in his life.

Finally, Fletcher stopped impersonating his overbearing father. "Shit, Rusty. We've been over this. It's my *duty*. My father expects a lot of me. The *clan* expects a lot of me."

And you expect a lot of me—without a lot in return. Rusty didn't say anything. He picked up the coffee cup and walked into the kitchen. The coffee maker's hot plate was still on, nothing but dregs in the glass pot. *Fletcher never did make more than he could drink himself.* Rusty turned off the machine before the dregs started to scorch.

"Rusty? Sylvie will be an important part of the clan. Don't you think you could make a bit of an effort?"

"I told you. It's on my schedule tomorrow. The materials should be delivered today. I'll have everything done by Friday. Definitely before the wedding, even if I run into delays."

"Why not start today, then, to be sure? If you worked late, set up fans to dry the mud, it would be ready sooner."

"I'm not willing to do that, Fletcher. You'll just have to delay the official tour, or explain that work is still ongoing."

"I don't see why—"

"Because," Rusty half yelled to make himself heard over Fletcher's strident tone, "I don't have *time* today. I've got to go back to Portland, to . . . uh . . . see a man about a wedding."

"That's all you've got? Really, Rusty. Now you're just being childish." The sneer in his voice matched the one on his face. "So tell me, whose wedding is it? Assuming it even exists, which I doubt."

Rusty held up his left hand and waggled his ring finger. "Mine."

Cas surfaced out of his usual dreamless sleep to the ringing of his landline. *Why is someone calling me on that dinosaur? If they want me to answer, they should call my cell— Oh.* He didn't have his cell phone. It was fucking *confiscated*.

He stuck one hand out from under his comforter and groped on the nightstand until he found the handset. "H'lo?"

"Hey." The voice on the other end of the line was vaguely familiar. Male, deep-ish. Laced with relief. "I was beginning to think you'd died."

Oh, if only you knew. "Who's this?"

"It's Matt. Matt Steinitz."

Shit. The tabloid photographer. Cas flung the comforter off and sat up. He hadn't spoken to Matt since the night Cas had royally screwed the pooch—and set in motion the events that led to his enforced marriage. "Um . . . How are you?"

"Been better. Say, I was hoping you might have another tip for me. I mean I know that last one turned into a total clusterfuck and got you lost on Mount Hood for two days, but the pictures I got—"

"No."

"But—"

"I'm sorry, Matt, but I have no desire to repeat that experience."

"Please, Cas. I'm desperate here. I've left *Scoop Weekly.* I'm freelance now and I've got nothing. Can't you throw me a few crumbs?"

"I haven't a crumb to spare, Matt. I'm sorry."

"Cas—"

"Good-bye." Cas hung up and then unplugged the damn phone.

What time is it? He had an app on his cell phone, an alarm app that pinged as soon as the sun set and it was safe to open his blinds. *But I don't have my cell because it was* confiscated.

The digital clock on the dresser read 5:57, so at this time of year, that should be safe. *Rise and shine, Casimir. Today is your wedding reception.*

He grinned, letting his fangs run out to their fullest extent. His wedding reception. His chance to prove to the council that he still had at least *some* control over his life. He tossed the covers back and got up.

But as he strolled into the bathroom, he started to remember Rusty's original misgivings. Would the council be so angry that they'd stake him on the spot? No. That would ruin the party for everyone else, and if there was one thing vampires held sacred, it was parties. Celebrations of any kind that meant they didn't have to sit in a dark crypt somewhere with nothing but their own blood-stained memories.

Besides, he had faith in their reaction to the elephant in the room. *Rusty.* He chuckled as he ambled into the bathroom and turned on the shower. Compared to the size of all the vampires —most of whom had Turned when average height was much shorter than now—Rusty would be a literal elephant. Although given his prodigious size, he'd have stood out anywhere except perhaps a troll sock hop. *The council is going to shit bricks indeed.*

It would be endlessly amusing to see them trying to hide their shock and horror behind their perpetual veneer of manners more suited to an eighteenth-century drawing room.

Cas couldn't wait.

After he showered, he threw on a pair of sweatpants. He wouldn't want to traumatize Rusty with his nudity after he'd been so adamant about the no-consummation clause. Cas ran a hand over his hairless chest, tweaking a nipple. *What would Rusty look like naked?* Given his size, his cock was probably in proportion, and Cas's ass cheeks clenched in a spike of desire. *I wonder if shifter semen is poisonous too?* No vampire in living (ha!) history had ever gotten close enough to find out. The stench of "bad blood" kept them at a safe distance.

Cas wandered down the hall. *Oh. Maybe I should turn on a couple of lights.* He could see in the dark, but could Rusty? Did beavers have night-adapted vision? Even if they did, would Rusty, as in Inactive, be missing that attribute as well?

Cas stopped with his hand on the dimmer switch. Rusty didn't stink of bad blood. Maybe this was an opportunity in disguise—disguised as a giant of a man who'd have no trouble manhandling Cas in bed. *If I seduced him, it would totally be research.* Condoms, of course, just in case, even though vampires, being dead, couldn't catch or carry human diseases. Could shifters? Once again, no vampire had ever thought to ask.

Yes. That was the tack he could take with the council if they gave him shit. A two-pronged attack: although he hadn't married *precisely* as the council had ordered, they hadn't played by the rules either when they'd channeled their inner feudal overlords and trapped him in a fucking arranged marriage. How could they blame Cas for doing an end-run of his own? After all, he'd tied the knot with a match facilitated by Supernatural Selection. Perhaps it wasn't exactly the one the council had intended, but he'd kept within the spirit of their edict if not the actual letter. Not only that, he'd taken one for the undead team and chosen a shifter mate—purely for altruistic research purposes, of course. Really, they should be thanking him.

He chuckled as he slid the switch halfway. In the dim light, he could see the guest room door was ajar. An invitation? He ghosted down the hall and peered inside. But the bed was made, its blanket so taut across the mattress Cas could probably bounce a quarter off it.

Of course. Rusty wouldn't have hung around in a dark house all day. He would have had the mother of all hangovers this morning, but that shouldn't have put him out of commission for long. What had he said before he'd shut the guest room door last night after scribbling his contact information on the back of their "commemorative" wedding certificate?

Oh. Right. He had to go home to get something to wear to the reception. Cas grinned as he pushed the button to raise the blackout blinds on his living room windows. Would Rusty show up in those work boots? A flannel shirt? That canvas jacket with the snap closures? *Gods, I hope so.* Nothing put the council's nose out of joint more than dress that was inappropriate to the occasion.

Cas turned toward the French doors that led to his backyard and— *"Awp!"*

A figure stood there, outlined against the solar lights that surrounded the deck. Not Rusty—the intruder was too small.

Cas's mostly nonfunctional heart spasmed, because adrenaline was one thing that vampires hadn't lost along with their lives. Then the intruder stepped forward, into the pale light cast by the dimmer. Dark wavy hair. Sharp cheekbones. Hooked nose.

Henryk fucking Skalding.

Cas strode across the room and yanked the door open, folding his arms across his bare chest to glare at his nemesis. "What the fuck are you doing here?"

"Is that any way to speak to someone who's doing you a favor?"

Cas snorted. "The day you do me a favor is the day Kristof Czardos goes sunbathing in Death Valley. Out with it."

Henryk held out his arms, displaying his body in its evening clothes. Henryk never let an opportunity pass to *expand* himself, emphasizing the point that he was taller and broader than Cas. But then, he'd been a stevedore on the New Orleans docks before he was Turned. Cas had been a silent film actor.

"Behold in me the council's messenger."

"You? I can't see Kristof trusting you with taking out the trash, let alone an important message." Although Kristof had cut both Henryk and Cas a wide swath of slack since they'd both been deprived of their sires so relatively soon after their Turns. Guilt—even for vampires—was a powerful motivator.

"Ah, but while you've been busy with your usual boundary-testing antics, I've been making myself . . . agreeable . . . to our estimable leaders. Besides, perhaps they consider a message to you as not only unimportant, but equivalent of . . . how did you so eloquently put it? Ah yes. Taking out the trash."

Cas snorted. "After a century, I'd think the relentless brown-nosing would have gotten old for you. Especially since it's all a fucking act."

"You'd think that someone who was literally an *actor* in his First Life would understand the value of a convincing pretense. What has your endless insubordination ever gotten you that my cooperation hasn't gotten me?"

"*Appearance* of cooperation."

Henryk shrugged, and polished his fingernails on his lapels. "It amounts to the same thing. Truth is in the eye of the beholder."

"We've got nothing to say to one another." Cas pointed to the gate. "Get off my property."

"Not so hasty, Moreau. Don't you want this?" He reached into the inner pocket of his tux jacket and pulled out—

"My cell phone." Cas held out his hand, but Henryk tucked his arm behind his back. "Come on, Henryk. I can't believe Kristof would ask you to deliver it, but since you're here, you might as well, you know, *deliver* it instead of playing some kind of juvenile keep-away game."

"You should know about juvenile. You're still pulling the same stunts you did in the early days of your Turn, and even before. Really, Casimir. Isn't it time to jettison the regret and indulgent wallowing in self-recrimination? You're a vampire. Embrace it."

"Like you have?"

Henryk inclined his head. "I like to think I have a certain flair."

Henryk's affectations drove Cas mad as usual. He'd tossed cotton bales for a living, for fuck's sake. He'd barely been literate. And now he was aping the old world aristocracy of the council's top flight. "Like making an unwilling fledgling?"

"A fledgling? Me?" Henryk widened his eyes. "But that would violate the Great War Evacuation Compromise and threaten the Secrecy Pact. Everyone knows I've never done *anything* to endanger our kind. Unlike some I could name."

Cas ground his teeth, his fangs poking the inside of his lip. "Speaking of *naming*." He took a step forward. "What do you think Kristof would do if I gave him the name of the person who hired that necromancer to curse him with blood aversion? In other words, you."

Henryk bared his fangs in a feral snarl. "Do that, and he'll discover you're the one who found the blasted necromancer in the first place."

Cas's belly turned over at the memory. *I'm sorry. Gods, I'm so sorry, Kristof.* "That was for a prank. Temporary. To prove a point." Although for the life of him, Cas couldn't remember what the point had been. But Kristof hadn't been the target. *Henryk* had.

"You think they'd believe it? With *your* track record?" He chuckled, the sound sending unpleasant shivers down Cas's spine. "A pity the necromancer himself can't offer testimony, considering the poor man died so suddenly."

"Died, my ass. You murdered him."

"As much as I despise you, Moreau—"

"The feeling is mutual, I assure you."

"You're useful to me at the moment as a smoke screen if nothing else. But your irritation factor is starting to outweigh your worth. I'd be careful, were I you."

"Gods, now there's an appalling thought. If I were you, I'd greet the sun tomorrow."

"Don't press me." Henryk's tone was loaded with menace. *Yeah, I know that trick too.* "My patience isn't endless."

Cas thrust out his hand again. "Just give me the fucking phone and get out, Henryk."

"Not until you invite me in. Your stupidly bucolic landscaping is giving me hives—or it would if I were still capable of getting them."

Cas held the door wide and jerked his head in grudging invitation. "Fine. Let's get this over with."

Henryk strolled inside, casting a sidelong smirk at Cas as he passed. "You've invited me across your threshold. You can't keep me out now."

"Stow it, Henryk." Cas shut the door. "You know perfectly well that's nothing but popular culture tripe. Now hand over the phone."

"Not so fast. I'm instructed not to pass it over until I see proof."

"Proof? That the phone belongs to me?"

"No, idiot. That you followed the council's orders and executed the mating contract at Supernatural Selection."

Oh fine. Now *he follows the council's commands.* Cas held up his hand and flashed his wedding ring. "There. Married. Give me the phone."

"Anyone can buy a gimcrack ring at the corner store. Show me the official paperwork."

No way was Cas letting Henryk see the contract with the *Temporary* watermark in giant transparent red letters splashed across it. *Ah.* He strode over to the breakfast bar—really, he should call it something different, since he had never and would never have breakfast or any other meal there. He picked up the fancy commemorative wedding certificate and handed it to Henryk.

"There. Satisfied?"

Henryk peered at the ornate writing, his alabaster brow knotted. *He can't read cursive.* Cas felt a little spurt of relief. *He can't report Rusty's name to the council. My surprise attack is still a surprise.* "I suppose. Now show me your husband."

"I can't. He had to run errands today."

Henryk leered. "Really, Casimir. You should know better than to let him escape. Who's to say he'll ever come back after enduring your insipid lovemaking?"

"You know nothing about my technique and you never will." Cas snatched the certificate back. "He had to run errands and he's not a vampire. *He* can go out in the daytime. He thought it would be better to do that while I was asleep so we can spend all the more time together after everyone gets to know him at the party."

Henryk set the phone on the granite countertop and slid it toward Cas with one finger. "I suppose you've met the terms for this to be returned. But if he's not on your arm at the reception tonight, you may find yourself in rather hot water."

Or hot sun. "Don't worry. We'll be there. I look forward to introducing him to you. I daresay he'll make quite the impression." Cas smiled, wishing a vampire's powers included shooting laser beams out of their eyes. "Now get the fuck out of my house."

Chapter Eight

Fletcher would not leave. He raged up and down Rusty's living room, punching his fist into the opposite palm. "I can't believe you'd do this to me."

"To you? How the hell does this have anything *whatsoever* to do with you?"

Fletcher stopped, disbelief twisting his face into a perfect impression of a goblin. "You're joking, right? Are you telling me you'd have done this if it weren't for *my* wedding?"

"Here's the thing, Fletcher. Regardless of why I made the decision, *your* wedding makes anything I choose to do in my love life *none of your fucking business*!"

A smirk displaced the goblin grimace. "I get it. You want to punish me, when I'm only doing my duty to the clan."

"I told you. This is not. About. You."

"You're lying." He stepped closer, inside Rusty's personal space. "I bet you're not even married."

"Oh yeah? If I cared what you thought—which I don't—I'd tell you to check the gods-bedamned registry at Supernatural Selection. Instead—" Rusty strode to the front door and held it open. "Give me a punch list of what you want done and leave it at the lake house. I'll deal with it when I'm back in town, but for now? Just get out of *my* house."

Fletcher sauntered out, never losing his smirk, making Rusty wish for his sledgehammer again. After Fletcher gunned his truck down the road—*I must have been out of it if I didn't notice his truck in the first place*—Rusty headed over to the Men's Wearhouse to pick up his new suit. The last time he'd needed one was a good twenty years ago, and aside from the old one being hopelessly out-of-date, his chest had expanded too much since then to fit in it.

Of course, when he'd ordered the new one, he'd thought it would be for his own wedding to Fletcher. He'd canceled the order once, when Fletcher had announced his engagement, then rebooted the purchase when he'd gotten matched with Ted.

But when he got to the store and tried on the damn thing, they'd made the pants *and* sleeves too short.

Great. Just fabulous. This to-do tonight was a party. A reception of some kind, although Casimir had been pretty sparse on the details. Since vampires were notoriously fussy about clothes, he could hardly show up in his jeans and work boots.

So he bought a new dress shirt and a pair of gray wool slacks off the rack, although they couldn't find a jacket to fit him. He'd have to wear his leather jacket. It at least fit well, and people— well, Fletcher—said he looked good in it.

He bought a new tie too, one with a discreet chevron pattern in shades of blue and gray. As Rusty was paying for his purchases, he stared at the color of the pants and the tie. He'd never owned a pair of gray pants. His new suit was navy blue and his old one was brown. Why had he picked gray?

Casimir's eyes are gray.

He cursed under his breath as he stowed his wallet in his pocket and slung the plastic-wrapped clothes over his shoulder. It didn't matter whether Rusty thought Casimir was beautiful, with his hair the color of caramel, his straight nose, his sharp chin, not to mention those incredible eyes. Casimir was a vampire and this relationship was temporary and for one thing only.

Revenge.

In less than a month, they'd both move on, never to see one another again.

But if that's the case, wouldn't this be a perfect time to take advantage of "optional consummation" for a little no-strings sex?

Sex? With a vampire? Gah! He slammed the heel of his hand against the hood of his truck, earning a startled glance from a man jogging past with a baby in a stroller. Rusty shrugged apologetically. "Sorry. Just forgot something." *Yeah, like my brain.*

He needed to focus on the objectives. Tonight, it was Casimir's party. Tomorrow, he'd start the repairs on the shambles he'd made of his—no *Fletcher and Sylvie's*—house. Then two weeks from Saturday, it was the rehearsal dinner, followed on Sunday by Fletcher's wedding, and it would be Casimir's turn in the awkward spotlight. *Just get through it, one day, one hour, one minute at a time.* Then, two weeks from Monday, he'd be golden.

He opened the truck and hung his new clothes on the hook in the extended cab. He checked his watch. *Damn. Was that the time?* Casimir's reception started at seven thirty. Casimir had said they should be fashionably late, but what did that mean? Seven forty-five? Eight? Ten thirty?

Whatever, better for Rusty to get up to Portland early and kick his heels in a coffee shop until it was time to roll out the deception than to hang around at his own house and risk not being there in time. Traffic between Eugene and Portland was always iffy around rush hour.

He drove home, showered, and packed a few things in his duffel so he wouldn't have to wear the new clothes on the drive home. But he put them on—everything except the leather jacket and tie—for the drive up. He checked himself out in the full-length mirror on the back of his bedroom door.

Hmmm. Not too bad. Yeah, he was still too tall. His shoulders were still too broad. But even though the new duds were off the rack, the shirt didn't strain across his chest, the sleeves reached all the way to his wrists, and the pants . . . He turned around and studied his rearview. *Damn.* Did his ass really look that good? A grin crept across his face. *Maybe I don't have anything to be ashamed of after all.*

He loaded everything into the truck and actually found himself singing along with the radio on the drive to Portland. Who'd have thought that going to a party with a bunch of vampires would put him in such a good mood?

Maybe because I'm supposed *to be different from them.* They'd be judging him, but not *him* specifically—more like him as an avatar of shifters in general. *Gaia. I think I'm actually looking forward to this.*

As he pulled off the highway into Portland, he activated his GPS. Casimir had texted him the venue address about the time Rusty had hit Salem. He'd been surprised to see that he recognized the location—more or less. It was a country club right next to the Pacific Northwest College of Arts and Sciences, where he'd taken a number of night classes in green building theory and techniques from a professor who'd turned out to be a druid. It hadn't surprised Rusty when he'd heard *that* piece of news—the guy was seriously tuned in to the earth—although apparently it had been a huge shock to Professor MacLeod himself.

Rusty had actually talked to him a few times since the big reveal. The professor was working with Rusty's therapist, Dr. Kendrick, to evaluate inactive shifter DNA and develop druid magic-based therapies. Rusty didn't hold much hope that his own condition could be reversed, but some Inactives, especially kids who were part of a bird shifter clan, had a lot of side effects that broke Rusty's heart to think about. Bad enough the poor kids couldn't fly. But the other stuff? *Man.*

Yeah, Rusty couldn't shift, but he could still swim. He could still build. He shared everything else that marked Fletcher or any of his other clan mates as shifters—higher body temperature, faster healing, longer lifespan. He just couldn't shift.

There were definitely worse things.

He pulled into the club's driveway, which wound through the trees to an oddly ill-lit parking lot. He aimed for the rear of the lot, where his extended cab pickup on its oversized tires wouldn't crowd any of the sleek sports cars that lined the aisles.

But suddenly, a stick-thin guy in a red jacket appeared in his headlights, motioning him toward the porte cochere next to the club entrance, where two other red-coated guys lurked. *Valet parking? Seriously? For a dinky little reception?*

His mouth went dry as he stopped the truck and threw it into neutral. He rolled down the window and forced a smile for the guy who slouched over to his driver's-side window. "Hey. I'm . . . uh . . . here for the party?"

The guy didn't say anything. He just held out his hand, apparently for Rusty's keys. *Okay then.*

He grabbed his tie and leather jacket. But then he caught sight of something that sent his stomach into free fall. A couple strolled through the nimbus of his headlights, the woman's floor-length gown sparkling in the high beams like it was made of diamonds. And the guy . . . was wearing a tux.

A freaking *tux. Fuck.*

The leather jacket was not going to cut it. Shirtsleeves wasn't going to cut it either, but at least he'd look like someone who might have left his suit coat on the back of a chair somewhere. He left the damn jacket in the cab and climbed out, dropping his keys in the valet's open palm. He stalked toward the entrance as he tied his tie, but when he got a load of the glittering, shifting throng of vampires in a gods-bedamned *ballroom,* he nearly turned around and bailed.

Only his promise to Casimir—and the fact that the valet had just zoomed off with his truck—kept him going.

Once inside the vestibule, however, his courage failed. He couldn't waltz in there on his own, dressed like the fricking waitstaff, the only shifter in a mob of vampires. That was asking too much. If he—

"Hey. I was beginning to think you'd gotten lost in the Sylvan wilds."

Rusty whirled at the sound of Casimir's voice. He was strolling out of the men's room, smiling like he hadn't just thrown Rusty under the bus, and he was wearing a freaking *tailcoat*. "I need to get out of here."

Casimir's smile faltered. "What? No. You can't. At least not yet. It's our wedding reception, and I have to introduce you to Kristof."

Wedding reception. How had Rusty missed that little detail? "There's gotta be a couple hundred people in there."

"People? You mean vampires?"

"Yeah. How big a deal are you, Casimir, that this many people care about your wedding?"

"Trust me, I'm the lowest of the low. They're not here for me, or not all of them are. But any excuse for a party. A vampire's life can be excruciatingly boring."

"How many vampires are there?"

Casimir held onto his smile, but it was clearly forced. "As you said. A couple hundred."

"I don't mean here. I mean everywhere. In the world."

Casimir held his gaze, his tongue flicking over his lips. "A couple hundred."

"That's *it*?"

Casimir shrugged. "The war to end all wars was nearly the war to end all vampires too."

"What—"

"Later, darling. It's a long and tedious story, which I will bore you with later if you like. Suffice it to say that we negotiated an extremely unfavorable contract for survival. Our population was severely reduced and there haven't been any new ones created since, well, me."

"Really? You're the last vampire?"

"Don't make it sound so terminal. As you see, there *are* a couple hundred, all waiting to meet you."

Rusty wiped his damp palms on his trousers. "I'm not dressed for this."

"Nonsense. You look great." Casimir leered. "Good enough to eat."

"Not. Funny."

Casimir shrugged. "Sorry. Just trying to lighten things up a bit." He cocked his elbow, inviting Rusty to take his arm. "Shall we?"

"You know," Rusty murmured through clenched teeth, "if you weren't already dead, I'd *kill* you for this."

He patted Rusty's arm. "You don't know how many times I've heard that, darling."

"At least tell me there's an open bar."

Casimir winced. "Not with the kind of drinks you're looking for."

"Dinner? Hors d'oeuvres?"

"Sorry. Vampires don't eat. We're actually very easy to cater for."

"So you're telling me I'll be sober, starving, and stick out like a sore thumb. Is that it?"

Casimir bit his lip. "That's about the size of it. Sorry."

Rusty heaved a sigh. "Fine. Bring it on. But I'm warning you. The night of the full moon? We're getting a divorce."

Cas maintained his smile in the face of Rusty's anger. Because his plan to prove that the council was wrong to force him into a marriage that was more about gatekeeping than companionship? That would go down the tubes if his gatekeeper spouse didn't, well, keep his gate. So to speak.

Since Rusty didn't take Cas's arm, Cas took Rusty's before the poor innocent bearded behemoth could lumber in amongst the piranhas. The muscles under Rusty's polyester-blend dress shirt felt damn good under Cas's fingers, and the furnace-blast heat of Rusty's skin warmed him on the outside the way a feeding did on the inside.

It gave him a little boost of courage, courage that had faltered badly and sent him scurrying to the men's room when he was afraid Rusty was a no-show. But now? As Rusty himself had said, *Bring it.*

Although this was less a party than a parole hearing for him, Cas intended to enjoy every last second of his peers' outrage and horror and social discomfort. *See, assholes? This was all your idea, and look how it turned out.*

As Rusty charged down the two steps into the ballroom proper, Cas clinging to his arm, the crowd parted before them as if they felt the need to keep a minimum safe distance. But when Rusty and Cas reached the middle of the room, the crowd closed around them, ringing them in, and Cas realized that the look on their collective faces wasn't shock or horror or indignation.

It was hunger.

Oh shit. He doesn't smell like a shifter. They probably think I've brought snacks. He clutched Rusty's arm tighter. Kristof was supposed to make the announcement, the introduction, after Cas presented his spouse, but Cas couldn't find him in the sea of avid faces.

He cleared his throat. "Good evening, everyone. Thank you for coming. I'd like to introduce my husband—Rusty Johnson, of the Dawson beaver shifter clan."

Almost as one, the crowd's expressions morphed from greedy to repelled. They drew back with an almost audible hiss.

"Way to make an impression, Casimir," Rusty muttered. "Even my own clan doesn't shrink away from me like I'm carrying the black plague." He glanced around. "You sure I can't get a drink?"

A commotion began near the ballroom entrance, and the crowd parted again, revealing Kristof Czardos in his impeccable evening dress.

"Casimir." He didn't shout. He didn't need to. The nearly inaudible voice pronouncing Cas's name with an old-world accent wouldn't have been more menacing if he'd bellowed it like a berserker. "May we speak privately?" He glanced at the surrounding vampires, and they turned away, averting their gazes as etiquette required. "Mr. Johnson can enjoy a glass of champagne in the meantime."

"Champagne?" Rusty said. "But I thought—"

"We expected Casimir's mate to be non-vampire. To offer refreshment is simple courtesy." He glanced to the side and lifted his brow a fraction of an inch. A waiter scuttled over holding a tray with a single glass of champagne and a gold-rimmed plate with a half-dozen morsels of food that looked like sushi run through a shrink ray. "Please accept these with my compliments while I exchange a few words with Casimir."

Rusty glanced between the tray and the waiter, who was practically genuflecting before Kristof, and then to Cas. "You gonna be okay?"

Cas's heart did that odd spasm again. Rusty was angry at him, uncomfortable, out of his depth, yet his first thought was for Cas's well-being. *It's almost as if he's really my husband.* Or else he was just a really nice guy whose feelings Cas hadn't considered before thrusting him into the most awkward situation imaginable. "Yes, darling. Enjoy your snack. I won't be long."

Cas released Rusty's arm—reluctantly, he had to admit—and turned toward Kristof. Of course, since this was Kristof, they didn't have to move away from the crowd to speak privately— the crowd moved away from them, like a wave retreating from shore, bearing Rusty along on its crest.

Once Kristof judged them at a safe distance, he fixed his implacable gaze on Cas. "I'm not certain what you are playing at, Casimir. Mocking the council's orders does nothing but prove we were right in our assessment of your risky behavior. I await your explanation."

Why did I ever think this would be a good idea? Maybe if I throw myself on his mercy now— But then, over Kristof's shoulder, Cas spotted Rusty watching him with concern as he tried to pick up his minuscule food with the hand holding his champagne flute. *Aaannnd there's that courage boost again.*

Cas straightened his spine and smiled blandly at the most powerful vampire on the planet. "But, Kristof, I complied with your instructions. I expected you to be pleased."

"Pleased? That you bring a *shifter* into our midst? Of all the supes in the known multiverse, shifters are the last option for a vampire's mate. *Worse* than the last. The foul stench of their tainted blood—"

"Do you notice any stench here?" Cas caught a glimpse of Henryk eeling his way through the crowd in Rusty's direction. "The only one I detect is from Skalding."

"That is enough. Mr. Skalding has mended his ways, as you should seek to do. He is sublimating his own needs and wishes to the council of his own volition, and is serving us faithfully. Perhaps *service* is what we should have decreed for you rather than matrimony."

Cas smiled tightly. "Indentured servitude? Surely that went out along with involuntary marriages."

Kristof's brow almost wrinkled. "It's not intended as a punishment, Casimir, but as an opportunity for betterment. You are young, the youngest of us." His gaze flickered, his lips tightening. *Probably remembering that there's someone younger now.* "Your own sire did not school you properly after your Turn, through no fault of your own. Despite what you may believe, we *want* you to succeed. Having Supernatural Selection seek an appropriate mate for you seemed the best, most humane solution. He was an ideal candidate. Selected for compatibility, and with his breeding and background, he would have blended in perfectly with our society—and eased your way as well. Why have you flaunted our choice?"

"Well, there was one slight problem with my perfect mate." Cas watched Henryk ease ever closer to Rusty, and his hands curled into fists. "Yesterday, he married somebody else."

Kristof's jaw sagged, his eyes widening. *Holy shit. An actual expression of shock!* Nobody had seen anything more intense than a slight frown from Kristof for decades. "But— But if that's the case, why didn't you inform us?"

"If you recall, you'd given me a time ultimatum. Midnight last night, or face the consequences." He shrugged, although his spine still prickled with alarm as Henryk said something to Rusty that resulted in both of them glancing in Cas's direction. "Rusty is also a Supernatural Selection client. His alleged perfect match married my alleged perfect match. So I guess 'perfect' isn't as absolute as we've always believed."

"But a *shifter*. Surely you could have picked a fae of some description, or—"

"Where would I have found one by midnight last night? I was complying with council orders. If *you* didn't consider the possibility of this kind of mismatch, then I think you'd appreciate my problem-solving ability. Isn't that one of the things you're always saying I lack?"

"I hardly think that allying yourself with an inimical species is an effective way to solve your problem, or to prove to us that your skills in that area are improving. A *shifter*, Casimir. You can't feed from him. You can't even consummate your union without threat of anaphylactic shock from his semen." As Cas opened his mouth to reply, Kristof held up a hand. "Before you say anything, may I remind you that condoms fail."

"I wasn't going to say that." *Yes, I was.* "We didn't activate the consummation clause."

Kristof gripped Cas's wrist, his fingers like steel. "A celibate marriage? Casimir, are you mad?"

"We're not consummating *with each other*, so we chose 'optional.' We've . . . uh . . . agreed to have an open marriage."

Kristof's fingers tightened for an instant, pressing tendon to bone under Cas's skin. "You cannot. Optional consummation refers to optional *with each other*."

It does? "Yes, but—"

"You cannot cheat on your husband with another, even if he agrees, because your contract stipulates that you cannot. Your only alternative is abstinence."

Cas frowned, trying to remember the exact words. "Wait. I'm sure that's not what—"

"We had your interests at heart, Casimir, balanced against the needs of our people. But it was my sincere wish that you be as happy and content as possible, which was why we contracted with Supernatural Selection. Yet again, you have made a bed of your own choosing without forethought." Kristof released Cas's wrist. "This time, however, that bed will be a cold and lonely one. I hope it brings you joy."

Cas flexed his fingers, trying to get blood circulating again. *It won't matter. It's just until the full moon, not forever.* Although it would be a good idea to check the fine print on that contract—if the optional consummation clause meant he couldn't feed from a live host (which so often led to sex), Cas had better make arrangements with the vampire blood delivery service, as much as he hated the taste of refrigerated blood. "We'll be fine."

But as Kristof shook his head and turned away, Cas caught sight of Henryk grinning in the face of Rusty's prodigious scowl. *What the fuck is that asshole saying to my husband?*

Cas dodged one of the council members who was approaching with her mouth pinched in disdain and plunged into the crowd to get to Rusty before Henryk could do anything stupid. Before he'd made it halfway, though, Rusty shoved his empty plate and glass at the hovering waiter and pushed past Henryk.

Cas reached Henryk just as Rusty hit the doors. "What the fuck did you say to him?"

Henryk smirked, and Cas had never wanted so badly to claw that expression off his face—preferably with face included. "I merely questioned whether any mate who truly cared for him would bring him someplace where he was clearly unsuited, unprepared, and uncomfortable—and then leave him alone. He seemed quite struck by the thought."

At least he didn't mention the damn necromancer. "One of these days, you bastard, I'll—"

"You'll what?" Henryk bared his fangs. "Fight me? A duel to the Second Death like in the old days?" He schooled his face into a bland smile for the benefit of a passing council member. "You wouldn't because *they* don't allow it. They don't allow us to do anything nowadays that they indulged in nightly for centuries. We should be able to—"

"Oh stow it, Henryk. I don't have time to listen to your recidivist shit for a second time today. And just so we're clear? Stay away from Rusty."

Chapter Nine

Rusty stormed out of the club, but he must have gotten turned around in the ballroom, because he wasn't in the parking lot. He was at the top of a wide swath of manicured lawn that sloped down to the street. He let his momentum carry him down, even though it was the wrong direction to reclaim his truck and get the hell out of Portland.

He needed to be back in Eugene tomorrow anyway, to get started on the lake house repairs, and the last thing he wanted right now was to be anywhere near Casimir Moreau. Would it have killed him to have given Rusty a clue about what they'd be facing? Gaia, if Rusty wanted to be sneered at and shunned, he could have just stayed home.

"Rusty." Casimir's voice nearly got lost in the windy dark. "Wait up."

"Why?" Rusty called, not stopping. "So you can maybe stick an apple in my mouth and lay me out on the buffet table? Oh wait. There isn't a buffet because none of you eat. Maybe you want me to tap dance. Do a magic trick. Tell a few jokes so your high-toned friends have something to *really* laugh at, or so when they do laugh I can pretend they're doing it because of my wit and charm and not at my expense."

Casimir was suddenly right next to him. "That's not what this was about."

"No? Could have fooled me." He smacked his forehead. "Oh wait. You *did* fool me. Or rather made a fool *of* me. I mean, I know we only got married for the shock value." *I just didn't think* I'd *be the one getting shocked.* "But what exactly were you trying to prove in there?"

Casimir peered up at him, meeting his gaze squarely, his eyes gone muddy yellow in the light of the retro streetlamps. "That I have a right to manage my own life. That the council has no right to deprive me of choice."

"Oh, so that Henryk guy was right. I was just a way for you to thumb your nose at the council. Make everyone gasp in horror at just how far you'd go to tell them to fuck themselves."

Casimir had the grace to look ashamed, his gaze falling to the middle of Rusty's chest. "I'm sorry. I admit that I was thinking more about the effect you'd have on them than the effect they'd have on you."

Effect. That was a good word for it. Like a flashback to every party he'd ever been to from puberty on, once it was clear he'd never shift. "You could have at least warned me that it was a black tie event."

"White tie, actually."

"Not the fucking point!" Rusty swung at a No Parking sign at the curb, connecting with a satisfying *clang*, but his hand caught on a jagged edge and pain lanced through his palm. "Shit."

"Are you okay? Let me see."

"It's all right." Rusty dug in his pocket with his other hand. *Double shit.* No handkerchief. He *always* carried a handkerchief, but he'd been in such a hurry to change into his new clothes. *Pretty funny that I thought I looked so damn good.* Compared to the vampires in their red carpet–worthy duds, Rusty looked like the accountant brought in to count the votes at the Oscars. *No, they wear tuxes too.* The accountant's second-tier mailroom clerk, then. No help for it. Unless he wanted to keep bleeding all the way back to Eugene, he needed to sacrifice his new shirt. He tugged his shirt tail out.

Casimir gripped his forearm. "What are you doing?"

"I need to stanch the blood, and I don't have a handkerchief. Shirt will have to do."

"Will you *please* let me see it? Stop being so stubborn."

Rusty heaved an irritated sigh. "Fine." He held up his palm, and blood trickled down his wrist onto his cuff. "There. Happy now?"

"You are such a—" Casimir grabbed Rusty's wrist, and before Rusty could figure out what was happening, he licked from Rusty's wrist to palm, finishing with a little extra suck against the cut.

Rusty jerked his hand back, but he couldn't break Casimir's iron grip. Talk about *effects*. Casimir's tongue on his skin, the suction as he pulled against Rusty's wound . . . "What the fuck?"

"Vampire saliva has a coagulant. I—" His eyelids fluttered and his knees started to buckle.

Rusty grabbed Casimir's shoulders, steadying him. "Shit, Casimir. I'm a shifter. My blood is poison to you."

Casimir wiped his mouth with the back of his hand. "I . . . forgot."

"You *forgot*? What's *wrong* with you? Wasn't your death wish satisfied by actually, you know, *dying*?"

"Sorry. But you don't *smell* like a shifter." Casimir blinked at him in the amber glow of the streetlight. "I—" He licked his lips. "Is poison supposed to taste this *good*?" He wobbled, and Rusty caught him around the waist as his knees gave out.

"When I said I wanted to kill you, I didn't really mean it. What happens? When a vampire bites a shifter?"

"I don't know."

"Well, *find out*. If we have to pump your stomach, or force a bezoar down your throat, or *whatever*, it would be good to know, don't you think?" Was there a vampire equivalent of an EpiPen? "Fuck. This is *not* what I need tonight." He glanced around wildly, searching for help, but the damn street was deserted. He wrestled his phone out of his pocket while supporting Casimir against his hip. Could the SMTs get here in time? How long would it take for Casimir to die? *Or die again.*

The lights of the college twinkled through the bare tree branches next to the club. *Dr. MacLeod. He's a druid.* And he kept night office hours.

Rusty decided to go for both options. He slung Casimir over his shoulder in a fireman's carry and called the supe emergency line as he hauled ass through the trees and up the path to the Environmental Sciences building.

"Supe nine-one-one. What is the nature of your emergency?"

"Yeah." Rusty staggered up the steps to the door. It was open, thank Gaia. "I've got a vampire here who's ingested shifter blood."

"Is he still breathing?"

Rusty rushed down the hall and around the corner. "I don't think he was breathing *before*. He's a *vampire*."

"Yes. Sorry. What is your location?"

"Off Barnes in Sylvan. Pacific Northwest College of Arts and Sciences, Environmental Sciences building, room 170."

Dr. MacLeod's office hours were posted outside the door. *Good. They're still the same. He should be here.* Rusty knocked, Casimir still slung over his shoulder. No answer.

"Sir?" the operator said. "Sir, are you still there?"

Rusty tucked his phone against his shoulder. "Yeah. Still here."

"Please stay on the line until the SMTs arrive."

"Sure."

Voices were approaching from down a side corridor, and the last thing he needed was to explain why he had an unconscious guy draped over his shoulder. Although Casimir didn't seem to be unconscious. Or not entirely. Was he humming?

And *shit*—was he petting Rusty's ass?

Fuck it. Rusty had installed enough doors and locks to gauge their strength, and this door wouldn't hold up to a shifter's blow.

Laughter echoed in the empty hallway. But it didn't seem to be coming closer. Yet.

He got ready to kick the door in, with a whispered promise to fix it himself tomorrow, when he remembered to try the obvious—he turned the knob.

It was unlocked. *Brilliant.* He slipped inside, careful not to bang Casimir's head against the jamb—although he might rethink that if Casimir didn't stop feeling him up. It was having the expected effect on Rusty's dick, and that was not what their "marriage" was about.

The office was empty. In one way, good—at least he hadn't barged in on a meeting between Dr. MacLeod and a student. The professor's glasses were on the desk, as well as a half-full mug of coffee which was—yep, still warm—so he had to be nearby.

In another way, bad. The SMTs were still a good ten minutes away and Casimir had started to convulse.

Rusty lowered him into Dr. MacLeod's battered desk chair, since it was at least padded, unlike the hard wooden side chairs, which were piled with cast-off clothing anyway. Casimir was so floppy and boneless that he nearly slid onto the floor. The convulsions—

Rusty peered more closely at his face. His pupils were blown and he had a manic smile. Then he giggled.

"Shit, Casimir. Are you *high*?"

He stared at Rusty with wide eyes. "I don't know." Another giggle burbled out of him. "But I know one thing," he whispered "I'm really fucking *hard*."

Rusty glanced down at Casimir's pants. Yep. Major tent pole, right there. Was this how anaphylaxis started?

"Sir? Sir? Are you still there?"

Shit. The emergency line. "Yeah. I am. Do you know what the symptoms are for—"

Rusty's ears popped like the pressure in the room had just changed, and then someone blurted "*Awp!*"

Rusty spun around, and found himself face-to-face with Dr. MacLeod.

A *naked* Dr. MacLeod.

"Hey, Rusty?" Casimir said, sounding like he'd just smoked his third joint of Blue Dream. "I think I'm hallucinating naked guys."

Dr. MacLeod hunched forward, his hands over his groin, and edged sideways to snatch something—which turned out to be his underwear—off the side chair. He nearly toppled over when he got his foot caught in the leg hole, but once he'd pulled them up and grabbed his chinos, he cleared his throat—although he still didn't meet Rusty's eyes. "Rusty. Not that I'm not happy to see you, but what are you doing here at this time of night, and for that matter, how did you get in?"

"The door was open. I'm really sorry, Dr. MacLeod, but it was an emergency. This is Casimir."

Casimir waved, that goofy smile still plastered on his face. "Hi."

"He's a vampire."

"Yes, I can see that. The fangs are rather a giveaway." Dr. MacLeod wrestled himself into a plaid button-down, but halfway through buttoning up—one buttonhole off—he froze, squinted at Casimir, then cursed softly, grabbing his glasses and shoving them on his face. "I recognize him."

"Yeah well, never mind that now. He just ingested some of my blood."

Dr. MacLeod's eyes widened. "You're kidding. And he's still ambulatory?" He motioned Rusty out of the way and knelt next to the chair, placing one palm flat on Casimir's chest.

"Well mostly. I had to carry him from the club next door. The SMTs are on their way but I thought I'd take a chance you'd be here."

"Good thinking." He pulled a set of keys out of his pocket and tossed them to Rusty. "Top drawer of the file cabinet. Black case. Hand it to me please?"

Rusty did as ordered, and Dr. MacLeod opened the case, sorting through a nest of cork-stoppered vials before selecting one. He unstoppered it and held it to Casimir's lips. "Drink."

Casimir frowned and pressed his lips together, turning his head away like a toddler presented with a forkful of spinach. "Don't wanna."

"Casimir." Dr. MacLeod's voice reverberated in the tiny office. *Whoa. Druid power voice.* "Drink. The. Potion."

Casimir's lips gaped like a baby bird waiting for a worm. Dr. MacLeod poured the potion on his tongue, and Casimir's jaw snapped shut, his face screwing up like he'd just sucked a lemon. *"Pfaugh.* Fucking druid poison."

Rusty's belly clenched. *No. Dr. MacLeod wouldn't—* "P-p-poison?"

"No. It's a broad-spectrum neutralizer, to alleviate the symptoms until the SMTs arrive, but it's not calibrated for vampire taste buds. However, I believe Casimir's comment was political rather than factual." Dr. MacLeod shot Rusty a crooked grin. "Vampires and druids have a rather ... complicated relationship."

"Complicated." Casimir snorted, his eyes still closed. "That's one way to put it."

"Indeed. Combining resentment and gratitude can do that." Dr. Macleod set the empty vial on his desk. "Druids and fae rescued the remaining European vampire population after WWI. But they didn't do it for free."

Casimir blinked rapidly and pushed himself up in the chair. "Whoa. Now *that* was a trip and a half." He stared at Dr. MacLeod, his eyes widening. "Oh gods. You're not just a druid." He covered his face with his hands. "You're Mal Kendrick's fiancé."

"Yes, I am." Dr. MacLeod's tone held buried laughter.

Cas peeked at him from between his fingers. "And I tried to hit on him the night you got engaged."

"Yes, you did." He rested one hand, nearly as big as Rusty's, on Cas's forehead. "Unsuccessfully, I might add."

"Yeah." Cas grimaced. "Sorry about that."

"Mm-hmm." He moved his hand to Cas's jugular. "Damn it. I can never judge temperature or pulse with vampires. But you're conscious. And seem to be coherent. So that's a good sign."

"What about my near-terminal embarrassment? Is that a good sign too?"

Dr. MacLeod chuckled. "Sure. You're reacting to stimuli. I'd call that a win."

Rusty sidled up behind Dr. MacLeod, who—now that Cas wasn't comparing him to Mal Kendrick's fae perfection—was seriously hot in his own nerdy way. "Will he be okay, Professor?"

"I haven't treated many vampires, but he doesn't seem to be suffering unduly." He folded his arms. "How do you feel?"

"Fine." *Although I felt better before Dr. Hot Nerd fed me that druid swill. Pfaugh!*

"That's a remarkably unspecific response."

"Well, that's what I've got." Hot *damn* but Rusty's blood had been a rush. Is that why feeding on shifters was a vampire taboo?

No, that couldn't be it. Most shifters stank like a manure bonfire to vampire noses, so they'd never be able to get close enough without retching. Rusty was the only one Cas had ever met who didn't. *Stupid. He's inactive.* Maybe his blood was more like a human's.

But no. That wasn't right either. Cas had tasted hundreds if not thousands of humans since his Turn, and none of them had tasted like Rusty—nor had any of them sent his senses flying.

"Casimir? Casimir!" The panic in Rusty's voice shook Cas out of his reverie.

"What?"

"You kind of went away there for a minute."

"I did?" Cas's nose twitched, a familiar aroma tickling his senses. It wasn't Rusty's spicy, earthy scent that had driven Cas mad on the way here from the club. It was . . . His gaze snagged on Dr. MacLeod's coffee mug. *Coffee. I smell coffee. I haven't smelled coffee in nearly a century.*

"Casimir!" This time Rusty sounded annoyed.

"Don't shout, Elmer. Vampire hearing is very sensitive."

"If it's so fricking sensitive, how come you didn't hear me the last seven times I said your name?"

"Um . . ."

"Mr. Johnson?" A guy in an SMT uniform stood at the door, a gurney and another SMT at his back.

"Yeah, yeah, that's me."

"I'm Ky and this is Pete. Can you fill us in?"

Rusty backed up to let the SMTs squeeze into the room. "That's the patient. The guy in the chair. Casimir Moreau, my . . . my husband. He ingested some of my blood."

"And you're a shifter, right?" Ky edged past Dr. MacLeod and knelt down next to Cas, running the same quick feel-up-the-vitals tests that MacLeod had done.

"Yeah. Beaver. But inactive."

Ky raised his eyebrows, but didn't take his attention off Cas. "Interesting. Mr. Moreau, could you please open your mouth and extend your fangs for me?"

"This is stupid. I feel fine."

"Since I'm here, though, could you humor me? Otherwise my supervisor will be on my ass like you wouldn't believe."

"Whatever." Cas opened his mouth, extending and retracting his fangs three times, just to . . . to do what? Show off? Prove he wasn't impaired? *But I can smell coffee. And Rusty's blood didn't kill me.*

"Well, those are clearly functional, and you're alert—"

"He's gone into a fugue state a couple of times," Dr. MacLeod said. "I dosed him with a druid neutralizer about ten minutes ago."

"That might account for the lapse in attention. Druid potions interact oddly with the undead."

Dr. MacLeod winced. "Sorry. I haven't been doing this long."

"No worries." Ky stood up. "But we'll take him in and have him checked out by a vampire specialist. Mr. Moreau, Pete and I are going to transfer you to the gurney now."

"This is stupid. And I don't need to go to the hospital. I feel fine."

"Sorry, man. The call was logged and we've got to follow protocol." Ky was a cute guy with his high-top fade haircut and wide smile. *Too small and wiry though.* Cas's tastes had just veered toward the big and brawny. *And beaver.*

His partner, another small, wiry guy, shouldered past Dr. MacLeod, and the two SMTs lifted Cas out of the chair.

"I can walk, you know."

They ignored him, as everybody seemed to be doing tonight, settling him on the gurney, the fluorescent lights of the hallway making him squint. Ky raised the side rail with a metallic *clink.* "I'm sorry, but we've gotta put the restraints on too."

Rusty took Cas's hand, and Cas felt it in his belly as well as his fingers. "Is that really necessary?"

Ky smiled apologetically. "Hospital policy for vamps. My hands are kind of tied."

"No," Cas said as Ky snapped the silver-laced cuffs on his wrists, immediately making him feel weaker. "That would be me." At least the chains attaching him to the rails were long enough for Cas to lace his fingers across his belly.

"This sucks," Rusty muttered.

"No, that would be me too, which is why we're in this predicament."

"If you're his husband, you're allowed to ride in the ambulance with him, but—" Ky scanned Rusty as if he were mentally measuring him for a suit "—it'll be a tight fit."

"That's okay. I've got to collect my truck anyway. You taking him to St. Stupid's—I mean United Memorial?"

Ky smirked at Rusty's slip. "Yep. Check in with admitting and they'll get you an escort. The vampire unit is in the secure wing." He tilted his head, glancing between Cas and Rusty as if he expected something. A sign of affection from the concerned spouse, perhaps? True, Rusty had taken his hand before, but Cas was under no illusion that he'd been forgiven for the reception debacle. *Perhaps the sign needs to come from me.*

Cas held out his hand in a rattle of silver chains. "I'm sure I'll be fine, darling. Although I'll feel *much* better once you're with me again." *Although perhaps not as good as I felt before that dratted druid potion. Gods, Rusty's taste . . .*

Glancing furtively at Ky, Rusty fumbled to lace his fingers with Cas's. "Uh, right." He leaned over, and Cas lifted his chin for a kiss. But Rusty veered north and pressed a kiss to Cas's forehead instead of his lips. *Damn it!*

"Don't worry, uh, honey. I'll be there as soon as I can."

Cas fluttered his eyelashes. "You're— You're not mad at me anymore, are you?"

Rusty glared at him, but his lips twitched as if he were trying not to smile. "Believe me, I'm still plenty pissed, and we'll definitely be discussing it later. But more because you could have died before I could get you any help than, you know, the other thing. After all . . ." He did smile this time, although it had a melancholy edge to it that made Cas's chest ache. *Unless that's the after-effects of shifter blood or druid potions.* "I'm used to being the odd one out."

As the SMTs wheeled Cas down the echoing hall, the ache in Cas's chest intensified, and he moaned.

Ky immediately bent over him. "What's wrong? Cramps? Vision going dark? Heart racing?"

No. Just wishing I wasn't such a flaming asshole. "Got anything in your med kit for regret?"

Ky laughed as they hit the doors and wheeled him out into the night. "I wish. Nobody's got a cure for that. But think of it this way." They'd reached the ambulance, and Pete opened the doors. "Regret is kind of like a vaccine to keep you from repeating the same mistakes in the future, right?"

"I suppose."

"Kinda makes you wish time-surfing was a real thing, doesn't it? So we could fix our mistakes in instant replay." The two men lifted the gurney and slid Cas into the ambulance, Ky climbing in after him. "Until then, we'll just have to live with 'em and learn from 'em."

"I've never been particularly good at that."

Ky clapped him on the shoulder as the engine started up. "Who is, my brother. Who is."

Cas fiddled with the edge of the unnecessary blanket covering him. "You realize this is a waste of everyone's time. I was a little disoriented for a while, but—"

"I know. You're fine. How much of Mr. Johnson's blood did you actually ingest?"

"Not much. He'd cut his hand and didn't have a bandage or anything to stop the bleeding. I just wanted to help."

"Uh-huh." Ky opened a locker at the foot of the gurney and took out something that Cas was only too familiar with—a blood test kit. "Let's just cross all our i's and dot our t's then, shall we?"

Cas scowled at the grinning SMT. "You've got that backwards."

"Have I?" Ky crossed his eyes. "You sure about that?"

"Great. A comedian. Just what I need."

"No, what you need is this blood test, so we can speed things along once we get you to the hospital. Finger, please?" Cas flipped him off. "Now, now. I'm just doing my job here."

Cas sighed and offered his hand. At least Ky was quick—a poke and a blot and he was done.

He peered at the test strip. "Hmmm. Your oxygen level and absorption rate look great, even a little on the high side. Had a big meal recently?"

"N—" A warning bell sounded in Cas's brain. "Why do you ask?"

"If you'd fed well and recently, it could insulate you against the effects of the shifter blood, especially if it was a small amount."

"Oh. I'm sure that's it." Except Cas hadn't fed for nearly a week. He should be on the very bottom of the absorption scale.

Ky studied him, his head tilted to one side. "You know, there hasn't been a case of a vampire ingesting shifter blood for . . . well, I don't know how long because it's outside of our recorded medical history. The doctors are gonna be really interested in what you have to say. They may want to run some tests."

"Tests? Forget it."

"Don't you want to know why you're not frothing at the mouth and vomiting up your entrails?"

Cas winced. "Thank you *so* much for putting that image into my head."

"Just sayin'. You're an oddity, my friend. They'll want to know whether it's something about you or something about Mr. Johnson."

Gods, the last thing Rusty needs after what I pulled on him tonight is to have more *people staring at him.* "You know, I'm not sure I had any of his blood at all. The cut was small." *It wasn't.* "And it had mostly stopped bleeding." *It hadn't.* "My last host was a swimmer." *He was an accounting clerk.* "They have crazy good oxygen capacity. Maybe it's just a reaction to that."

"Hmmm. Still trying to skive off the trip to the hospital, eh? I promise we're all nice people. Well, except for Dr. Hyde. Watch out for him."

"Is that another joke?"

"I wish."

"I don't suppose you could just let me out at the next intersection?"

"Nice try, but no."

"But I'm really okay."

"If that's so, they won't keep you long. Just relax. It's still early, not even midnight, but they always prioritize vampire patients so they can get home before dawn. I'm sure you'll be out of there in no time."

"But—" *Wait a minute.* They were taking him to the vampire unit, the one place in the hospital where he'd been banned since last summer, when Henryk's spite and Cas's own negligence had left an innocent person near death. But this time, he had a reason to be here, one the guards couldn't gainsay.

Cas relaxed, not bothering to hide his smile. Tonight, he'd end up where he'd wanted to be since that one dreadful moment under Mount Hood, when he'd finally realized the full extent of Henryk's hatred and thirst for power. Tonight, he would cross the threshold of St. Stupid's at last—for a completely stupid reason, but all the better. He'd be released quickly once they realized he was perfectly fine, and he could somehow make his way to the VICU.

And then . . . *and then.* He could *truly* be free. Released from the sentence of permanent mating. Released from the threat of meeting the sun. Released from his guilt and regret.

Yes indeed. Maybe encountering Rusty had been the luckiest thing that had happened to him since the day he'd served lunch to D.W. Griffith and gotten his first film role. Once in the VER, he'd redirect the doctor's questions, keep Rusty's name out of it, and spring himself from medical captivity in time to sneak into the VICU.

Cas laced his fingers over his stomach, nestled into the pillows, and decided to enjoy the ride.

Chapter Ten

Rusty gnawed on his lip as the gurney disappeared around the corner under the curious gazes of a couple of students. He hadn't taken a deep breath since Casimir licked his palm—and he couldn't completely blame fear for that. *He was hard. For me.* And Rusty had to admit he'd had twinges of his own arousal until flat-out terror had taken care of it.

He turned to Dr. MacLeod, who was locking his office. "Do you think he'll be okay?"

Dr. MacLeod pocketed his keys. "He seemed to be lucid and not in any distress."

"But I thought shifter blood killed vampires."

"As I understand it, it's more of an extreme allergic reaction." Dr. MacLeod regarded Rusty intently as if he could see through his skin—or wanted to. "You're an Inactive. It's possible that the factors in your genetic makeup that prevent your shifts also damp down the allergens in your blood."

"I'm, uh, not sure how I feel about that. I mean it's one thing that *I'm* broken, but to break other people too?"

"You didn't precisely break Casimir, and I wouldn't say you're broken either. You're a fully functioning adult with a large number of supernatural attributes. Shifting shape simply doesn't happen to be one of them." Dr. MacLeod glanced down and noticed that his shirt was buttoned wrong. He fixed it, a blush creeping up his neck under his scruff. "Really, it's surprising that *any* shifter is active. The required DNA combinations are very fragile and subject to damage by congenital or environmental factors."

"I guess."

"This opens up a new testing path for me in the work I've been doing with Alun—Dr. Kendrick, that is—on palliative therapies for Inactives." He patted his shirt placket and looked up. "Do you suppose you and Casimir might be interested in participating?"

"I can't speak for him, but I'm happy to help any way I can. Right now, though, I need to get to the hospital."

"Of course. Would you like me to come with you? Answer any questions that the medical staff might have about the potion he ingested?"

"Would you? That would be great. My truck's this way."

Dr. MacLeod fell into step beside Rusty, and the two of them booked it down the hallway. "I'm actually quite surprised to find you in such close proximity with him, let alone married to him. As I understand it, most vampires find that shifters stink like cow manure steeped in sulfur."

Rusty wrinkled his nose. "Ugh. No wonder they always have that look on their faces. But Casimir said I didn't stink. Maybe that's another thing that's broken—my vampire repellent."

Dr. MacLeod chuckled. "Perhaps. But that seems to be an advantage if the two of you found enough affection and common ground to commit to one another." His voice sounded strained, and when Rusty held the door for him, he was blushing again. "I know how problematic that can be when two species are hereditary adversaries."

"I think it's more that shifters are opposed to being dinner. Especially the smaller species. Too many flashbacks about predators." He led Dr. MacLeod into the sparse woods. "And vampires probably object to dying."

"Yes. There is that, isn't there? But I've had personal experience with the way rumor, anecdotal history, and deliberate information suppression can hide the true source of an interracial conflict." As they threaded through the trees, Rusty noticed that Dr. MacLeod patted all of the trunks within his reach. "Fake news. It's a thing, even among supes. Although it's much easier to bury the truth when there's no written evidence."

Rusty rubbed the back of his neck, glancing sidelong at the professor. "If you don't mind my asking, Doctor—"

"Call me Bryce. Please. You're a colleague. Not an undergraduate."

"Bryce, then. Why were you naked when you showed up?"

Bryce blinked. "Uh . . ."

"And for that matter, where did you come from? I know the door didn't open."

"We need to talk. But—" Bryce slowed as they reached the edge of the parking lot. "I'd . . . ah . . . appreciate it if you didn't mention this incident to Mal."

"Because he doesn't want you flashing your junk at other guys?"

"Because he doesn't like it when I test my hypotheses on myself. That's why I had to try this here rather than at home."

"Try what? And if it's so dangerous, maybe he's right. Maybe you shouldn't do it—whatever it is." Rusty raised his eyebrows. "Er, what *is* it?"

Bryce glanced down, fiddling with one button, then took a deep breath and met Rusty's gaze head-on. "Time-surfing."

Rusty's jaw dropped. It took him a good thirty seconds to come up with something to say. "Fuck me sideways."

A smile glimmered on Bryce's mouth. "No, thank you."

"But—but in all the stories about time-surfers I've heard, they're treated like their own species, like shifters or druids or fae."

"No. They're simply the people who have figured out how to surf time. And are able to do it without irreparable harm to their DNA." He stopped talking when the valet shuffled over and handed Rusty his keys, raising his eyebrows when the guy ambled away. "How'd they know which keys were yours?"

"Take a look at the other cars. I'm the only person at this shindig who looks like he drives a pickup." As they headed for the truck, Rusty turned over Bryce's revelations in his head. "DNA damage, you said? That's not good. I mean DNA mutations are what cause inactive shifters."

Bryce climbed into the cab as Rusty slid behind the wheel. "Yes. That's why I'm conducting my experiments here."

"But . . . but why? If it's so dangerous?"

He stared out the windshield, his expression dreamy, as Rusty started the engine. "My besetting sin—my tragic flaw, I suppose you could say—is curiosity." He met Rusty's gaze again, and the spark, the fire in his eyes was the same enthusiasm that had made his classes so interesting. "I've been a scientist for years, a druid for months, and a dreamer for my entire life. When I discovered that the tales my grandmother used to tell me were true? You can't imagine what that did to me."

Rusty backed up, careful to avoid the fancy vampire-mobiles, and drove out of the lot. "Life-changing, huh?"

"You have no idea. So now, I approach every myth, every legend, every rumor, with the idea that it could be real, and then peel away the inaccuracies until its central truth is revealed in all its amazing, shiny glory."

"Some of those tales aren't all that shiny, you know." Like some of the early ones about shifters. The way the demons had been beaten down and confined to Sheol. The way the djinni had been persecuted and then enslaved for their abilities. "I'd rather they *weren't* true."

"Yes. We're always balancing instructive history with discovery. But—" He turned in his seat to face Rusty, the headlights from passing cars glimmering on his lenses. "After I found out about my heritage, that I'm a supernatural being myself, I went back through Gran's old journals. And I found her descriptions of time-surfing." He grinned. "It's real. I just proved it."

Rusty took the ramp onto I-5. "You went back in time? To what? Some big scientific event? Or political—like to prevent an assassination or—"

"Nothing so dramatic. For one thing, you saw how I was dressed, right?" Rusty nodded. "You can't take anything with you when you surf because you can't take anything that didn't exist at the time you're seeking—although there may be other restrictions related to the molecular displacement . . ." He paused, his eyes going unfocused for a moment before he waved a dismissive hand. "But anyway, showing up at the *Challenger* launch naked wouldn't accomplish anything except horrifying the crowd and getting me arrested."

"That would be a drawback, I guess."

"You think? People fantasize about being able to travel back in time and kill Hitler, or prevent political assassinations, or warn the captain of the *Titanic* to look out for the fucking iceberg. But it doesn't work that way. Uh, Rusty? You might want to slow down. There's no point in beating the ambulance to the hospital after all."

"Sorry." Rusty eased up on the gas. "But time-surfing. It *does* work?"

Bryce nodded. "Yes, although until I found some cryptic notes in Gran's journal, I was convinced it wasn't real."

"Hate to tell you, but most people think *we're* not real."

"Fair point. Time-surfing *is* real, but it's limited. If you think of actual surfing, you're traveling across the water on your board, propelled by a wave, which will eventually break or dissipate. But that wave is local to your beach."

"Um . . . so?"

"If all of time might be analogous to the ocean, say, the time that you or I or anyone can traverse is the equivalent of the waves on the local beach. You can't decide to catch a wave in Waikiki if you're surfing at Rockaway."

"So what you're saying is..." Rusty scrubbed a hand through his beard. "What are you saying exactly?"

"You can only access a point in time that exists within your own lifespan, and around events that have some direct connection to you. Your local beach."

"What made you believe it?"

Bryce hesitated, and Rusty had a feeling that if there had been enough light in the cab, he'd have seen Bryce blushing again. "In Gran's journal, she described seeing me as an adult. Er, naked. So that's where I went. To visit her."

"And you did it? You saw her? What did she do?"

Bryce chuckled. "She told me to put some pants on."

"She told you—" Rusty let out a crack of laughter as he slowed down in front of the hospital. "Listen, I really want to talk to you more about this, but right now I need to get in to see Casimir. But I think Mal is right. Don't do it alone anymore, okay?"

"Very well."

It was only when Rusty pulled into a spot in St. Stupid's parking garage that he realized something. "Uh, Bryce? I'm not sure when I'll be able to leave. I should have thought of that before. I just assumed you'd ride with me, and—"

"Don't worry, Rusty. I'll call Mal and have him pick me up. He'll leap at the chance. He dearly loves making me ride behind him on that stupid motorcycle of his." Although Bryce's tone was tart, his smile was decidedly fond.

Huh. Guess you can care about someone and still be annoyed by their behavior.

"And Rusty?" Bryce gripped Rusty's shoulder. "Don't worry. I'll head over to the medical director's office and let her know the details of the incident, shall we say, discreetly?"

Rusty let out a relieved breath. "Thanks, Bryce. I really appreciate it."

"Anytime."

They parted inside the lobby, Bryce heading to the elevators that led to the administrative wing and Rusty to the admitting desk. He recognized the clerk—Alice was a grandmotherly werewolf who'd been here as long as Rusty could remember.

"Mr. Johnson." She smiled up at him, and then her smile faded. "I didn't know we were expecting you. Your regular blood work isn't scheduled for another month, is it?"

"I'm not here for me. My husband was brought in. I'd like to see him, please."

Her smile bloomed again. "Your husband? I didn't know you'd gotten married."

"Yeah, well, it's new. Just yesterday in fact." Unless . . . was it after midnight yet? It must be, because this day had felt endless.

"Newlyweds. How lovely. Congratulations!" She bit her lip. "Although I'm sure this isn't where you want to spend your honeymoon. What's his name? I'll locate him for you." She turned to her monitor and typed something.

"Casimir Moreau."

"Casi—" Her gaze flew to his, her mouth agape. "But—but Mr. Moreau is a—"

"Vampire. Yes, I know."

"You can't— I mean, the *health* ramifications. For you both. It's—"

Rusty sighed and propped his hands on the counter, leaning in to keep his voice low. "Look. I just want to see him, okay? Can you arrange that, Alice?"

She shook herself as if she were shedding water. "Of course. Forgive me." She typed something else, then her hand disappeared under the desk. "I've called for security to take you down to the vampire unit." She opened a drawer and withdrew a red badge on an alligator clip. "You'll need this."

"Thanks." He attached it to his shirt pocket, then noticed he had blood on his cuff and a little bit of dried blood on his wrist underneath it. *Casimir didn't catch it all.* For some reason, the memory of Casimir's tongue on his skin set off a buzz along

Rusty's veins. *Not appropriate. Not here. Not now. Not ever. That's not what our contract is about.*

Rusty headed for the restroom to scrub his hands before heading downstairs. *Because shifter or not, walking into a vampire ward with obvious evidence of what's in my veins is probably a really lousy idea.*

After the security team at the vampire unit checkpoint waved Ky and Pete through, they took Cas down the elevator to the VER.

Ky grinned at Cas when he unlocked the restraints. "Thanks for not making us initiate the full Van Helsing protocols." He and Pete transferred Cas to a bed in a curtained cubicle.

"Entirely my pleasure, I assure you." Cas rubbed his wrist where the silver had raised a pink rash. "I rarely fly into a psychotic blood frenzy before 3 a.m. at the earliest."

Chuckling, Ky patted him on the shoulder, and the two SMTs left Cas to the mercy of St. Stupid's medical staff, who were apparently in no hurry. Boredom set in, despite all the medical pokes and prods.

Ting ting ting. Cas tapped his fingernail against the bed rail. The nurse, entering something in her laptop, didn't even glance at him. He tried clearing his throat. Still no response. *Screw it.* "Excuse me, I'd like to leave."

She looked up. "Not until the doctor clears you."

"But you've taken three test strips. They were all good, right?"

The nurse—her name tag read *A. Donovan*—closed the laptop and faced him. "They were all excellent. They were all perfect, as a matter of fact. But that doesn't mean the doctor doesn't want to speak with you. The information from the SMTs and the transcript from the emergency call doesn't match your own story of what happened."

He smiled, calling on the epic practice he'd gotten in schooling his expression as an actor and then as a newly fledged vamp trying to lure in his next host. "Who are you going to believe? Them or me?"

She didn't crack an answering smile. "Them." She pulled aside the blue flowered curtain, its rings clattering on its rod. "The doctor will be with you shortly."

Damn it. Nurse Donovan was a tough audience. Witches were like that, just as bad as druids. They had such sticks up their asses—witches about natural consequences, druids about the fucking balance of nature. Neither one of them were fans of vampires in general, since the natural consequence of dying should be, well, death. And every living host who died or was incapacitated for the benefit of the undead tipped the cosmic scales further out of whack.

He wondered if she resented working in the vampire unit. He wondered whether the hospital had resisted installing the unit at all—underground, gated, and guarded, with specialized equipment. It was expensive to maintain for such a tiny patient population.

Luckily, the vampire council had money. Lots of it. And they were quite generous in donations to the hospital—with stipulations.

Tapping the railing, twiddling his thumbs, flexing his feet. Cas couldn't stay still and damn it, he felt fine. He wasn't about to sit around here until the doctor decided to show up. Luckily they hadn't made him change into a hospital johnny, so he slid to the end of the bed and dropped softly to the floor, wincing when the heels of his dress shoes tapped against the tiles.

Nurse Donovan didn't stage an intervention, though, so he crept to the curtain and peeked out. She was at the nurse's station, her back to Cas. He measured the distance between his position and the safety of the elevator vestibule. *I'm a fucking vampire. I've got a stealth mode.* Although he usually didn't make the effort to engage it—Cas's whole life had been about being seen, not being invisible—he could do it when he tried.

He waited until Nurse Donovan opened a cabinet over her computer station, then whisked himself to the elevator in the blink of an eye. Some vampires could do it in less than a blink, but Cas was still young.

He debated calling the elevator—Ky hadn't needed a keycard to activate it after they'd cleared the security checkpoint, and had even joked about the hospital only preventing anyone from going up, as opposed to down to the deeper levels of the vampire unit. But Cas decided on the stairs instead, to avoid the telltale ding of the arriving car and the swish of its opening doors. As he ducked into the stairwell and headed down two flights, past the vampire general floor to the VICU, he extended a claw and ripped the hospital ID bracelet off his wrist.

He eased the door open and peered into the lobby. It was empty, with a nurse or maybe an administrator sitting at a desk, peering at a computer monitor. Behind her were three glass-fronted cubicles, only one of which was occupied, its banks of equipment beeping and flashing. *Drat.* He'd never actually been down here. He hadn't realized it would be so . . . devoid of hiding places.

He approached the desk with his best nonchalant—although vaguely concerned—air. He had no idea if the staff down here had been apprised of who he was and that he'd been explicitly barred from the place, but he didn't have much choice.

She looked up at him and smiled. *At least they don't have my face plastered around down here as public enemy number one.* "Hello." Her voice was low and pleasant. *Another good sign.* "May I help you?"

"Yes. I'm—" Cas clasped his hands together so they wouldn't tremble. "I'm here to see Archie Ellis."

Her smile faltered. "I'm afraid Mr. Ellis isn't receiving visitors. He's—"

"Unconscious. I know. I'd just—" He gestured toward the left-hand cubicle, where a still figure lay under pristine white blankets. "May I just watch him for a bit? Outside the windows of course."

"Well . . ." She glanced back at the window, then down at the red badge the SMTs had clipped to his jacket when they'd dropped him in the VER. "I suppose it wouldn't hurt. He doesn't get many visitors, you know."

"I imagine not."

"Just for a few minutes." She waved him on. "I'll let you know when time's up."

"Thank you."

Cas walked past the desk, his steps slowing to near stop-action speed as he approached the window.

Archie was so still. An IV stand next to him held a bag of saline and another of blood. He didn't need a cannula, of course —he wasn't breathing anymore, his chest unmoving, which was another reason he looked so still. The horrible burns of his first panicked flight into a stray sunbeam still disfigured his face and arms. How long would it take for them to heal? It had been nearly eight months since that day, a day Cas still regretted.

Cas had been so sure Henryk was up to something, something intended to make Cas look bad in front of the council again. Not that it was hard to do. Cas managed that quite efficiently on his own, chafing against the rules the council insisted on, rules that might have been the height of necessity back in the middle ages, but that had nothing to do with the modern world. Hell, half of the council had never even seen a movie. How nuts was that?

Henryk resented the rules even more than Cas did, but he was sneaky about his rebellion—and always managed to frame Cas to take the fall, holding the necromancer blackmail over Cas's head to keep him from telling the truth.

That day, Cas had come better prepared. He'd cultivated the acquaintance of a tabloid photographer, one whose work was skewed toward cryptid hunting. The guy—Matt Steinitz—had published multiple pictures of Bigfoot sightings. Cas lured him in with the promise of a real-live (dead) vampire clinging to the ceiling of a cave under Mount Hood.

Safe in the unrelenting dark, they'd waited, from the wee hours of the night when Cas had led Matt into the warren of caves and caverns, until well into the morning. Cas had started to get sleepy, and Matt had been snoring, their early start and the tedium getting to them both.

Then Cas heard it. A rustle of clothing. A scrape of boot against stone. A stifled moan. He nudged Matt awake, tapping his arm three times with their agreed-upon signal, then positioned Matt's hand in the direction of the noise.

He waited, ears straining, for the perfect moment, the moment when Henryk took to the walls, to roost among the stalactites as he'd bragged about, as he'd claimed *real* vampires ought to do, as if living in comfortable houses with wi-fi and indoor plumbing was somehow a crime against their natures.

"Now!" Cas said.

But the powerful beam of his flashlight and the glare of Matt's own equipment only illuminated poor, bewildered Archie, his features distorted by his Turn. He covered his distended eyes with his clawed hands, scraping his own face, and stumbled away—directly toward the cave entrance, and the deadly sun.

Cas killed the lights.

"Hey!" Matt shouted.

Cas raced with all his vampire speed. But his own vision was slow to adjust and he missed a turn. By the time he corrected, Archie had just stepped into a finger of sunlight and begun shrieking in agony. Cas took him down in a flying tackle, rolling them back into the sheltering darkness.

But the damage was done, to Archie's body and soul, and to Cas's reputation. He'd been unwilling to leave the poor boy, nor to expose him further to Matt's merciless camera. He'd hidden them both, listening to Matt alternately cursing and calling Cas's name as he stumbled out of the cave.

The instant night fell, the council leaders had found Cas sheltering behind a fallen boulder, still cradling a whimpering Archie in his arms.

They'd all assumed he was Archie's sire, demanding *why* Cas had violated the Evacuation Compromise rather than *if* he'd done so. Cas hadn't thought what it would mean when he didn't answer, when he *couldn't* answer, with Archie sobbing against his chest and his own outrage tangling his tongue. The council hadn't even questioned how Henryk had discovered Matt's hastily posted online photograph of Archie mid-Turn. It was so easy for them to believe Cas would follow in his own sire's footsteps that they hadn't found it *at all* suspicious that Henryk was able to lead them straight to the spot.

In a way, Cas was grateful to the bastard. If he hadn't intended to frame Cas, setting him up to be caught with the evidence, so to speak, Archie would have died.

Although looking at him now, with wounds that might never fully heal, Cas wondered whether Archie might not have preferred that. They'd met as Grindr hookups, but Cas had liked him. Had intended to see him again because he was nice as well as beautiful. He'd been an athlete. A star at one of the Oregon universities. An Olympic hopeful in multiple swimming events. They'd called him the next Michael Phelps.

He'd never swim again. And he'd probably never be beautiful either.

There was no way his Turn was voluntary, and Cas had no illusion that Henryk's choice had been random. He'd chosen Archie precisely because there was evidence linking him to Cas.

He's got so fucking much to answer for. And to be fair, if Cas *had* been responsible for this, the council's verdict would have been incredibly lenient.

Cas rested his palm against the glass. "I'm sorry," he whispered.

"You know him?"

Cas turned sharply at the male voice at his shoulder. Another RN, this one male. *J. Derricks*. "Slightly. Has he..." Cas swallowed. "Has he awoken at all?"

Nurse Derricks gazed through the window at Archie. "Once. For a few minutes. But he was in such pain." He sighed. "We put him back into a healing trance."

"Did he— Did he say anything? Call for anyone?"

"No. He cried."

"Because of the pain?"

He looked at Cas like he was an idiot. "Because he wanted to see the sun and we told him the truth."

"Will he get better?"

"We hope so, although his resistance to the Turn is troubling. We'll be reducing the strength of the spell over the next weeks before introducing a host to the environment. Once he senses an irresistible food source, we believe he'll return to consciousness and learn to accept—"

"Casimir Moreau! Step away from that window. Immediately."

Cas whirled to see Kristof, a team of hospital security guards, and hovering behind them, Rusty, of all people.

Cas lifted his hands and backed up. "I wasn't doing any harm. I was only—"

"You are barred from this unit specifically because you're not allowed any contact with Mr. Ellis." Kristof advanced on him, the security guys cracking their knuckles at his back. Really, what did they think they could do that Kristof couldn't? He could probably kick all their asses in ten seconds or less.

"I didn't have contact. I merely observed."

"You are far too inclined to engage in solipsistic hairsplitting, and we have had enough of that. You—"

"Hey." Rusty stepped around the security guards—he was taller than they were, which gave Cas an unexpected ping of satisfaction. "He said he was just observing. Give him a break.

Although—" Rusty narrowed his eyes at Cas "—he really should be upstairs, waiting for the doctor to check him out. I mean, maybe wandering around the hospital is, you know, a side effect of his, uh, condition. He was pretty loopy earlier."

Kristof's silver-eyed glare flicked from Cas to Rusty and back. "You and your . . . husband will wait there—" he pointed at the tiny lobby "—until we have ascertained that Mr. Ellis has sustained no harm. Then you will return upstairs for your own treatment, whatever it is."

"He—"

"Fine." Cas cut Rusty off before he blurted out the damning truth. Until he knew what had happened himself, he didn't want to tell anyone about it. Who knew what it meant? It might just have been a one-time anomaly. And if it wasn't? He'd deal with that when the time came. In the meantime, he refused to think about it.

If there was one thing Cas was good at, it was denial.

Chapter Eleven

Rusty expected Casimir to come to him, but instead he walked right past, his spine as straight as a two-by-four. Rusty caught up with him in one stride, catching his arm. "Casimir. Hold on."

Casimir looked down at Rusty's hand as if it were some kind of alien tarantula. "I would take it as a great personal favor, *Elmer*, if you would stop calling me *Casimir*."

Rusty frowned down at Casimir's averted profile. "But that's your name."

"That's what *they* call me." He jerked his head toward the vampire leader and his security entourage. "Especially when they're getting ready to kick my ass."

"Okay." Rusty was the last person to blame somebody for wanting to go by an alternate name. He let go of Casimir's arm. "What do you want me to call you?"

"Cas. Just Cas." He crossed to the corner of the waiting area and sank down into a chair. "How did they find me?"

"Security cameras."

"But security cameras can't pick up vampire movement. They're not sensitive enough."

"It's a vampire unit, Cas. Don't you think they'd upgrade to equipment that's calibrated for vampires?"

"I suppose." He closed his eyes, pinching the bridge of his nose. "Damn. I should have thought of that."

Rusty took the neighboring chair, peering past the reception desk at the only occupied patient room. "Cas, if you don't mind my asking, who's in that bed?"

Cas twisted his fingers together in his lap. "A young man—or should I say vampire—named Archie Ellis."

"Archie Ellis?" Rusty's eyebrows climbed up his forehead. "There was an Archie Ellis in the engineering school at OSU, but he got recruited for the Stanford swimming program and transferred after his freshman year. But then he disappeared right before the NCAA championships."

Cas flicked a glance at him. "Keep track of your Beavers, do you?"

"He was kind of a big deal. There was a big foofaraw when he disappeared since he'd been up here visiting his family at the time."

"He didn't disappear." Cas's shoulders slumped. "He became a vampire."

"But—but you said you were the last vampire."

"The last one before him. But he's never *practiced*, if you get my meaning. He hasn't been out of this hospital since his Turn, and it's all my fault he's here."

Rusty's stomach twisted, his gorge rising. "Did you . . . *Turn* him?"

Cas snorted a laugh. "No. Not that they'll ever believe me."

"Then how is his condition your fault?"

Cas turned on him, snarling, his fangs fully extended. "Because I decided to pull a thrice-damned *idiotic* stunt to prove to the council that Henryk wasn't as perfect as they imagined. It shouldn't have hurt anybody. It *wouldn't* have hurt anybody if I'd been able to stop the photographer in time. *Mesmer*ize him into forgetting the incident, then present the photographic evidence of Henryk's recidivist habits." He pressed his fingers against his eyelids, and his chest actually expanded with a breath. "I didn't know Archie was there. How could I know? It's against vampire law to create fledglings."

"It is? But I thought—"

Cas winced. "Shouldn't have said that. The moratorium is supposed to be secret."

"Why?"

"What happens with vampire business *stays* vampire business. It's a thing."

"Got it. Don't worry. I won't tell."

Cas studied Rusty, his head tilted to one side. "No. I don't believe you will. Malice isn't really your gig, is it?"

Rusty glanced down the hall at Archie's room, then back at Cas, who'd risked a lot just to visit someone who he felt responsible for. "It's not really yours either."

Cas smiled crookedly. "I do try not to be selfish. When I remember." He traced a pattern on his knee with one finger. "I really am sorry about blindsiding you with the reception. I obviously didn't think it through very well."

"Yeah, well . . ." Rusty shrugged. "We both went into this with that shit-bricking motive, so I suppose I can't be too outraged. Just would have been nice to get a heads-up. Since we're on the same team and all."

"Are we?" Cas's remarkable eyes were hopeful. *So pretty.* "On the same team?"

"Sure. We're married, aren't we?"

For a few minutes, the two of them sat in silence, watching the little clot of people backlit by the medical equipment. Rusty longed to put an arm around Cas. Comfort him somehow. But they didn't have that kind of relationship. Did they?

What the hell. Guess we do now. He laid his arm on the back of Cas's chair, just a little pressure against his back, and his breath hitched when Cas leaned against him, putting his head on Rusty's shoulder.

Archie Ellis. Damn, it was hard to believe. There hadn't been a whisper of a rumor in any of the supe gossip channels. "So Archie. Will he get better?"

"Define 'better.'"

"Will he recover? Get his old life back?"

"You don't 'recover' from vampirism. One of the requirements is death, and last I checked, there wasn't a cure for that."

"Right." Rusty concentrated on the feel of Cas's hair, soft against his neck. "Were you afraid? When you were Turned?"

Cas shook his head, ruffling Rusty's beard. "No. Is that stupid? My sire made it seem so glamorous, so powerful, so *exclusive*. He told me not everyone could be chosen for such an honor." Cas snorted. "He didn't bother to tell me it was also illegal as hell."

"Illegal? For you?"

"Not exactly. My existence was illegal, but he's the one that got sanctioned by the council for the crime." Cas wilted against Rusty, so Rusty tucked him closer. *He's my husband. I can do that.* "Did you know that the entire vampire population used to live in Europe?"

"It's safe to say I know nothing about vampires. Shifter, remember? Not only don't we meet socially, but we pretty much ignore the other race's existence."

"Vampires don't like to travel. Not just because it's difficult, what with the whole can-only-be-out-after-dark thing, but because they're nearly as bad as dragon shifters about their homes, their possessions, their *turf*. They started out in central Europe, and that's where they would have stayed, nursing their own little empires forever. They had wealth, power, social influence—most of them had fucking *castles*, for pity's sake. They'd weathered wars before, even revolutions. But that one—the Great War and its aftermath—where whole countries became spoils of war? That one broke them."

"'They'? Don't you mean 'we'?"

Cas lifted his head and smiled crookedly. "Not me, darling. I'm one of only two American-made vampires." He nestled against Rusty again. "Henryk is the other."

"Ah."

"They refused to see the signs until it was almost too late. Then some of them refused to leave anyway. But others—" he pointed at the cluster of people standing outside Archie's room "—led by Kristof, brokered a deal with the fae to evacuate them through Faerie to America. The only problem with that was that vampires couldn't pass the Faerie threshold without druid magic."

"So the druids outlawed fledglings?"

"Not at first. But one of the earliest émigrés was, shall we say, imprudent and not at all appreciative of his new country's hospitality. He not only Turned Henryk and attacked a half dozen people in a very indiscreet way, he also wrote a letter to the newspaper claiming not to be human. He called himself the Axeman of New Orleans." Cas smiled bleakly. "He was quite the local celebrity. Visibly invisible."

"Shit."

"As you say. The fae . . . took care of him in 1919. That was the birth of the Secrecy Pact, you know. The druids insisted on a fledgling moratorium and the fae required a no-kill policy or the vampires could sit in Europe and rot."

Rusty craned his neck to look down at Cas. "I take it they agreed."

"Not all. They weren't excited about trying to rebuild their lives from nothing in the uncouth New World." Cas smoothed the crease on his trousers with one finger. "But everyone who refused was . . . eliminated by the newly elected council."

"Gaia," Rusty muttered, studying Kristof's pale profile. "Did they . . . um . . . eliminate your sire too?"

"Not at first. They just gave him a stern warning—seconded by the druids—and monitored his activities rather casually. But in 1947, he kicked over the traces in a very shocking way."

"What did he do?"

"I'd rather not say. But look up the Black Dahlia murder if you want the details." Cas folded his hands on his knee. "They staked him for it. Although I was never sure whether it was the murder they objected to or the fact that he taunted the police and thereby threatened the Secrecy Pact."

Rusty ran his hand up and down Cas's arm. "Do you think Archie chose to Turn?"

"What do you think? He was a swimmer. A champion. An Olympic contender. That's not something you can do when you're undead."

Anger swirled in Rusty's belly, and he tightened his grip on Cas's arm. "You mean he was turned against his will?" Cas nodded. "Who?"

Cas glanced at Czardos. "Henryk. He knew I'd fed from Archie, and he set me up to take the fall."

"What would be the point of that?"

"Henryk and I have been rivals since my Turn. I'm not sure why it started, whether he resented that I didn't lose my sire immediately, or because my First Life was more privileged than his. Our own little vampire class war. He's framed me for things before, but in the past few years, it's escalated."

"You think he wants to . . . to eliminate you?"

"No." Cas's tone was uncertain. "I don't think even he could pull that one off. The council doesn't like to exterminate vampires, except under extreme circumstances, since there are so few of us left. Consider my own sire, and Henryk's. They both had to do something completely egregious, including threatening supe exposure, before they got shut down. Fledgling and sire would be safe, even if the sire was punished. And said sire—definitely *not* me—would have something none of the currently surviving vampires have."

"You're kidding. *None* of them have fledglings?"

"The old master vampires were very territorial. They didn't allow their fledglings to make fledglings. None of the old masters emigrated, with the resulting consequence." Cas's shoulder moved under Rusty's arm. "Ergo, with the moratorium, there are no more masters. Going by my own feelings, I suspect the others rather enjoy their independence."

Rusty folded his arms, studying the group across the room. "What happens when Archie wakes up?"

Cas smiled grimly. "What I *hope* happens—and within the next two weeks—is that he tells the council I didn't Turn him. That way, my mandatory marriage sentence will be dismissed and Henryk will be outed as a conniving bastard. But right now, he's the council's white-haired boy and I'm the black sheep." He frowned down at his hands. "I probably made everything worse by coming down here. They'll think I was trying to exert a sire's influence over Archie. Force him to incriminate somebody other than me. So even if he tells the truth now, they might not believe him." Cas threw himself back in the chair. "*Fuck.*"

"So why *did* you come down?"

"I wanted to see how he was doing. If he'd woken up and said anything to the medical team."

"And had he?"

"No. He was conscious briefly. But he just . . . cried."

Rusty's heart squeezed in his chest. Shit, what a mess. "So they're blaming you."

"Yes."

"And you feel really bad about it."

"You think? I mean, I've pulled some stupid shit in my day, but I've never done something like this." He scrubbed his hands over his face. "As the council frequently tells me, I'm a disgrace, an embarrassment, and a disaster waiting to happen."

"Seems a little harsh. Haven't they ever done anything stupid?"

"If they have, they're not telling."

"Trust me, everyone does boneheaded shit."

Just then, Czardos came striding over to them. "You are incredibly fortunate, Casimir, that the nursing staff can vouch for you having no contact with Mr. Ellis."

Cas put on that arrogant expression he'd worn when Rusty had first seen him at Supernatural Selection. "Lucky me."

"Your actions in the past few days have not supported your claims of innocence. If you were serious about making amends, you wouldn't have flaunted our orders so flagrantly. If—"

Rusty stood up. "Sorry. I'm afraid you'll have to catch up with my husband later. Cas here needs to go back upstairs and check in with the doc up there. Cas?" He held out his hand, and Cas took it, bemused. "If you'll excuse us?"

Rusty led Cas to the elevator, expecting Czardos to sic the security guards on them at any time. But when they stepped into the car, the vampire leader was still staring at them, stone-faced.

As the doors slid shut, Cas turned to Rusty. "What did you just do?"

Rusty shrugged. "You don't need to stand around here and get shade thrown on you by these assholes. Let's get you checked out and I'll take you home."

The trip back to the VER didn't take long, thank the stars. Although it wasn't the stars he should thank, apparently, but Bryce MacLeod.

The VER doctor peered at the results of yet another blood strip. "You seem perfectly fine now. Dr. MacLeod explained that the discrepancies in the earlier accounts were the result of your husband's unfamiliarity with the symptoms of oxygen depletion."

"He did?" Dr. MacLeod was not an average druid.

"Yes. I'd advise you not to abstain so long between feedings in the future." The doctor signed Cas's discharge paperwork just as they paged him over the intercom. "I've got to go. Give this to the guard at the checkpoint on your way out."

Cas returned to the waiting area, which was empty except for Rusty. He was leaning against the counter over the admitting station, chatting with the clerk, both of them laughing about something. As soon as Rusty saw Cas, though, he straightened up.

"Hey. All set?"

"Yes. I shall live—more or less—to die another day. Or night, as it were."

Rusty's brows drew together—not a full on frown, but *concern* maybe? Annoyance? Who knew? "Right." He patted the countertop. "See you next time, Fran."

"Take care, Rusty. Don't forget to leave your badges at the checkpoint." She waved to them as Rusty punched the elevator call button.

"You two seemed cozy."

"She's usually stationed upstairs in the lab, so I see her every month."

"Every month? What for?"

He shrugged. "Blood work."

Cas's fingers tingled and his middle tightened. "Are you sick?"

"Nah."

"Then why do you have to get regular blood work?" Cas licked his lips. *Don't think about blood.* "That's a little invasive, isn't it?"

"The shifter councils are still freaked out about that inactive werewolf who attacked Dr. Kendrick's office manager. They put a lot more controls in place to make sure we don't all go off the rails." Rusty rubbed the back of his neck. "And I, um, may have had an extreme reaction when Fletcher told me he was marrying somebody else."

"'Extreme'?" Cas's grin exposed both fangs, but who cared? "You? What did you do?"

"I'd rather not say."

"Oh, come on, Rusty. You can't really be as boring as you seem."

"Boring? You think law-abiding is boring?"

"Well. Yes." Cas nudged his shoulder. "What's life without a little risk to spice things up? Come on. You know my most shameful secret."

Rusty looked at him with those serious dark eyes, and Cas wanted to squirm, but that would be unbecoming for a vampire. *And that's stopped you when?* "I don't think I do. But that's beside the point. It's embarrassing."

"Oh if it's just *embarrassing*, then you have to spill." The elevator doors slid open and Rusty held them for Cas to enter. "Rusty? Give."

Rusty waited until the door shut, then his shoulders lifted in a sigh. "I took a sledgehammer to the walls in his bedroom."

Cas's jaw dropped. "You did what?"

"I took—"

"I heard what you said, I just can't believe it. Was he in the bedroom at the time? Please tell me he was in the bedroom. Preferably in bed. Naked."

Rusty's lips twitched as if he were about to smile, but he pressed them together, nostrils flaring. "Why is that important? It has nothing to do with the destruction."

"Who cares? It makes a better mental picture. It'd be a *great* scene in a movie."

"As a matter of fact, nobody was in the room. Or the house. New construction. It was the house I was building for—for—" He hung his head.

Cas's heart—such as it was—pinched. "For the two of you?"

Rusty nodded. "It was supposed to be a wedding present."

"A surprise?"

"No. He knew about it. Earl—his father, the clan leader—bought the lot for us. Well, for him."

"And they let you build the house thinking it was for both of you? What kind of assholes are they?"

Rusty smiled wryly, although he didn't lift his gaze from his boots. "The assholes who run the clan. Who have to consider the clan's good. Needs of the many and all that."

"Bullshit. They can wheel and deal in all the politics they want. It doesn't give them the right to make you think you were building your own house."

"To be fair, I think Earl probably believed Fletcher had told me before construction ever started. The match was arranged almost a year ago. They just didn't announce it until the engagement party last month, and Fletcher was never openly affectionate to me in front of his dad. Or anyone, for that matter."

The elevator reached ground level—finally. Why was the thing so slow? And why wouldn't the damn doors open?

Cas punched random buttons until Rusty caught his wrist, brandishing his red badge.

"Stop trying to break the elevator panel. There's an exit spell." Rusty tapped his red badge against the sensor, and the doors slid open. "See?" He stepped out. "Now you."

"Wonderful. It's like a vampire roach motel. We can check in, but we can't check out without fucking permission." Cas smacked his badge against the card reader, then stalked out to toss the damn thing to the bored guard at the checkpoint. His heels struck the tile with extra force as he strode across the lobby toward the parking lot.

"Cas. Hey. What's the hurry?"

Cas stopped as the lobby door whooshed open, letting in a blast of chilly air from outside. He checked over his shoulder— he'd outpaced Rusty, despite the man's mile-long legs. He'd just been—

Angry.

Yes, angry. He never got angry anymore. Anger could be deadly for a vampire because it interfered with their control, which led to bad choices. Even when Henryk had baited him— time and again, year after year, decade after decade—Cas had never let himself get truly angry except over Archie.

But that some asshole would let a man like Rusty—and even Cas, with his questionable morals, could tell that Rusty was a good man—build a *whole fucking house* believing that he'd be living in it with the love of his life, knowing that it would never happen?

Cas wanted nothing more than to face down this *Fletcher* asshole and show him what *bad decisions* were really about.

They reached Rusty's truck, and Rusty held the door for Cas to climb in. He circled the front of the truck while Cas was still fuming, then climbed in and started it up. "I'll drop you at your house. I promised Fletcher I'd start on the repairs tomorrow. Or today, I guess, since it's past midnight. He wants them done ASAP, but I'm aiming for the rehearsal dinner a week from Saturday."

"The rehearsal dinner. Don't you need your husband on your arm for that?"

Rusty smiled crookedly, his usually ruddy complexion greenish in the dashboard light. "I didn't really hold up my end of the bargain tonight. So don't feel obligated. I'll manage on my own."

"Nonsense. A Moreau always keeps his promises."

Rusty cut a glance at him as he took the ramp onto the Morrison Bridge. "Really? Is that your family motto?"

"I have no idea. *Moreau* isn't really my name anyway. The studio thought fans would be confused by *Mateusz*, so they changed it for me. It seemed as good as any other, since I had no remaining relatives to object." He grinned at Rusty. "And it means I can make up my own family mottos."

Rusty chuckled, as Cas had hoped. "That could be fun. 'A Moreau always comes out swinging.' 'A Moreau never wears brown shoes with black pants.'"

Cas rested his hand on Rusty's shoulder. "A Moreau never lets a friend face an enemy alone."

"I wouldn't call them enemies, precisely."

"Really? I would." He squeezed Rusty's shoulder and then let it go. "And much to my surprise, a Moreau never lets a friend repair drywall on his own. I'm afraid I've cultivated a deserved reputation for being decorative rather than useful, but I could probably wield a paintbrush or a Shop-Vac. Do you need any help?"

Rusty smiled for real this time. "Thanks. I'd like that."

"That's settled, then." Cas peered out the window at the dark. "It was barely two when we left the hospital. We have time to stop by my house, let me pack for a few days, and still make it to Eugene before dawn."

Rusty glanced at him worriedly. "Yeah. Dawn. That's gonna be a problem for you, right? Don't vampires conk out during the day?"

"We ordinarily sleep—when we *do* sleep, which isn't as necessary as it is for the living—during the day because we can't *go* anywhere, and daytime television before cable sucked." Although Cas had gotten quite involved in *Guiding Light* back in the fifties. "If we haven't fed in the last week or so, we get sluggish and drowsy anyway, so why not? Boredom sets in and a stretch of unconsciousness, free from deciding what to do next, is a relief."

"Okay. But sunlight. That's a no-go, right?"

"Sadly, yes. It's so inconvenient."

"Hmmm." Rusty tapped his steering wheel with one thumb. "The lake house has vampire-grade blackout shades on all the windows—that's standard for any Johnson Construction project—but it doesn't have any furniture to speak of. There's an air mattress that I used to catch a nap sometimes when I was working late or—" He cleared his throat and suddenly became very interested in the street signs.

"Don't tell me your asshole ex actually had sex with you. In that house. Without telling you it wasn't yours."

"We, ah, might have done. Once or twice. Or more."

Anger surged again, heating Cas's blood. "When was the last time?"

"Kind of a personal question, don't you think?"

"*Elmer.*"

Rusty sighed. "Fine. The day before the engagement announcement."

Red tinged Cas's vision, turning the landscape stark and flat. *Is that still anger or—gods forbid—jealousy?* Perhaps a little of both. He closed his eyes and tried to exercise some hard-won control. He wasn't particularly successful. He was still angry. Still jealous. But at least he wasn't about to punch out the window of Rusty's truck. "Well." He unclenched his fists, finger by finger. "I hope you washed the sheets."

Rusty cracked a laugh. "You are— I don't know exactly *what* you are, Cas."

"A vampire?"

"We're not only our natures, you know. But *I* know I've never met anyone like you."

"Trust me, Rusty, that's a very good thing."

Conversation fizzled after that, and they were both silent— although not uncomfortably so—until they pulled into Cas's driveway and Rusty stopped the truck in front of the gate.

"Should I park out here?"

"The gate code is three-two-six-four."

Rusty rolled down his window and punched in the numbers. "Three-two-six-four. FANG? A little obvious, isn't it, Cas?"

"*You* wouldn't have guessed it."

"Probably not." Rusty pulled through the gate after it swung open, silent as the grave (so to speak). "Nice tech. Who'd you get to install it?"

"A supe security firm. They handled the light-blocking protocols and my panic room too."

"You have a panic room?"

They both climbed out of the truck, and Cas led the way to the front door. "All vampires have a panic room. In case, you know, the house should suddenly be consumed by alien locusts and possibly expose our fragile flesh to the sun."

"Cas." Rusty's tone held reproach—although Cas dared hope it was edged with affection, not resignation. *He knows me too well already. Certainly better than the council, despite nearly a century of opportunity.* The least Cas could offer in return was a de-escalation of snark.

"What can I say? The Great War and near-extinction made cowards of us all." He paused on the front steps and cleared his throat. "Thank you, by the way. For standing by me tonight, even though I was a complete dick to you about the reception."

Rusty shrugged. "That's okay. If I had a chance to score off Fletcher, I'm not sure I'd have been able to resist it myself." His eyes, already a deep brown, darkened. "They had no call to treat you like that. Like an embarrassment. Like a liability. Believe me, I know what that's like, and it sucks."

"Yes. Yes, it does, doesn't it?"

Rusty smiled then, his lips a perfect crescent, his eyes crinkling at the corners. And Cas couldn't help it. As if Rusty were a magnet to Cas's cold lonely steel, he leaned forward and kissed Rusty's delectable mouth, his lips so soft, his flavor delicious under the slight flick of Cas's tongue.

Rusty moaned, angling his head, and for an instant, it was perfect. The way they fit, the way Rusty's heat met Cas's coolness.

Then Rusty broke away, backing up so Cas practically fell forward off the steps. "Sorry. I'm sorry. I shouldn't— The whole poison thing."

Cas touched his tingling lips. "No, my dear. It is I who am sorry. I should have asked rather than imposing on you with yet one more thing."

He turned to the door, digging in his pocket for his keys, but Rusty was suddenly *there*, a warm wall behind him, his fingers gripping Cas's wrist gently.

"Casimir. You need to listen to what I'm about to say."

Cas nodded, his gaze riveted by Rusty's fingers ringing his flesh, the flash of gold on his ring finger. "I'm listening."

"You're beautiful. And funny. And surprising. But I will not endanger your life. I'd like nothing more than to kiss you, but I'd want more then. And I don't know what's safe."

"You don't have to make excuses. I'm—"

"Stop. You're incredibly sexy when you're not trying to be a jerk on purpose." Then Rusty brushed Cas's hair away from his neck and his lips were there, warm—almost hot—against Cas's skin. And oh gods was that his tongue tracing the vein under Cas's ear? "But you're a vampire. I'm a shifter, even if I am a broken one. We can't go any further without hurting you. And I won't do that. Not ever. Besides, this is a temporary marriage. A fake marriage. No consummation, remember?"

"I believe it was consummation optional, but I take your point." Cas leaned against Rusty for a second, allowing himself a moment of weakness. "Thank you." *But I'm going to do everything I can to get you to take a risk or two.* Because if the bulge pressing against Cas's ass right now was any indication? It would totally be worth it.

Chapter Twelve

Damn that consummation loophole anyway. Rusty lurked in Cas's unused kitchen, hands in his pockets, trying to convince his erection to stand down. There was no way Cas could have missed it, since it had done its best to lead the way into the house. *Into Cas.* Rusty gritted his teeth. *Not going to happen.*

Cas disappeared down the hall. "I won't keep you long."

Don't say "long." Rusty propped his hands on the counter, head down, and breathed through his nose. The front of his fancy-ass dress pants—which had been about sixty times *less* fancy-ass than anyone else's at the party tonight, including the valets—didn't do as good a job at keeping his dick under control as his usual jeans.

But then his gaze snagged on the blood edging his shirt cuff.

Cas could have died.

That settled things *down under* PDQ.

What a difference forty-eight hours could make. Two days ago, Rusty wouldn't have given a shit if all the vampires on the planet disappeared. Frankly, he wouldn't have noticed, since vampires and shifters did *not* intersect, and for good reason. Hard to like somebody when the whole time you were talking to them, their nose was scrinched up like you smelled worse than an open sewer.

Thing was, when you thought of people as nothing more than a group, a herd, a mob with similar characteristics instead of as individuals, it was easy to fall into asshole behavior. *All vampires are elitist snobs. All vampires are bloodthirsty psychopaths.* Or *All shifters stink like an open sewer.* It definitely went both ways.

When he'd sat across the lobby from Cas at Supernatural Selection, all he'd wanted was for the annoying guy who was obviously judging Rusty from his beard to his boots to GTHA— get the hell away.

But now? Cas was a person. A person with flaws, sure. A person who, without warning, had exposed Rusty to the kind of public humiliation that was all too familiar. But then he'd apologized. *And felt me up.*

Was that why Rusty was having these . . . these . . . *feelings*? Because he hadn't had sex with anybody since before Fletcher's engagement announcement, and Cas had *touched* him and then kissed him, despite the enmity between their species?

Or was it the look on Cas's face when they'd been in the hospital? His regret, his self-recrimination, his devastation at Archie's condition, at the way that Czardos dude treated him?

Rusty wasn't the only one fighting prejudices. Sure, Cas might have done some things in the past to warrant his reputation, while Rusty had done nothing but get born, but still. Cas said he hadn't done *that thing*, that really horrible thing, and Rusty believed him. Because one thing Cas had never done—as far as Rusty could tell—was lie.

He didn't always deliver the *full* story—witness the significant missing information about the reception—but he didn't try to replace the real story with something else.

He didn't *redirect* like Fletcher did—simply skirting the issue and pretending the decision he didn't want to make was all the other party's fault.

If Rusty had asked for more information, would Cas have given it?

Yeah. Yeah, I think he would have.

Cas deserved to have the vampire council believe him about his innocence. Of course, before they could believe him, they had to *ask the fucking question*. And from what Rusty had seen, they were all about assumptions and appearances. That smarmy Henryk guy was a case in point. He was like that Wormtongue guy in *Lord of the Rings*, pretending to tell somebody something for their own good, but really serving his own long-view agenda.

And *damn*. When it came to *long view*, nobody could beat vampires. *Death* didn't even stop them.

The tiny splotch of blood on his cuff caught his eye. *Cas could have died for real.* He rolled up his sleeve so he wouldn't see the evidence of the most terrifying moment since his first swim as a kit, when he hadn't shifted like the others and had flailed around in the water, forgetting all about the swimming lessons they'd all endured—whining—since before they could walk.

He visited the bathroom, and when he emerged, Cas was in the living room with a rolling suitcase and a garment bag. He'd changed out of his tux, but his jeans had to be a designer brand, and his sweater looked so soft that Rusty's fingers twitched with the urge to touch.

"You, uh, won't want to paint in clothes like that. They're bound to get trashed."

Cas glanced down at himself and shrugged. "Eh, I've got some other stuff in the bag, but it doesn't really matter." He grinned. "I can always paint naked."

Rusty ran a hand over his face, ending by tugging on his beard. Hard. "Casimir. You're killing me here."

Immediately, Cas turned serious. "I'm sorry. I don't mean to make you uncomfortable." He gazed up at Rusty from beneath his brows. "Well, mostly. But we've got two weeks until we're locked into our *long-term*—aka, *for-freaking-ever*—marriages, so I'm just saying—if you want to have a little fun, where's the harm? It may be temporary, but our mating contract is still binding."

Right. Temporary. Don't get attached. "Just get in the truck, Cas. We need to get to the lake before dawn."

Cas gave him another cheeky grin before sashaying out the door, trailing his suitcase in a purr of high-end casters. Rusty tried to relieve Cas of the luggage to stow it in the truck, but Cas wouldn't let go.

"Elmer, need I remind you that I'm a *vampire*? My strength is the strength of ten ordinary humans."

"Yeah." Rusty wrested the case out of his hand. "But my strength is the strength of a shifter." He tossed the bag in the rear of the cab. "So suck on that."

"I'd like to suck on something," Cas muttered as he hung his garment bag on the hook inside. "Someday, we're having an arm-wrestling contest, and I'm giving you fair warning." He paused with one foot on the running board. "I will wipe the floor with you, Mr. Beaver."

Rusty grabbed the door handle as Cas settled himself in the cab. "Is that so? Know what I say about that, Mr. Bloodsucker?"

"What?"

"Bring it." Rusty slammed the door on Cas's laughter and circled the truck to climb in the driver's door. The gate opened smoothly behind them as he backed the truck onto the road.

Cas patted the dashboard. "So. This is one big honkin' truck. I'd ask if you were compensating for something, but based on earlier evidence from this evening, I know that's not the case."

"Yeah. Um. Sorry about that. Didn't mean to be inappropriate."

"The only thing *I'm* sorry about is that we didn't take it further. But let's leave that behind us, shall we?" Cas muttered something else about *behind* that Rusty didn't catch. "Tell me a little more about where we're going."

"It's a lake in the hills west of Eugene. The clan owns the land, but the idea is that the property is held in trust for its members. Any of us can visit whenever we want. There's a communal lodge. But likewise, any of us can purchase a lot for our own use."

"Which is what— What's the leader's name again? Duke?"

"Earl."

Cas snapped his fingers. "I *knew* it was some sort of lesser nobility."

Rusty cast a sidelong glance at him as they merged onto the 405, but Cas was looking out the window, so Rusty couldn't tell if he was sporting his usual smart-ass smirk. "The lake's a big place, and the clan isn't large. There's still plenty of open plots."

"But now the one you wanted is taken."

"Actually, no. That spot isn't my favorite. The one I'd have picked—the one I still plan on buying someday—is about a third of the way around the lake, on the north side. I can situate a house there so it gets light all day, plus great sunrise and sunset views." Cas made a noncommittal grunt. *Ah shit.* "Sorry. I guess natural light isn't something you want to think about."

"I can't experience it, no, but the mere thought of it doesn't send me into a maidenly swoon, so you may wax as rhapsodic as you like about your future housing plans."

Rusty took the ramp to I-5 south. "That's the thing. I'm not sure when that'll be. Ted—the guy I was supposed to marry—has a cabin in the Coast Range. It's next to a lake too. I think his idea is that we'll live up there, at least at first. I'm taking a month off from my business as kind of a honeymoon/adjusting period. Although since the wedding is delayed, I won't have quite as long."

Cas was quiet for a long time, until they reached Woodburn. "Are you sorry? That you have to spend the time with me instead?"

Rusty whipped his head to the side, but Cas was staring out the window at the outlet mall. *Kinda doubt he's all that interested in the Eddie Bauer store.* "No." Rusty returned his attention to the nearly empty road. "I'm actually okay with this. I mean, the reasons we went into it are kinda sketchy. But you're an okay guy, Cas." Rusty poked him in the arm. "Even if you are technically dead."

"You're a laugh riot, Elmer," Cas said, his voice dry.

"That's not something anyone's ever accused me of before."

"Really? Why? Your supply of comedy material is limited because rude beaver jokes are off the table?"

"You're the one who told me I was boring." *Stable.* Gaia, he was as exciting as a dentist's office.

"Yes, I did, and I'm sorry for it. Clearly anyone who'd take a sledgehammer to his asshole ex's bedroom walls—after having *just finished them*—is very far from boring. Whacko, maybe," he said, his tone sly. "Perhaps borderline psychopathic. But not boring."

And even though Cas was probably just being polite—assuming anything connected with Rusty's rampage could be considered polite—it warmed Rusty's heart. Somebody saw him as exciting. Even if it wasn't true.

"I'll remind you that you said that after three days of watching mudding compound dry."

"What was it you said earlier? Oh yes. I remember." Cas settled back against the seat. "Bring it."

It took them another two hours to reach the lake. They pulled into the gravel drive next to the dark bulk of a house at a little after five. *Thank the stars it's November.* If it were June, dawn would already be threatening on the horizon. But this close to the solstice, they had another hour or two before Cas had to retreat to the nearest black box.

In the meantime, he climbed out of the truck and wandered down a slope of draggled grass until he could see the lake. Even under the wan starlight, the water sparkled in his enhanced vision. A boathouse stood next to a pier, and several similar structures dotted the edge of the lake as far as he could see.

"What kind of boat does the evil ex have?"

Rusty's steps crunched in the gravel behind him before being muffled on the grass until Cas felt his warmth—that furnace-blast of heat—at his back. "None."

"Why not?" Cas moved sideways so he could look up at Rusty's profile. "Still trying to scope out what the neighbors are floating so he can one-up them?"

Rusty nodded at the next boathouse along the shore. "None of those are for boats."

"Seriously? Why have a boathouse, then?"

"That's where we—they—shift before they go into the water. They keep towels, extra clothes, even TVs and refrigerators sometimes." He grinned down at Cas. "There's enough room inside them that if beaver instinct suddenly gets to be too much, they can build a reasonable-sized lodge." He tucked his hands into his pockets. "That's usually what the kids do while the adults watch TV and drink beer."

"So what you're saying is . . . beaver kids build their own tree forts."

Rusty laughed, just as Cas had intended. "I guess they do. Although rather than building the fort *in* the tree, they use the trees—or parts of them—to build the fort in the water." He jerked his head toward the wide porch on the front of the house. "You want to look around out here while I make sure the house is sunproof for you?"

"No. I'll come in with you." He faked a shudder. "The wide-open spaces. Brrr. It's enough to give a fellow claustrophobia."

Cas followed Rusty up the broad porch steps. He paused for a moment to look back over the lake. The view here would be stunning when sunlight gilded the water or tipped the fir trees on the hills. *Stunning for anyone who could still see the sun, that is.*

He hurried through the door in Rusty's wake and closed it behind him—only to be faced with another panoramic view past the deck outside the French doors off the great room. He was tempted to sigh, because the house was so clearly not meant for anyone with light sensitivity. But he didn't waste the effort, because *of course* it wasn't. The house wasn't for him—it wasn't even for Ted, Rusty's perfect Supernatural Selection mate.

It's for an asshole who doesn't deserve him in a million years.

Cas wandered across the gleaming hardwood floors, past a fieldstone fireplace with an oak mantelpiece. This wasn't any slapdash construction job. The crown and base molding was reminiscent of early Craftsman houses—as Cas had reason to know, since he'd been born in one, back when birthdays had meant something to him.

"Your company built this place?"

Rusty joined him in the middle of the echoingly empty room. "Yup. Although I did most of the finish work myself. I wanted to—" He shrugged, his cheeks ruddy above his beard. "Never mind."

Cas wrapped a hand around Rusty's arm. "You thought it was going to be your home. You wanted to be a part of it in a more personal way. I get it."

Rusty looked down at him. "Do you?"

"Mm-hmm. That's also why you went all *Thor: Ragnarok* on the bedroom walls, I bet. He didn't deserve a personal gift from you."

Rusty shook his head. "I shouldn't have done it. Even though it wasn't gonna be *my* home, it was still a Johnson Construction project. I thought I had more pride in my work than that."

"Pride *always* takes a back seat to heartbreak, darling. No need to be ashamed."

Cas wandered through the kitchen—not his favorite room in a house, usually, since he had no reason to be there. This one, though, looked like a place you'd want to hang out even if you had no excuse. The big center island was obviously meant as a gathering place, with a bar-height counter on two sides.

Rusty followed him in. "Since the appliances at your house have never been used, I'm guessing you don't spend a lot of time in the kitchen. Can you— That is, *do* vampires eat anything? Anything other than . . . you know."

"Other than the hot, thick blood coursing through throbbing human veins, you mean?"

Rusty gave him a cheeky smile. "I wouldn't have put it quite that way."

"It's what you were thinking though."

"You're not getting me to admit that, one way or another."

Cas chuckled. "We prefer arteries anyway. More oxygen content." He paced around the island, trailing a finger along the smooth counter. "Granite?"

"Recycled glass. You're avoiding the question. Does it make you uncomfortable?"

"No. But it does make me a little . . . nostalgic. Our sense of smell changes when we're Turned, optimized for identifying, well, *prey* to put it bluntly. We *can* eat, although we don't absorb any nutrients, and since without a functioning sense of smell, we can't really taste anything, there's not much point."

"You really can't smell anything?"

"Our olfactory nerve is very practical. Nothing that doesn't serve survival. All those other frivolous things—like the smell of flowers or a seductive perfume or the aroma of a decent bourbon—are inconsequential, so it seems they were prioritized right out of the species." He finished his circuit of the island and walked his fingers up Rusty's chest. "On the other hand, I can smell a shifter from ten paces." He gazed up into Rusty's eyes. "Everyone but you."

Rusty cleared his throat and edged away. "That's good, I guess. Since we're stuck with each other for a while."

Temp-or-ary, Casimir. Don't hit on the possibly poisonous guy who's getting married to somebody else in two weeks. "Do you mind if I look around?"

Rusty gestured expansively. "Be my guest. Not much to see."

Cas peeked into a room that was probably going to be an office. "So why *is* the place empty? If it's supposed to be occupied soon—"

"Fletcher wanted to wait to choose the furniture. Until he got a better feel for the house."

"Uh-huh." *A better feel for his spouse, you mean.*

"Beavers build their home together."

From the wistful look on his face, Cas had no doubt that's what Rusty had thought he and Fletcher the Fuckhead were doing here. Cas strolled past Rusty and mounted the stairs to the second floor. "So how is he going to check off that box with his new little wifey? She wasn't down here finishing the hardwood floors or grouting tile in the bathroom, was she?"

"I expect they'll pick out the furniture together," Rusty said from right behind him.

Cas glanced into an obvious bedroom, then paused, his dark-evolved vision picking out a long bulky shape, about waist high, covered in a mover's pad. He switched on the light and walked across the room to pull off the pad, revealing a cherry-wood headboard, decorated with delicate scrollwork. "Looks like Fletcher was jumping the gun on that little adventure."

Behind him, Rusty's breath caught as if he'd just absorbed a body blow. Cas whipped his head around. "Rusty? Are you okay?"

"Yeah." His voice shook, and his usually ruddy cheeks had gone pale, so he clearly was *not* okay.

"What is it?"

"The headboard. It's by a local artist. I—" He licked his lips, his gaze bouncing everywhere except the unscheduled furniture. "A few months ago, we ran across it at the guy's studio when we were out poking around different artisan sites. I fell in love with it. Told Fletcher I wanted it for our house. But he said—he said he didn't like it. He wouldn't let me buy it."

It was a damn good thing Fletcher wasn't here, or Cas would have been tempted to remove his head. Or possibly other parts of his body. How dare he? How *dare* he?

"So," Cas said with forced brightness as he shoved the pad over the top of the headboard, "is there any more demolition to do, because I could get behind that right now."

"No. Everything's clean and ready for repairs." Rusty's voice was subdued, and Cas really wanted to punch something, preferably Fletcher.

"Damn it," he muttered. "Well at least show me the site of wallmageddon, because I need *something* to feed my chaotic vampire spirit." He stuck his nose in the air and put on his poshest accent. "In the absence of actual death, don't you know, we'll settle for untold destruction."

As he'd hoped, Rusty chuckled. "First, don't you think we should lightproof the house so you don't go crispy on me?"

"Oh. Good point."

Cas trailed Rusty from room to room as he either lowered the blackout shades—nice!—or closed doors on rooms that lacked them, stuffing the cracks under the doors with rags he'd brought from the truck. Cas wanted to linger in the master bedroom, to savor the sight of exposed studs and insulation, but it obviously upset Rusty, so he allowed himself to be hurried along.

"I'll walk through after dawn before you come up, just to make sure there are no light leaks."

"Up from where?"

Rusty grinned, the first real Rusty-grin since they'd entered the place. "Someplace you haven't seen yet. Come on." He led the way back to the kitchen with its massive island. He walked to one of the short ends, the one nearest the refrigerator. "Watch."

He flicked something under the counter and *holy shit*. The counter slid aside, and the end of the cabinet opened to reveal a staircase.

"You're kidding me? A secret wine cellar?"

"Yup."

"Rusty Johnson, you would have been a *god* during Prohibition!" Cas peered down the stairs. "Imagine the bathtub gin you could store down there." He glanced up at Rusty. "May I?"

"Be my guest. It's where you'll be sleeping today, given it has the only thing approaching a bed in the house."

Cas paused on the top step. "Where will *you* be sleeping?"

"I can, ah, bunk down in my truck."

"Pardon my ignorance, but don't you have a house somewhere nearby?"

"Back in Eugene, yeah, but I don't want to leave you here alone, in case . . ."

"In case Fletcher the Fuckhead stops by for a micromanagement tour?"

Rusty glanced down at a piece of paper crumpled in his fist. "It could happen."

"What's that? I didn't see you pick it up."

"The punch list for the house. It was, uh, taped to the mirror in the master bath."

"What's there to do? The place looks great—other than the obvious issue in the master bedroom."

"Fletcher decided he didn't like the paint choices. He wants the living room and all the bedrooms repainted. The tile in the master bath replaced. And some built-in library shelves in the office."

Cas held out his hand and waggled his fingers until Rusty handed him the paper. "Is this normal for a new house?"

"A walk-through with the owners is pretty standard. Verifying that everything works, that the contract was fulfilled as agreed upon before the final payment."

"So Fletcher the Fuckhead is holding out on paying you until you do all this stuff?"

"Not exactly." Rusty rubbed the back of his neck with a grimace. "I didn't charge for labor, only materials. I mean, I paid my crew, of course, but—"

"Out of your own pocket?"

"Yeah."

Cas's earlier anger flared again, heat blooming in his veins. "Because it was going to be your home. Because it was a wedding present for the two of you."

"I didn't feel right billing for my own place."

Cas had seen far too much victimization in his time. Back in his living days, when the studios had held the power to make or break a career, to make or break a *life*, all of the players, even Valentino, were afraid to stand against them. Billy Haines was the only one in those days who'd had the balls to tell Louis B. Mayer to go fuck himself and stick by his boyfriend. For life. Even in those chaotic first years after his Turn, Cas had admired the man and wished he'd had the guts to make a stand himself.

Well. As it happened, all he needed was the right incentive.

"You know what?" Cas folded the paper once, twice, three times, then ripped it in half. "Fuck this list. We'll fix the damage, but anything over and above that? Fletcher the Fuckhead and his blushing bride can handle it themselves. It'll be a beaver bonding experience for them. Making a home. You said it was a thing, right?"

"Yeah, but—"

"And forget sleeping in your truck. Until your house is vampire-safe, you'll sleep down here with me—I promise I won't take liberties."

"I'm not worried about that. But if I want to get my house vampire-safe, as you call it, I've got some work to do. I need to get over there—"

"Elmer. You have been up all day and all night. I don't care if we have to crash here during the entire repair process, you are *not* allowed to do extra work just for me. Because I may be undead, rebellious, and a 'risk to the supe community at large,' but I am not now, nor have I ever been—" he slapped the paper scraps on the counter "—a fuckhead."

Chapter Thirteen

Spending time with Cas was more enjoyable than Rusty had anticipated. The guy was hopeless at any real construction work, of course. Rusty hadn't expected any less. But he was surprisingly good company. The stories he told about Hollywood in the silent era? Man, Rusty had never realized what a different world it was for queer people there, compared to the rest of the country back then or after sound came along.

Rusty's plan had been to power through the repairs as quickly as possible. But you couldn't rush drywall mud, and they'd gotten a string of cold, rainy days that had put a literal damper on everything and slowed the curing process way down.

He hadn't expected Cas to stick it out, actually. He'd thought, yeah, maybe a day or two, then Cas would ask to go back to his fancy house in Portland, close to the nightlife that was his literal night *life*. But he'd surprised Rusty there again.

"If you're staying, I'm staying."

"It can't be that interesting for you here. No clubs. No bars. No anything, really."

"First, I don't drink, so the bars aren't really a loss. Clubs? Eh, I can take or leave them. And second, this place has something very interesting indeed." He smiled with a hint of fang—which was happening more frequently as the days wore on. "The company."

Rusty snorted. "Oh yeah. I'm really interesting."

"Don't sell yourself short. You're a great listener, for one thing, and in case you haven't noticed, I dearly love to talk."

"You could find a listener in any of those bars."

"Those people listen only until you leave them a big enough conversational gap so they can leap in and talk about themselves. They're not listening. They're *waiting*. You're an active listener. You take it in. You ask questions. You want to learn more."

"The stuff you've done is way more interesting than my life. I went to college, sure, because what else was I going to do?"

Cas set down his paintbrush. "You act as if going to college is a trivial thing. That it denotes a failure on your part, but it most assuredly does not. You took your instinctive aptitude for building and learned enough to build for *anyone*, not just your fellow beavers. You have a successful company."

"How do you know?"

"I googled you, of course. Do you know how unusual it is for any construction company to have *no* negative customer reviews? I also know that you have the best employee retention rate of any contractor in the state."

Rusty shrugged as he poured more paint into the roller pan. "It makes sense to pay good people to stick with you. Otherwise you'd end up with those negative customer reviews, right?"

"Mm-hmm. So tell me. Why don't you have any beaver shifters on your crews?"

Rusty nearly dropped the paint bucket. "What? How do you know that?"

"When Fletcher the Fuckhead—"

"Cas. You can't keep calling him a fuckhead."

"I'll stop calling him a fuckhead when he stops acting like a fuckhead. I mean, seriously, Rusty? Why are we painting this room again? It was perfectly lovely the way it was."

"You know why. When Fletcher brought Sylvie through to see it—"

"I still think we should have hung around for that instead of hiding out at your house."

"We couldn't. Or at least you couldn't. They came in the middle of the day and all the blinds were open."

"Well, *you* could have hung around."

Rusty's neck heated as he tapped the lid on the can. "I didn't want to leave you alone," he mumbled.

"What was that?"

"I said I didn't want to leave you alone."

"Yes, I heard you. I just wanted to make sure you heard yourself, because I don't think that's what you mean." He sashayed over to Rusty, his paintbrush making a figure eight in the air. "You'd rather spend time with me than with Fletcher the F—"

"Cas."

"F-f-future clan leader."

Rusty caught Cas's wrist before he could fling the trim paint all over the walls. "What if I do? Is that a problem?"

Cas smiled up at him—no fangs in evidence. "Not at all, darling. Not at all."

The sincerity in Cas's voice, in his expression . . . *Does he mean what I mean?* Since Rusty didn't know how to answer that question—or even what the question *meant,* he went back to the repairs, which were taking longer than he'd planned because he had more than his sledgehammer meltdown to address.

Despite Cas's—rather arousing—dismissal of Fletcher's original punch list, Rusty had insisted they repaint after Fletcher had brought Sylvie by for a visit. He stood firm on not retiling— Cas was right about that, and besides, tile wasn't Rusty's strong suit and he wasn't about to ask his guys to come in and redo their perfectly beautiful work just because Fletcher had changed his mind about a color.

But in addition to the added tasks, Cas contributed to the schedule slowdown personally. He refused let Rusty work at his usual pace. They'd work for three or four hours, then head over to Rusty's house—which he'd managed to lightproof with the aid of a shit-ton of blackout cloth—and watch a movie or just hang out. Cas was a cuddler. He'd cozy up next to Rusty on the sofa and make snide comments about the actors.

Why did Rusty feel more comfortable with Cas than he felt with any of his clan—or any other shifter for that matter? Was it because Cas didn't see him as defective? Would Ted, who was a fully functional bear shifter, look at Rusty like his clan did, or like Cas?

He was afraid it would be the former, and his brief time of feeling *whole* would be over. *Maybe it makes sense to rip that Band-Aid off now rather than later.*

"Hey, Cas?" Rusty called from the stove as he was making himself a bacon sandwich before they left for their evening shift. "You know, if you'd rather go back to Portland until the wedding, it would be okay." *No, it wouldn't.* "I could drive you up anytime."

Cas strode in from the hall, toweling his hair dry. "Under no circumstances. I'm standing by my man. So get used to it."

Unfortunately, Rusty had gotten rather more used to it than he wanted. "Okay. But just so you know, the offer's on the table."

"Elmer, you ... you ..." The towel dropped from Cas's fingers, and he caught himself on the edge of the counter as his knees buckled.

"Whoa." Rusty flung the bacon tongs into the sink with a clatter and grabbed Cas around the waist. "Steady there. What's the ..." He stared at the bacon, spitting in the pan, and wanted to kick himself. "Cas, when's the last time you fed?"

Cas pushed irritably at Rusty's chest. "Unhand me, Elmer. I'm not some fragile Victorian rose."

"Answer the question."

He stuck his nose in the air, but the effect was spoiled when his knees wobbled. "That's my business."

"It's mine if you wipe out in my kitchen. When, Casimir?"

His brows bunched together, and he pouted like a kindergartner. *Did they even have kindergarten when he was that age?* "The day before our wedding, if you must know."

"What?" Rusty shouted. "That was ten days ago. What do you think you're doing, starving yourself this way?"

"I can handle it. Vampires can go a *long* time without feeding. Kristof went— Well, I can't tell you that, but it was a really long time."

"Yeah, but he has some kind of medical condition, right? He didn't have a choice. Why have *you* put it off?"

"I've had other things on my mind, Elmer, in case you haven't noticed."

Since Cas didn't meet his gaze, Rusty was pretty sure that wasn't the entire story, but prying the reason out of him could wait. "Get in the truck. We're going to Portland."

Cas continued to pout all the way into town, returning monosyllabic answers to Rusty's comments and questions, until Rusty surrendered and pulled up a *Wait Wait . . . Don't Tell Me!* podcast on his sound system. He caught Cas smothering laughter several times, so he counted it as a win.

"Where do you want me to drop you off?" He waited, but Cas just stared out the window. "Casimir. Stop being a prima donna. The Pearl? Old Town? Where do you usually, er, hunt?"

"Just drop me at my house. I'll take it from there."

"If you say so." Rusty complied, but as Cas disappeared into the house, he was consumed with an unreasonable spike of jealousy. *If I wasn't a shifter, he could use me. And I'm not even a proper shifter.* Of course, if he were fully active, Cas couldn't stand to be near him anyway, so Rusty was screwed from both directions.

Why the hell did it matter? Gaia bless, did he *want* to be vampire chow?

He drove around aimlessly for a couple of hours, stopping for coffee at a Starbucks in Beaverton, just because he could imagine Cas's eye roll at his choice of city. When he got back to

Cas's place, he expected to have to wait, but Cas was standing on the porch, shifting from foot to foot, when Rusty pulled through the gate.

Cas hurried over and climbed in the truck, setting a small duffel on the floor at his feet.

"All set?"

"Yes. Can we go now?"

Rusty tried to tap down his curiosity. He failed. "So where did you find your, er, dinner."

Cas glared at him. "We call them *hosts,* Elmer, as you very well know." He folded his arms and looked out the window— apparently his new favorite pastime—and mumbled something that Rusty didn't catch.

"What?"

"I said I didn't feed from a host. I called a blood delivery service." He nudged the duffel with his toe. "I got some extra to keep at your place so we don't have to come back."

For some reason, that lightened Rusty's mood so much that he whistled halfway to Eugene, until Cas told him irritably to shut up or pick a song other than "Stagger Lee."

After they got back to Eugene, Rusty made Cas rest until the following evening. They returned to work then, but with their leisurely schedule, they didn't finish painting until the day before the wedding.

Rusty tapped the lid on the last paint can and stood up, stretching his back until it popped. "That's the last one. Just in time."

Cas huffed. "We would have been finished last week if you hadn't given in to Fletcher the Fuckhead's demands to repaint the entire interior."

"It wasn't a demand," Rusty said mildly, hefting two paint cans in each hand. "It was a request. A very nice request. From Sylvie."

"Right. If this was all Sylvie's idea, I'll eat my Jag."

"Best pretend it was, anyway. It's their wedding day tomorrow. Let's cut them some slack. Weddings can be stressful. Don't you remember your reaction two weeks ago?"

"Yes, but that was understandable. That wedding wasn't *my* idea."

Rusty swallowed against a lump in his throat. "I thought it was a mutual decision."

Cas dropped the paint roller pans with a clatter and rushed over to him. "I don't mean *our* wedding, darling. I meant the first one. The one where I got left at the altar." He patted Rusty's chest. "This one has been just lovely. I'm grateful you agreed to be my temporary husband. It's too bad—" He bit his lip and winced. "Ow. You'd think after ninety-two years I'd remember the fangs."

A swarm of butterflies swirled in Rusty's belly. *Was Cas regretting the end of their arrangement the way he was?* "What's too bad?"

"Nothing. Never mind."

Butterfly mass extinction. "Let's load this stuff in the back of my truck. We've got some time before the rehearsal dinner—"

"Rehearsal dinner? You're *in* the wedding?"

"Hell no. But I'm invited—*we're* invited to the dinner. It's not until eight thirty." He glanced at the paint speckling his arms. "So I'm going for a swim in the lake to get rid of all this paint."

Cas stared at him, mouth agape. "What the fuck, Elmer? For some incomprehensible reason, you have not one, not two, but *four* perfectly functional showers at your house. Are they only there for show? Why not make use of several of them?"

"Sue me. I like to swim."

"In November?"

Rusty shrugged. "I'm a—"

"Beaver shifter. Yes, you may have mentioned it."

"Come on. It's great. Vampires aren't affected by the cold, right? You can come too."

Cas plucked at a spot of paint on his jeans. "Vampires can't swim. Our body composition changes during the Turn. Little things like bone density." He sniffed, but his smile lacked its usual edge. "Don't let my svelte appearance fool you. I weigh more than your average refrigerator."

"Don't exaggerate. I've carried you, remember?"

"Yes, but you're such a fine, strapping fellow, you probably fling refrigerators about on a regular basis and think nothing of it."

Rusty grinned at Cas's snooty tone. "Seems like you'd be great divers, though. No need for tanks since you don't have to breathe."

"However, since we sink like very fashionable stones, we tend to panic. Panic leads to gasping, and gasping leads to lungs full of water."

"I imagine that's not a good thing."

"No. It's not. We may not need to breathe, but we can still drown."

Rusty's grin faded. *But that means . . .* "Archie. He won't ever be able to swim again, will he? Not even at night?"

Cas shook his head. "No."

"Damn," Rusty muttered. He nudged the fallen pans with his boot. "Let's get the last stuff cleared away. I'm ready to be done with this place, aren't you?"

"Hell yes."

Rusty blocked the door, looking down at Cas. "But then, I'm taking you for a swim."

"But—"

"Don't worry. I'll hold you up."

Cas complained all the way to the truck—both trips—and then all the way to the boathouse.

"Do we really need to do this?"

"It's a tradition," Rusty said, checking the supply of towels that every beaver shifter kept stocked in their boathouse. "I come up here to swim after every construction project. Most of the time, the project is somewhere else, though, so the close proximity this time is a perk."

Since the boathouse wasn't actually for boats, there was more decking than in a usual slip. Cas peered into the dark water. "I wouldn't call this a perk. More like a water hazard."

Rusty strode down the side walkway and unbarred the doors. "Come on, Casimir. You're the risk-taker here. You telling me you can't handle a little personal tour of the lake? You've spent enough time mooning at it."

"Yes, because it's picturesque. That doesn't mean I want the full-body immersion experience."

Rusty faced him across the slip, the gentle lake waves lapping at his feet. "Don't you trust me?"

"Of course I trust you." Cas kicked one of the pilings. "But —"

"I won't let you go under. I promise."

Cas stared at him, throat working. Finally, he nodded. "All right."

Warmth bloomed in Rusty's belly. "Good." He took off his boots, shed his shirt, and stripped off his pants, all under Cas's watchful eyes—which had an unfortunate effect on his dick. Luckily, slipping into the frigid water took care of that. He treaded water, looking up at Cas. "Ready when you are."

Cas nodded and removed his own clothing. *Gaia strike me blind.* The man was beautiful. Not stocky and hairy-chested like Fletcher or any other beaver shifter. Long. Lean, with smooth alabaster skin, the only color a faint tinge of pink in his cheeks. His cock lay flaccid between his legs as he sat on the edge of the deck and eased his feet into the water.

He grimaced, but didn't shriek like a human would have. "It's definitely brisk."

"Oncoming winter'll do that. Come on in." Rusty held out his arms. "I'll catch you."

"All right." Cas slid into the water, transferring his grip from the edge of the dock to Rusty's neck.

Rusty choked out a laugh. "No need to throttle me. I've got you."

"Sorry." Cas loosened his chokehold, but he trembled against Rusty.

"Are you cold?"

He reared back and gave Rusty some serious stink-eye. "I'm *dead*. Of course I'm cold. But I don't *feel* cold."

"So the trembling? Fear?"

"You think?" Cas's tone was tart, but he pressed up against Rusty, his body slick and sleek under the water, and his expression turned sultry. "Or maybe it's proximity to you."

"Hold that thought. I'm taking you out now." Rusty turned Cas in his arms so his back was to Rusty's front, and kicked out through the boathouse doors, Cas resting on his chest. They cleared the roof, and the stars spread out over them, no moon to dim their glory.

Cas breathed a soft, "Oh," and relaxed against Rusty's chest, his head nestled on Rusty's shoulder.

Since Rusty had been swimming in this and other bodies of water from the time he could toddle, he was able to keep them afloat and moving with just the power of his legs. But as he frog-kicked farther into the lake, he became uncomfortably aware that his dick was tucked into the cleft of Cas's ass, and the motion of his kicks was creating more movement and friction than was really appropriate for a swim with his fake husband.

He tried to concentrate on the night instead, on the wind soughing in the firs along the shore, on the call of an owl in the trees, on Cas's wordless hums of joy. But Cas's skin was silk under Rusty's callused hands, and compared to the lake water, *warm*. At first, it was only the stroke of his index finger along Cas's rib. Nothing too invasive. He wasn't even moving his hand.

But what would it feel like if I did move my hand? So he tried that. Just a little pet, the curve of those ribs so perfect they deserved a statue in marble or bronze.

Cas didn't seem to mind the petting. He nestled his head tighter under Rusty's chin, relaxing his grip so his hands barely skimmed the hair on Rusty's arms—which made it stand straight up, as his dick was attempting to do, despite the chill of the water.

If his ribs feel this good, what about his chest? His . . . his nipples? Keeping one arm firm around Cas's waist so he wouldn't feel insecure, Rusty drew his hand up over each ridge of that delicate rib cage until he could splay his big, clumsy paw over Cas's pec, and feel the brush of an erect nipple. He let out a breathy moan and moved his hand in little circles, mesmerized by the *difference*. The smooth skin of Cas's chest under his rough fingertips. The tiny firm flesh of the nipple against his palm.

They'd reached the center of the lake, and Rusty was barely moving his legs now. Just enough to keep them afloat. Just enough to keep his growing dick docked in Cas's cleft.

"Elmer."

Cas's voice shocked Rusty out of his trance. He kicked out wildly, splashing both their faces, and moved his hand—*bad hand*—back to Cas's waist. "Sorry. I'm sorry. I—"

"*Elmer.*" Cas grabbed Rusty's hand and placed it firmly back on his pec. "I wasn't complaining about that. Not necessarily, anyway, as long as you don't get so distracted that we both drown."

"I wouldn't—"

"I know." Cas kissed the side of his neck, right over his jugular, adding a little flick of his tongue, and Rusty's cock pulsed. "But I prefer my foreplay to be less water-borne. Do you suppose—" this time he sucked on Rusty's skin, and Rusty buried his groan in Cas's hair "—we could continue this on land?"

Chapter Fourteen

Rusty shuddered under him. "We shouldn't."

His skin thrumming from Rusty's touch, his ass clenching to hold that lovely expanding cock in place, Cas pressed his mouth against Rusty's neck, the heat, the pulse, the *smell* making him so dizzy he could have slid off Rusty's chest and sunk to the bottom of the lake and he wouldn't have minded.

Well, not true. He'd have minded *a lot*, because he wanted Rusty inside him, and he wanted it *now*.

"Why not? It's not like we're cheating on anybody. We're married."

"But I'm a shifter." Rusty's voice, rumbling in his chest, vibrated Cas's bones. "Isn't it dangerous for you?"

"It's dangerous for me to be out on this lake with you feeling me up—"

"I'm sorry. I—"

"Stop. I said I didn't mind. Well, I didn't mind the feeling up, but as charming as this little watery interlude was, I can do without the lake. Can we go back now? Can we please please *please* make love?"

Rusty hummed deep in his throat. "I shouldn't. I don't want to hurt you."

"Look, if you were *that* poisonous, I'd have been dead two weeks ago from that little blood amuse-bouche. If you were poisonous—" Cas closed his eyes and inhaled "—you wouldn't smell so fucking good. Vampires are calibrated for self-preservation. That's why the only thing we can smell is whether someone will be a tasty host." Except he'd smelled coffee. Right after he'd tasted Rusty, in Dr. MacLeod's office, despite the druid neutralizer. He'd smelled *Rusty* too, and until now he hadn't realized how peculiar that was. *What the fuck does it all mean?* Cas licked the side of Rusty's throat. "Besides, my life, my choice. I've got condoms in my pants—"

"You do?"

"Of course."

"But you don't need them. Supes don't. Not with humans."

Cas nuzzled the hinge of Rusty's jaw. "Who says they're for humans? Maybe they're supe semen insurance."

"You mean you— That is, you want me enough to *plan* for this?"

"Darling, why sound so astonished? You can't blame me for wanting to take advantage of our optional consummation clause. You're incredibly hot." He wiggled a bit, enjoying the tickle of Rusty's truly fabulous chest rug against his shoulder blades—and of course, the extra pulse of that giant cock. His own mast was raised too. All they needed was a sail. Or a less stubborn beaver. Rusty's skin, fever hot, was a delicious sensual contrast to the chill of the lake. "In fact, so hot that the lake may be the only thing not sending us both up in flames. Now." Cas raised one hand and pointed to the boathouse. "I believe land is thataway."

"I'm going to regret this," Rusty muttered, but scissored his legs in another powerful thrust through the water—*stop thinking about scissoring and thrusting*—sending them back toward shore.

"I hope not. What better way to prepare for Fletcher the Fuckhead's wedding than to move on in action as well as in theory?"

Once Rusty put his mind to it, he could be mistaken for a motor boat. Unfortunately, with his attention focused fully on speed, his lovely wandering hands stayed anchored on Cas's waist. *Oh well. We'll get there again. Soon.*

In an astonishingly short time, the boathouse roof loomed over them. Rusty let their legs fall and used one arm to keep their heads above water. They bobbed next to the dock. "Can you pull yourself up?"

"Darling, vampires are like ants. We can lift fifty times our weight."

"Yeah, but can you actually lift your weight when it's, you know, you?"

"Don't be fresh." Cas grabbed the edge of the dock and boosted himself out of the water. "See?"

Rusty grinned up at him, wet and sleek as an otter. *No, not an otter. A beaver.* "Towels on the shelf."

Although Cas's legs were unsteady from the residual effects of Rusty's hands on his skin, he managed to stroll over to the shelves with a little wiggle to his ass. *Take that, Mr. Sexy Water God.* He teased a towel off the shelf with slightly more flair than was necessary and draped it over his back. It was a huge, extra-fluffy bath sheet that fell nearly to his feet. "I see that beavers like the finer things in . . ." His mouth dried at the sight of Rusty levering himself out of the water and standing on the deck. *Oh my stars. Talk about the finer things.*

Cas had seen full-frontal Rusty not half an hour ago before he went into the water. He'd *felt* full-frontal Rusty during their swim. But neither of those had prepared him for the sight of full-frontal Rusty as water sheeted off his skin, as he slicked back his hair, eyes closed, as he rolled his shoulders and stretched.

Then he opened his eyes and smiled at Cas, stalking forward with heat in his eyes like a lion stalking a gazelle. *Beaver, my ass.*

Cas pulled another towel off the shelf and held it out. "T-t-towel?"

"Thanks." Rusty wiped himself down, never taking his gaze off Cas until Cas felt warmer than he'd felt in almost a century. He was probably burning up that nasty take-out blood, but it was worth it.

It was *so* worth it when Rusty dropped his towel and eased his fingers under the edge of Cas's, his hands nearly searing Cas's skin in the best possible way.

Rusty dropped his gaze then, watching his hands skate over Cas's body. Throat, shoulder, pec—nipple!—ribs, hips, *ass*. He dipped his head and took Cas's mouth in a kiss surprisingly gentle for such a huge guy—lips soft, edged with the springy hair of his beard and mustache, tongue teasing Cas's with flicks and curls. *His taste. Gods preserve me, his taste.* Like fire and air and lust. He drew back, breathing fast. "You're cool. Like lake water."

"And you're hot." *Like blood.* Cas nuzzled the wiry hair between Rusty's pecs. "I love the fur."

Rusty's laugh rumbled under Cas's lips. "Good thing. I've never been much for manscaping."

Cas glanced up. "You . . . you don't mind that I'm not? Hairy, that is?"

Rusty nudged Cas's belly with his *extremely* impressive dick. "I think it's pretty obvious I don't mind anything about you."

Cas nudged back. "Likewise." His voice was strained because he couldn't make himself remember to take in air. "But I told you what I want. Can we please go up to the house and fall onto that stupid air mattress and—"

"Don't have to." Rusty nodded at the corner of the boathouse. "There's a double cot over there behind that screen."

A laugh caught Cas by surprise. "Seriously? Beavers keep beds in their boathouses but no boats?"

Rusty grinned, and the crinkles at the corners of his eyes made Cas's knees go weak. "What can I say? We have our priorities."

"Then let's go." After snatching his pants off the floor, Cas took Rusty's hand and led him to the cot. He nudged it with his bare toe. "Seems sturdy."

"It better be. I built it for me."

Cas jerked his head up. "You built— Shit, of course you did. This was supposed to be *your* house. I'm sorry. I—"

"Hey." Rusty cupped Cas's jaw in his big square hand. "I'm over that, okay? I've spent the last couple of weeks making it into somebody else's house, with your help. I think we've both earned the right to christen this cot." He kissed Cas again, slow and hot and thorough. "And then I'm taking it back. Fletcher the Fuckhead can build his own boathouse cot."

Cas laughed, twining his arms around Rusty's neck. "That's my fierce warrior beaver. Gods, please kiss me now before I say anything even *more* sappy."

"Am I? Yours?" Rusty's eyes were black in the dim boathouse light, and the expression on his face . . . *Vulnerable.*

Cas couldn't lie. "For now. For tonight. For tomorrow and the next day, you absolutely are, just as I'm yours. Let's not worry about anything beyond that. Okay?"

Rusty nodded, his shoulders lifting in a sigh. "Okay." Then he cupped Cas's face in his gloriously warm hands, and dove in for a kiss. And another. And three more. And with each meeting of their lips, each stroke of their tongues, Cas learned something new.

Beard hairs are soft and springy, but mustache hairs are sharp, like tiny vampire fangs.

Rusty's taste is as forbidden and intoxicating as a speakeasy cocktail.

Fletcher Dawson is a fucking idiot if he had this and threw it away.

Rusty lowered Cas onto the cot, breaking their kisses long enough to run his hands over Cas's skin, skirting his cock, damn it, but cupping his balls. *Ah.* "Your skin . . . I've never seen anything like it." Rusty pressed his open mouth against Cas's throat, sucking the skin over his carotid, and Cas's hips bucked, out of his control. Rusty raised his head and grinned. "Like that, do you?"

"Try it again and see."

He kissed his way to the other side, with a stop at the base of Cas's throat, and then zapped the other carotid until Cas had to grab the base of his cock to keep from coming.

"Wow. Guess vampires have a thing about necks."

Cas flailed on the blanket until he found the lube. "We have a thing about being fucked too."

Rusty glanced at the little tube. "You sure? I mean, kisses and spit don't seem to poison you, but—"

"We've got a condom, Elmer. Just get me ready."

The snick of the cap was as loud as a thunderclap. Whether that was because of vampire hearing or relative significance, he didn't care, because Rusty's finger was circling his hole, teasing, tickling, tormenting. Then he pushed, waiting for Cas to let him in and *there*.

"Can you make—" Cas sucked in air as Rusty hit his prostate "—your fingers do the same thing your legs do in the water?"

Rusty inserted a second finger, stretching, burning, *perfect*, and Cas keened his approval. "You mean like this?" And he did it—the sinuous roll and flick that nearly sent Cas up to the ceiling. "Gaia, Cas, your gland is—" He brushed it with his knuckle. "Do all vampires have such extra-large ones?"

"I wouldn't . . . know. I've . . . never conducted any . . . nnngh! Researrrch!" Cas's back arched and he scrabbled for Rusty's arm. "Stop. Stop. I don't want to come yet. I need you inside. I haven't been topped since 1926."

Rusty's fingers stilled. "You what?"

"History lesson later, Elmer. You in me now."

"Don't have to ask me twice." Rusty withdrew his fingers, accompanied by Cas's whimper, and knelt at the end of the cot to snag the condom from the blanket.

Foil crinkled as Cas clenched his eyes shut and counted Keystone Kops. Rusty swore, and Cas's eyes flew open. "What's wrong?"

"Nothing." Rusty was scowling down at his dick. "Haven't worn one of these in a while. Don't remember them being this . . . snug."

Cas regarded Rusty's cock with approval. "Well, you are a rather *gifted* man." He pulled his legs up to his chest. "And I *really* want a present. So how about a little regifting, hmmm?"

Rusty finished rolling the condom on, and when he looked up at Cas, his eyes widened, tongue darting out to wet his lips. "Gaia, but you're beautiful."

So are you. Cas didn't say it though. Somehow, he didn't think Rusty would believe it, not after the way he'd been treated all his life. "Come here."

He didn't. Instead he slid his hands under Cas's ass cheeks and drew him forward, tilting him up so the angle was right and then— *Oh gods, then . . .*

Rusty breached him, so wide, so *hot* that Cas was sure he'd be reduced to ash. But then he held there, just at the entrance, until Cas was panting with the need for *more, damn it, more.* So he asked for it. "More, damn it, more."

"I don't want to hurt you. You're not— Ah!"

Cas relaxed and Rusty entered on a smooth thrust that seemed to go on for days, yet wasn't nearly long enough. The wide head of Rusty's cock brushed his prostate, and Cas threw his head back, mouth wide, gasping for air he didn't need.

And then Rusty's lips were on his, Rusty's tongue in his mouth, as his rhythm—*their* rhythm—beat like the pulse of a dragon's heart. *Gods.* He remembered bottoming feeling good, but not *this* good. Not top-of-his-head-may-blow-off, spine-may-spontaneously-combust, dick-may-shoot-the-moon good.

"Cas. I'm—"

"Me too. Now. Please. Touch me."

So Rusty did, clasping Cas's dick in his fist, and that was all it took. That touch. That grip. The smooth palm and callused fingers. Hard and soft and hot and *his.* He shot over Rusty's hand, and Rusty grunted, as if in surprise, but then he groaned, his back muscles tight under Cas's hands and Cas could *feel* it— that pulse inside him, no hotter than Rusty's body but so much warmer than his own skin, his own heart.

Rusty shifted his weight onto his elbows, as if he were about to pull out, but Cas wrapped his arms and legs around him, holding tight.

"Mmm. Don't go."

Rusty chuckled. "I should take care of the condom at least."

"In a minute. Stay here for a little longer. You're so warm." *And you feel so good. I feel so good. In fact, I haven't felt this good in decades.*

"We really need to get back to my place to shower and change for the rehearsal dinner."

Cas snuggled closer. "We can be late."

"We'll already be late."

"We can be later. It's not as though you're in the ceremony."

"I know. But—" Rusty kissed the spot underneath Cas's ear, making him shiver. "We might as well reduce our outrage footprint where we can, since just being together is likely to set off a clan explosion."

"Interesting combination of metaphors." He patted Rusty's chest. "Fine. I bow to your superior social conscience."

"Hold on. I'll try to pull out gently." He grabbed the base of his dick and the edge of the condom, brow furrowed in concentration, and withdrew slowly. Cas closed his eyes, the better to savor the sensation. *He really is the dearest man.*

"*Fuck,*" Rusty growled, causing Cas to open his eyes again.

"What?"

He looked up, his face bleak. "The condom broke."

Chapter Fifteen

Rusty leaped off the cot and raced across the deck to where he'd left his clothes. He grabbed the whole pile, feeling for the telltale hard rectangle of his phone. "Where the hell is the damn thing?"

Cas sat up on the cot, blinking at him with a blissed-out smile on his face. "What are you looking for?"

"My phone. To call Bryce. I came inside you, Cas. There was nothing left in the condom. It was way more than the little bit of blood you ingested." Rusty cursed and threw his shirt down, then shoved his hand into his pants pocket. *Keys, not phone. Damn it.* "Bryce said you could go into anaphylactic shock."

"Oh." Cas's tone held zero concern. "Kristof said that too."

Rusty glared at him. "Then why aren't you freaking out?"

"You're doing a good enough job for both of us. Besides . . ." He raised his arms and fell back on the cot, spread-eagle. "I feel *fantastic!*"

"I must have left my phone inside. Put your clothes on so we can go back to the house."

"I don't want to. I feel too warm. I haven't felt this warm since I died." He made some kind of freaking snow angel on the sheets. "It feels like summer. In fact . . ." He sat up, eyes sparkling. "Maybe we should go for another swim."

Screw getting dressed. Rusty shoved his feet into his boots, then clomped over to the bed. "Let's go."

Cas licked his lips. "Okay." He reached for Rusty's dick.

"*Not now*, Casimir."

He peered up at Rusty through his lashes. "Your mouth says no but something else is saying yes yes yes."

The twisted thing was that Cas was right. Just being this close was making Rusty's previously flagging cock perk up. Rusty sent it a stern *Down, boy!* "Fine. If you want to play it that way . . ." He'd carried Cas once, he could do it again. He grabbed Cas's wayward wrist, and with a stoop, heave, and grunt, slung him over his shoulder.

Cas giggled as Rusty stomped up the hill. "The boots are an interesting touch. Kinky." Cas giggled harder. "Kinky boots. Get it?"

"I get that you're higher than a kite." He wobbled as he took the porch stairs, and had to steady himself with one hand on the handrail.

"Ruuusssty," Cas crooned. "I smell like you."

"More likely you're smelling, you know, me," Rusty said between clenched teeth as he wrestled the door open one-handed, "since you're licking my back. Stop it."

"No." Cas's voice took on a dark, wicked edge. "I've got your spunk running down my leg."

Gah! Rusty's cock *really* liked that image. He should have just used the damn thing to batter the door down instead of fucking around with this— *There.* Finally. He pushed inside. *Shit. No furniture.* The cooler he'd brought over to hold drinks while they'd worked was still sitting in the vestibule. He lowered Cas onto it and pointed a finger at his face. "Stay."

Cas faked a nip, his fangs flashing in the entryway light, but at least he didn't get up.

Rusty clomped into the kitchen, and sure enough, his phone was on the counter next to a handful of paint chips. He grabbed it, thanking Gaia he'd asked for Bryce's emergency number after Cas's last trip to la-la-land.

Bryce answered on the second ring. "Rusty? Is something wrong?"

"Yeah. It's Casimir again."

"Did he ingest more of your blood?"

Great. How was he going to explain this without going up in flames of embarrassment? "No. Not exactly. But—" From the vestibule, Cas burst into song, something Rusty didn't recognize, and Rusty wanted to smack his head against the countertop. "We were, um, and the condom broke."

"I see." Rusty could swear Bryce was trying not to laugh. "So we're talking semen incursion rather than blood ingestion."

Rusty clenched his eyes shut and took a deep breath. *Semen incursion.* What a way to describe the most incredible sex he'd ever had in his life. "Yeah." He walked back into the vestibule to see that Cas hadn't followed directions—*shocker*—and was dancing around the great room, still humming the same song.

"Does Casimir seem lethargic? Disoriented?"

Rusty watched Cas shimmy across the floor, shaking his perfect ass. "Um. No."

"Hives or skin discoloration?"

Other than the hickeys on his throat? "No." Rusty sat down on the cooler.

"What about swelling?"

Cas turned around, and his cock was fully erect, leaking a bit at the tip, and Rusty's mouth watered. *Don't think that's the kind of swelling he's talking about.* Cas grinned and stalked toward Rusty. "He looks great, actually. Perfectly healthy. En—" Cas straddled Rusty's lap and nuzzled his shoulder, grinding his cock against Rusty's belly. "Energetic."

"It sounds like he's okay for now. Can you get him to a VER?"

"There isn't one anywhere in this county. We don't have a vampire population." *Probably because there are only two hundred of them in the entire world and the county is lousy with shifters. Why would they want to live here?*

"Hmmm. Okay, here's what we'll do. I'll call in a favor from a druid circle at U of O. I've tweaked that neutralizer he took at my office the other day, altering the formula for vampire genetic markers, and I'll give them the formula. I'll put a rush on it, so you should be able to pick it up in ten minutes."

"Ten minutes where? We're up at the lake house, half an hour from anywhere."

"Shit," Bryce muttered. "Where's the lake house located? Can you text me a map?"

With Cas pressing open-mouthed kisses on his neck—*Damn, why did his fangs feel so sexy?*—it wasn't easy for Rusty to focus, but he managed after only fumbling twice. "Get it?"

"Yes. Okay, you're not far from a Faerie gate. Mal's not here, but I've got a bauchan friend who can lead me there. They'll probably like poking around in the woods while I check Casimir over. I'll be there as soon as I can."

Rusty heaved a sigh of relief, letting his head *thunk* against the wall, which unfortunately, Cas took as an invitation. "Thanks, Bryce. I appreciate—" But Bryce had already disconnected.

Cas hummed against his throat. "You smell good enough to eat."

Rusty gritted his teeth, gripping Cas's waist with both hands, and standing both of them up. "I asked you before not to say that."

He put one hand over his mouth. "Oops."

"Come on, babe. Bryce and his friend will be here soon, and I don't think we want to meet them as a naked flag twirling team." He took Cas's hand and led him toward the door.

Cas skipped to keep up. "Are we going for another swim?"

"Not a swim. But I may dunk you in the lake just to cool you off." *I could use cooling off too.*

Once on the porch, Rusty glanced down at Cas's bare feet. "I'd better carry you. The ground is rough. It'll hurt your feet."

"Pish. I'm a vampire." Cas grinned up at him. "Race you!" He launched himself off the porch, not bothering with the steps, and took off down the hill in a blur of white skin.

"Shit." Rusty glumphed after him in his untied boots, hoping he wouldn't take a header and roll into the lake.

Cas was already inside the boathouse when Rusty reached the shore, but he wasn't getting dressed. He was peering into the dark water, dipping his toe in. He kicked a few drops at Rusty. "Are you sure we don't have time for a swim?"

Rusty glanced down at himself. He didn't have the evidence of their lovemaking trickling down the inside of his legs like Cas did, but he probably smelled of sex, which didn't seem like the best way to greet Bryce. Or his bauchan friend. Bauchans had notoriously sensitive noses. He eyed the lake. *That may be the fastest way to get us both reasonably clean.*

"Not a swim."

"No?" Cas pouted. "But I want to go in the water again."

Rusty toed off his unlaced boots. "Oh trust me. You're going in the water."

"Yay!"

He stalked over, took Cas around the waist with one arm. "Don't panic."

Cas blinked at him. "What?"

Rusty blocked Cas's nose and mouth with his other hand. And jumped.

Cas froze in his arms until they surfaced—they were only submerged for a few seconds—and then he smacked Rusty in the chest with a surprisingly steely fist.

"You *asshole*. You said you'd hold me up. You *promised*."

"I am holding you up." Rusty rubbed his chest. He was going to have a beauty of a bruise. "I never said I wouldn't dunk you."

"It was *implied*." Cas turned his head away, exposing that spot behind his ear that Rusty found too delectable to resist.

So he didn't. Instead he kissed the soft skin, tickling it a bit with the tip of his tongue. "I'm sorry. But Bryce will be here any minute and we need to get clean—more or less—and dressed."

"You're really harshing my buzz, Elmer."

Rusty barked a laugh. "Does anyone say that anymore?"

"I do. Can we get out now? I'm cold."

"Now you're just whining." But Rusty let Cas lever himself out of the water. He waited until Cas had wrapped himself in a towel before he followed. He toweled off quickly and got dressed with his back to Cas. "I'm gonna wait for Bryce outside. You stay in here. It'll give you some privacy during the exam."

Cas sniffed. "I don't need an exam."

"Please, Cas? For me? I couldn't live with myself if I hurt you."

"Oh fine." He plopped on the cot. "Let the druid do his worst. But I'm still mad at you."

"Yeah, I get that." Rusty hesitated, tempted to cross the deck and give Cas one more kiss, but he sighed and went outdoors instead.

And just in time—Bryce was standing inside the tree line, talking to a creature who came up to his waist, and who blended so seamlessly into the undergrowth that Rusty could barely make them out.

Bryce glanced up, the lenses of his glasses flashing in the light of the rising moon. He raised a hand in greeting, and with one last remark to his companion, strode across the grass to meet Rusty.

"Hey. I got here as fast as I could."

Rusty shook his hand. "Thanks." He nodded at the boathouse. "He's in there. If the lighting isn't good enough, we can go into the house, but—"

"I'm sure it will be fine." He held up a hand and a little ball of blue light appeared in his palm. "I carry my own anyway."

"I'll stay out here while you— I mean, I want to give him some privacy, you know?" *And I'm afraid of what I'll hear.* Better to have it filtered through Bryce's viewpoint later.

"Very considerate. I doubt it will take long." After Bryce disappeared into the boathouse, Rusty wandered closer to the lake.

He stared at the water, where such a short time ago he'd been so happy. *And horny. And look where that got Cas.* The moon rose higher, clearing the tops of the trees, and it occurred to Rusty that they'd definitely missed the rehearsal dinner.

Fletcher will be pissed. Earl will be annoyed. The clan will feel justified. A week ago, any one of those things would have sent Rusty into a spiral of apology and self-recrimination. But now?

Screw 'em. None of those things mattered as much as the fate of one particular vampire.

Gaia, please let Cas be okay.

He stood on the shore, watching the moon rise, his hands clenching and unclenching, until Bryce finally slipped out of the boathouse. Rusty waited, holding his breath, but Cas didn't follow him out. He met Bryce halfway up the slope.

"How is he? Is he okay?"

"Yes. He appears to be fine, although he's still rather angry with both of us. I expect that will last for a while."

"I don't care. As long as he's not going to die. I mean die again."

Bryce tucked his hands in the pockets of his pants—well, one of the sets of pockets. His pants and his khaki vest both had multiple pairs. "I've been doing some research since you showed up in my office, and I'm not sure that vampires are technically dead."

"I know. They're *un*dead."

"That's a colloquial term, coined by a very unscientific community, legends of Van Helsing notwithstanding. I'm beginning to believe that what we're looking at is an alternate form of life altogether, based on different principles. Granted, the procreation method is vastly dissimilar, but when you come right down to it, it's still the merging of two separate sets of DNA into a new individual. The sire's contribution to the fledgling's creation never goes away. It will always be part of him or her. A type of inheritance, if you will." He tapped his lower lip. "I've lately begun to think that vampires are proof of alien life."

Rusty goggled at him. "You're kidding."

Bryce's eyebrows quirked above his glasses. "Not at all. This may be the only way the alien species can propagate—by merging their DNA into a human host to create a hybrid with altered viability parameters."

"That's a little far-fetched, don't you think? Are fae and shifters little green men too?"

"No. And don't disparage little green men anywhere where *they*—" he nodded at the woods, where something with huge yellow eyes peered out of the underbrush "—can hear you, since they are literally green. At least parts of them." He took off his glasses and polished them on his shirttail. "We already know the elder gods were instrumental in creating the fae, using already evolved human DNA. They're very practical, the elder gods. They see no point in creating something entirely new when they can cobble it together from spare parts."

"How do you know?"

"Well, the scientific evaluation of the evidence, for one thing. For another, I've talked to one."

"You've . . . talked. To an elder god?"

"Yes." Bryce frowned, his eyebrows drawing together. "Although he was less than forthcoming about a number of things. He's not especially sociable these days." He put his glasses back on, settling them on the bridge of his nose with one knuckle. "But *anyway*. All supes—fae, druids, shifters, demonic and angelic hosts—everybody I've been able to test—we all have what my grandmother called the 'wee center' and what some supes call the *calon*. We all have it, even the Inactives like you. All of us—except vampires. Instead, they've got something else, something that's piggybacked on their DNA, something that doesn't exist in any other species on this planet." He shrugged. "So, if it doesn't exist on *this* planet—"

"It must have come from another one?"

"QED."

Rusty ran his hands through his hair. "Okay. Can*not* think about this right now."

"You don't need to be freaked out about it. I don't think an alien invasion is imminent. In fact, I think they're probably extinct. Vampires might be the only legacy that remains of them."

"That doesn't exactly make me feel better," Rusty muttered.

Bryce didn't seem to hear him as he gazed out over the lake, rocking from his toes to his heels. "I hadn't thought of this before, but maybe ... maybe poisonous blood and scent aversion is the result of natural selection for shifters. Perhaps the original hybrids—whom we'll call vampires for lack of a better term—were the early shifters' primary predators. Perhaps all shifters began as Inactives—their shifting ability only unrealized potential—but then as a result of ... of ..."

"Overgrazing?" Rusty said with a lift of his eyebrow.

"I was trying to be sensitive. Mal says I have a problem with being too blunt."

"Don't hold back on my account. I've developed a pretty thick skin."

"Overgrazing, then. From Cas's reaction to you, and the effects feeding from you seem to have, Inactive shifter blood stimulates the vampire pleasure centers to a, er, considerable degree."

"No shit," Rusty muttered.

"Every species has the desire to be okay, to survive, and more, to feel good. Since vampires can't get drunk on alcohol, you can imagine how they might want to pursue something that has such a pleasurable effect."

Great. I'm the equivalent of a pitcher of margaritas. "That's why he's seemed so high both times."

"Exactly. In a more primitive time, they'd have had no concept of how to maintain their—" he cut a sidelong glance at Rusty "—herds. They'd have been more prone to, well, gorging, with the result that the inactive population diminished as the active population was selected for survival. Vampires had to move on to the food source that also happened to be their source of procreation. Humans."

Rusty's stomach rebelled. "So they're what? Cannibals?"

"Eh . . ." Bryce held out one hand and waggled it back and forth. "Only if you classify vampires as human. And I don't think they are. Not anymore. But you—and all the other Inactives? I think you're throwbacks. Inactive shifter blood is like human blood plus. High octane, but it can still go in the tank without destroying the engine."

"That makes me feel even worse, thanks."

Bryce colored. "I'm sorry. Still struggling with that sensitivity issue. If it helps, I think Cas's reaction may diminish a bit over time as his body adjusts. There may also be other effects that could deliver a more tangible advantage, effects we haven't seen yet. For instance . . ." Bryce cleared his throat, shuffling his feet in the bedraggled grass. "Casimir told me he's able to smell things other than optimal or unfavorable food sources. He was able to smell the coffee in my office, which hasn't been the case since he was Turned."

"Can he still smell other things?"

"He said it faded fairly quickly. He couldn't detect any hospital smells when he got to the VER for instance. But he told me that tonight, after the, er, event, he was able to smell the lake, the forest, and, well, you—although that might be because you're the most optimal blood source. He, ah, wasn't particularly complimentary about my scent in comparison, even though there's no chemical contraindicator in druid blood."

"So it lasted longer this time. Was it because it wasn't blood? Because there was, um, more of it?"

Bryce scrubbed his hands in his hair. "God, I wish I knew. But let's just say this. Your semen didn't appear to do anything other than make Cas really happy and able to smell the roses, er, fir trees. He was pretty pissed at me when I made him take the neutralizer. Oh." He dug in one of the many pockets of his vest, and pulled out half a dozen little vials. "Here. In case it should *accidentally*—" His lips quivered but he didn't smile. "—happen again. One dose is all it should take to offset the euphoria."

"What about—" Rusty rolled the vials around in his palm, not sure he wanted to know the answer to this question. "What about lasting effects? Could this hurt him in the long run?"

Behind the shimmer of his glasses, Bryce's eyes were kind. "I don't know. We don't even have anecdotal evidence about this situation. But based on discussions with my druid circle, coupled with my research into epigenetics, I'd say prolonged exposure could very well alter his expressed genetic profile permanently."

"Is that— I mean, could he die?"

Bryce shook his head. "Unknown. The changes to the vampire genome are precariously balanced, as are those of all supes. Who's to know what alteration will tip it over into unviable."

"Unviable." Rusty's heart tried to stop. "You mean dead for real this time."

Bryce jerked his chin down in a single nod. "It's possible. I'm sorry. If there's anything I can do—"

"Thanks, Bryce. You've done plenty." Rusty took a deep breath. "The rest is on me."

Alien. Shit on a stick, as if being a *vampire* wasn't bad enough.

When Cas finally beat down his temper sufficiently to emerge from the boathouse, Bryce was gone and Rusty was staring stonily at the lake.

"I, um, guess we've missed the rehearsal dinner?"

"Mmmphmm."

The noncommittal grunt wasn't promising in terms of Rusty's state of mind, but a whole night and day together before they had to be at the wedding had to be a good thing, right? He crept up to press himself against Rusty's back. "Then we have time for that swim."

Rusty sighed, his shoulders slumping. "I know what you mean when you say 'swim,' Casimir, and it has nothing to do with getting in the water, does it?"

Oops. "Well, it doesn't *have* to. Not that I'd mind. But as romantic as the boathouse is, with the lovely spider webs festooning the corners and the bats flying around outside, I really think your house and your bed might be a much nicer place to spend the rest of the night."

"I agree."

Cas blinked, peering up at Rusty's profile. *You'd think a beard would soften the jut of that stubborn jaw, but no.* "You do?"

"Yes."

"Thank the gods," Cas breathed. "Because I really want—"

"To sleep. Separately. No sex."

Cas gaped at him. "No sex?" His voice squeaked on the last word. "But—" He took a step back. "I get it. You're freaked out."

Rusty pivoted and glared at him. "You're damn right I'm freaked out, and you should be too." He ran both hands through his hair. "I mean—" He gestured to Cas. "And—" He flung a hand toward the boathouse. "Not to mention—" He smacked himself on the forehead.

"Elmer. Use your words. Because I have no idea what's going on in your head." Cas twisted his fingers together. "Are you revolted because I might be a little bit extraterrestrial?"

"What? No!"

"Then what?"

"Didn't Bryce tell you? My blood. My—" There he went with the gestures again, pointing both index fingers at his crotch. "I could screw up your body so much that you die."

Cas leered. "But what a way to go."

"You—" Rusty grabbed him, his fingers flexing on Cas's biceps. "Don't. Joke. I can't—" He dropped his gaze, shoulders heaving. "I can't take it."

Cas reached up to stroke Rusty's beard. "I'm sorry, darling. It's a defense mechanism. When death is essentially the reason you exist, you tend to get a bit cavalier about it. I'll try to do better. I promise."

Rusty let go of him and stepped away, swiping a hand under his eyes. "Okay. Thanks."

"Let's clean up here and go home."

Rusty nodded and turned to trudge up the hill. Cas hurried to catch up. It wasn't much past midnight. Once they got back to Rusty's place, with half the night and all of tomorrow ahead of them before they had to be at this stupid wedding, Cas was confident he could shake Rusty out of his funk and convince him to make love again.

He was wrong.

As soon as they got to the house, Rusty hustled him inside and into the bedroom—which Cas took as an excellent sign. However, Rusty did nothing except stand with his arms folded while Cas undressed and climbed into bed.

Cas fluttered his eyelashes and patted the bed next to him. "Join me?"

"No. I've got to go out."

"Now?"

"It's an emergency. Leaky pipe. Under the, uh . . ."

Cas narrowed his eyes. "Under where, darling?"

"The house. Under the house. I have to go out to the store. Get some plumbing supplies."

"At one in the morning?"

"It's an all-night . . . Home Depot."

Seriously? "Can't it wait? I mean, water isn't gushing out of the faucets. The tides aren't rising up the stairs. Just come to bed, for pity's sake. You need your rest before weddingmageddon tomorrow."

"I can't. I'll be back."

"When?"

"Later."

He left, closing the bedroom door softly behind him. Cas lay in bed, fuming, for an hour before he got up and went into the living room. He binge-watched the entire first season of *Sense8* —almost twelve hours' worth—and Rusty *still* wasn't home. They had less than two days until their temporary marriage was over. Didn't Rusty want to spend some of that time with him, even if they didn't spend it in bed?

Finally, he lay down on the sofa and went to sleep out of sheer frustration, and was awoken by an incoming call. He groped for the phone on the coffee table and saw that it was four in the afternoon. "H'lo?"

"Where are you?"

"Rusty?" Cas sat up, rubbing his eyes.

"Yeah. Where are you?"

"On the sofa."

"I'm about to come inside. Go into the bathroom and shut the door."

"But—"

"I mean it, Cas. I'm not risking the light leak. I'll stay out here until dark unless you get yourself somewhere safe."

"Fine." After being alone for more than twelve hours, Cas had hoped for a little more *Honey, I'm home*, and a little less *Prisoner, back to your cell*. He stomped down the hall. "Hear that? I'm going into the bedroom." He slammed the door. "Door's closed."

"Now the bathroom."

"For pity's sake, Elmer, it's not as if the sunlight is a sentient super villain. It can't creep down the hall and—"

"Just get in the damn bathroom, Cas."

"I'll get in the damn bathroom," he muttered. He waited until he heard the front door close. "Can I come out yet?"

"No! One more trip. I'll tell you when." Rusty cut the call.

Cas turned around and flopped against the door. "This is stupid. I *hate* being a vampire."

He slid down the door until his ass thumped onto the floor. *I really do. I hate being a vampire. I think I've hated it from the beginning.* Yes, he had eternal life—*if this qualifies as a life*—but at the expense of others. He had wealth, but couldn't flaunt it too ostentatiously for fear of attracting too much attention. He'd had countless sexual partners, but never a lover. *Until now.*

If I wasn't a vampire, I could be with Rusty. I could swim with him in the lake, in the daytime. We could cook dinner together, eat together, build a life together.

But if I wasn't a vampire, I'd be decades buried.

Besides, did Rusty want the same thing? Maybe his disappearing act today was his way of ending their temporary relationship early. Cas could hardly blame him. *If I were him, I wouldn't want to date a vampire either.*

Yet this was the life Cas had chosen, that he continued to choose every day. How awful would it be for someone who didn't have the choice? *Or what if I decide to make a* different choice?

The door opened and closed again. "Cas?" Rusty called. "You can come out now."

What if I don't want to? He wrapped his arms around his knees, scowling at the floor. *Maybe I'll just stay in here.* Alone. The same way he'd ended every day of his Second Life until Rusty. *That's not a different choice, damn it!* It was the same song, different verse.

Besides, he'd already spent all night and half the day in a pissy mood because he was by himself. He'd be cutting off his balls to spite his dick if he refused company now that he had it.

He exited the freaking airlock Rusty had insisted on and joined his soon-to-be-ex-husband in the kitchen. The breakfast bar and island were covered with bags and several lengths of galvanized pipe. Cas studied it silently for a few seconds, then turned to meet Rusty's gaze.

Rusty had the grace to blush and look away. "I told you I was going to get some plumbing supplies, so I decided I'd better actually do it."

"Do you *need* plumbing supplies?"

"Not right now. But you know. Construction company. I'm sure we'll need them eventually."

"Rusty—"

"I'm sorry, Cas. I know I was a dick. But I didn't trust myself. When Bryce said that prolonged exposure to my . . . bodily fluids . . . might hurt you, I couldn't risk it. I mean, what if spit is dangerous too? I couldn't be in the house with you and not want to kiss you. Not after— Not after the lake."

Cas's sharp vision picked out a familiar logo inside a semitransparent Walgreens bag. "If that's the case . . ." In a flash, he dipped his hand inside and pulled out the box of condoms. "Why do you need these?"

Rusty winced. "Like I said. I don't trust myself. So they're . . . insurance?"

Cas's annoyance vanished, shot down by an arrow of pure affection. "Good thinking." He strolled around the island, making sure to brush Rusty in passing. "What else have you got in here?" Cas tugged the edge of a plain brown bag.

"Don't look in there!" Rusty tried to snatch it out of the way, but Cas was vampire-quick, and running on twelve-plus hours of irritation.

He whisked the bag out of Rusty's reach. "More shameful than magnum XL condoms? What could it be? Unless it's something you . . ." Cas reached into the bag, eyes burning, and lifted out a plastic florist's box containing a white rose boutonniere. "Is this— You got this for me?"

Rusty scuffed his boot against the tile floor. "Yeah. I thought it might, you know, help mask the shifter stink. I mean, tonight's not gonna be pleasant for you."

"That is so incredibly sweet. But it's not necessary."

"Oh. Okay. You don't have to use it. We can just leave it here.

Rusty reached for the box, but Cas clutched it to his chest. "No. I want it. I love it, and I'm going to wear it because it's beautiful and you gave it to me."

"But if you don't need it—"

"'Need' and 'want' are two very different things, darling. To manage the shifter stank—since it would be the height of rude to tell the bride that she reeks, and vampires are *never* rude—I brought my secret weapon."

"What? Stealth air freshener?"

"No. Garlic nasal spray. Stings like a son of a bitch, but it kills my sense of smell for at least an hour. I'll be fine, although I'll probably smell like an Italian restaurant."

"Probably? Don't you know?"

Cas tapped the side of his nose. "No sense of smell except as it relates to vampire feeding, remember? Sadly, lasagna and pasta e fagioli are not on the regular menu."

Rusty's cheeks reddened, and he gazed down at his hands clutching the edge of the counter. "The reception is at a historic hotel. It'll probably go pretty late, but I've got a room reserved. It's our last night together, so even if we decide to do, you know, something, it can't very well turn into *prolonged* exposure."

Cas sidled up and bumped Rusty's hip with his own. "Are you saying you want to do 'something' with me tonight?"

Rusty met his gaze, and the naked *want* in those gorgeous brown eyes lit a fire low in Cas's belly. "More than you'll ever know."

"Then pack your 'insurance,' darling, because we will definitely be doing 'something'—more than once. I don't suppose we can skip the whole wedding and just go straight to the hotel?"

Rusty laughed and kissed the top of Cas's head. "That'd kind of defeat the purpose of my half of the wedding contract, wouldn't it?"

"I suppose. But I'm holding that thought in reserve, just in case."

Chapter Sixteen

Rusty tugged on his collar as he and Cas stood at the back of the church, waiting for the ushers to seat them.

"Will you relax?" Cas whispered.

"I can't help it. They're all gonna judge both of us, and when —" Rusty's stomach lurched as he stared at the stained glass window over the pulpit. "Shit." He grabbed Cas's arm. "Can you even *go* in a church?" Cas simply stared at him, face expressionless except for a slight quirk of one eyebrow. Rusty winced. "Right, right. Popular culture hype. Not reality."

They stepped to the front of the line, and the usher—Donald, one of Fletcher's cousins Rusty'd known all his life—stared at Cas with his mouth hanging open.

Cas smiled, and Rusty didn't blame him for showing a hint of fang. "Groom's side, please."

When Donald didn't tear his gaze away from Cas, Rusty reached out and nudged his shoulder to turn him around. "For Gaia's sake, Donald, show us to our seats."

"But, Rusty, he's—"

"My husband. Now show us to our seats. Please."

Donald stumbled up the aisle and flung his arm out randomly in a gesture that could mean any one of six different pews. Rusty chose the unoccupied one nearest the rear of the church, and guided Cas into it with a hand on the small of his back.

"Sorry about that," he murmured.

"Are you kidding?" Cas whispered back, wiggling in his seat and wrapping his hands around Rusty's arm. "The fun is just beginning."

They'd cut it close in terms of timing. Donald and the rest of the ushers only had a couple more trips down the aisle with other guests—all of them shifters, as far as Rusty could see, and from their general sizes and coloring, probably all beavers too. He didn't recognize the people on the bride's side, but that wasn't surprising. His clan didn't parade him around at interclan gatherings, for obvious reasons. They'd done it while he was still a teenager, because it would have been disrespectful to his mom to exclude him while dragging all the rest of the teens along—most of whom would have been just as glad to stay home and swim in their own lake. But once he'd started college, and then later his own business, Earl had made only a token protest about clan duties before accepting Rusty's excuses about being too busy.

After all, beavers admired nothing quite so much as industriousness.

Rusty glanced down at Cas, who was gazing around him with barely concealed amusement. *I wonder if that's one of the reasons they don't like vampires, even though there's no threat. Because none of them do any work.*

He leaned down to murmur into Cas's ear. "What do you do?"

Cas's eyebrows lifted in those cute double peaks. "Do?"

"For a living?"

"Haven't you heard? Vampires are parasites, feeding off the underbelly of supe society."

"No, really. What do you do?"

Cas sighed. "If you must know, I sit on the board of a foundation dedicated to the restoration of old films. Although I've missed this month's meeting."

Rusty grinned. "Really? That's so cool! Not missing the meeting, but the whole film-restoration thing."

"It's rather disheartening, actually. I remember so many films that have been lost forever. Beautiful things. Inspiring things. Things that would break your heart. Gone now. All gone, just like the artists who made them."

"Except you. You're not gone."

Cas smiled a little sadly. "I was a very minor cog in that wheel."

"I don't care. I'm glad you're not gone."

Cas's shoulders hitched, another unexpected breath. He laced his fingers in Rusty's beard and brought his head down for an achingly sweet kiss. *Who needs wedding cake?*

But then the organist pounded out the opening chords of the wedding march, and they had to stand up along with the rest of the crowd. This put Rusty at least a head taller than everyone else in the church—and put him in direct line of sight to Fletcher, who was glaring at *him* rather than gazing down the aisle at his bride.

"Uh-oh," Cas murmured. "Watch out, darling. That man is *not* ready to let you go."

Rusty tucked Cas's hand through his elbow. "He'll have to. Because I'm taken."

Cas chuckled and cuddled closer, and stayed that way throughout the ceremony. Afterward, the ushers cleared the pews from the back of the church forward, so they were among the first outside and were directed toward the back of where the crowd would wait for the bride and groom to emerge. The bridesmaids handed out birdseed for them to toss, but Cas looked at the little net bundle tied up with peach and green ribbons, and handed his and Rusty's to a nearby child who looked thrilled to have scored the extras.

"Let's head to the hotel. I've never liked the tradition of pelting the bride and groom with foodstuffs. It reminds me too much of my days in Vaudeville."

"Suits me." Since they'd parked in the hotel's underground lot and checked in before walking to the ceremony, they could go directly to the reception. But Rusty was in no hurry. The evening was chilly but dry, and since neither he nor Cas was bothered by the cold, he took Cas's hand. A little park lay between the church and the hotel, so Rusty headed there.

"You know what I was thinking while Fletcher the Fuckhead —"

"Cas. It's his wedding day."

"Exactly. But don't worry. I've gotten that off my chest and can be civil for the rest of the evening. Anyway. Do you know what I was thinking, in that lovely old church, decorated with masses of flowers that included far too many sticks of sharp-ended curly willow for my peace of mind, with the men in their tuxes, and the bridesmaids in those seasonally inappropriate colors, while Fletcher lied his ass off to that poor woman who's now stuck with him forever?"

"What?"

Cas looked up at him, and what Rusty saw in his face made him stumble to a stop under a bare maple tree. "That our wedding was a hundred times nicer. And I wouldn't trade it for anything else."

Rusty laughed, although his chest was almost too tight to let it out. "Casimir, we said our vows to a pissed-off witch in a slate-lined chamber that smelled of an exorcism, with nobody but a nervous demon and a smug AI as witnesses. How could it compare?"

"Like I said. A hundred times nicer. It was honest, for one thing. And at the end of it?" Cas twined his arms around Rusty's neck. "I got you."

Rusty's hands tightened on Cas's waist. "Cas—"

"Shhh. I know. I only have you until tomorrow. But Elmer? I wouldn't trade it. Not for anything. Not if D.W. Griffith himself rose from the grave and offered me the lead in his next picture."

Even though they were standing in the dark, in a park full of bare trees and skittering leaves, November wind ruffling their hair, Rusty could swear it was spring. *Who needs sunlight when I've got this face shining at me?*

But not for much longer. One day, and then their contract would be up. Ted would be free. The idiotic vampire council would force Cas to marry that incubus, someone higher class than Rusty could ever be. But even so, even though that knowledge cast a shadow over them that made Rusty shiver, it couldn't take away from this moment.

"Neither would I, Casimir. Neither would I."

He wrapped his arms around his husband, his vampire, his . . . his . . . Gaia preserve him, his *love*, and leaned down for a kiss. Cas's lips were soft and cool, a balm against his own warmer-than-human heat. Rusty lost count of how many kisses they shared, never too hot, never going too far. But each one a benediction.

Then he pulled Cas against his chest, tucking Cas's head under his chin, and simply held him while the rest of the world revolved around them as if the park, this tree, this patch of grass, was the only place that mattered.

Eventually, Rusty sighed. "Everybody's probably at the reception already. In fact, we've probably missed the receiving line."

"Good." Cas burrowed closer, his fingers playing with Rusty's hair.

"We already missed the rehearsal dinner. If I don't at least greet Sylvie, it'll seem like a slight. She's part of my clan now, and Fletcher's actions aren't her fault."

"Sadly, you're correct, my noble beaver knight. Let us sally forth."

When they entered the hotel lobby, Cas stopped Rusty before they could head upstairs to the ballroom where the reception was being held. "Wait a moment. You look like you've been out kissing some random vampire in the park." He reached up to run his fingers through Rusty's hair, holding up a curled brown leaf. "Debauched by nature, darling. What can I say?"

"You look perfect, as always. I think you intimidate nature. It wouldn't presume to muss you up."

"Is that so?" He grinned and took Rusty's arm. "In that case, I'll have to depend on you for that."

Something about the idea of *mussing* Cas sent a pulse of heat to Rusty's groin. "Count on it," he growled as they mounted the stairs.

When they got to the top, though, Cas's face pinched, and he tugged his arm free. "Hold on. I have to duck into the men's room to refresh the garlic spray."

"Should I come with you?"

Cas grinned, no fangs. "If you come with me, we might never come out, which would totally defeat the purpose of being here. Besides, I'm fully capable of conquering my own sinuses."

As Cas strolled away down the mezzanine, Rusty admired the way his suit accented his shoulders, even though the tails of his jacket hid that stellar ass.

I'll see it tonight though. He licked his lips.

"Rusty."

He nearly bit his tongue at Fletcher's harsh tone. He took a moment, smoothing the front of his jacket, breathing through his nose, and then turned. The two of them were alone on the mezzanine, like two ink blots on the red carpet, although one of the bridesmaids was peeking at them from the open ballroom doors.

"Fletcher. Congratulations."

"Cut the crap. Where have you been?"

"We decided to walk over from the church. Cas hasn't seen this part of the city before, and I wanted to show him the park. I hadn't realized we'd taken so long."

"That's not what I mean and you know it. No one's seen you for almost two weeks."

Rusty was tempted to roll his eyes. "That's because I've been busy repainting your entire house. If anyone wanted to see me, they could have found me there."

"You weren't at the rehearsal dinner."

"No. I wasn't." Rusty smiled blandly although his belly was roiling.

"Why not?"

"Something came up. I apologize. I hope it didn't upset your seating arrangements."

"That's not the point."

Rusty heaved a sigh. "Then what is the point, Fletcher?"

Fletcher stepped closer, close enough that he invaded Rusty's personal space, just like he'd always done. That wasn't unusual for clan leaders, of course. They used proximity to exert their authority. But Rusty wasn't falling for it tonight. He didn't back away, but he crossed his arms.

Fletcher glanced behind him at the ballroom doors. The nosy bridesmaid looked away quickly, but Donald was there to goggle in her place. Fletcher gestured peremptorily and Donald scrambled to shut the doors.

He turned back to Rusty. "The beaver council is concerned about you. This kind of recalcitrance and violence was what presaged that werewolf's breakdown last year. You're acting out of character."

"I don't know. Maybe this is my real character for the first time."

"You married a fucking vampire. How is that normal?"

"You lost the right to object to my choice of partner when you dumped me, Fletcher."

"Aw, come on." His voice turned cajoling, the same tone he'd used from the time they were kids to argue that his own actions, no matter how selfish, were perfectly reasonable and that Rusty's objections weren't. "This is politics. Clan duty. You know that. It doesn't have anything to do with how I feel. It doesn't have anything to do with us."

"I'd say it does."

Fletcher advanced until his chest was within a double hand span of Rusty's. "You're pissed. I get it. I should have told you about the deal before."

"You think? I built a whole fucking house, Fletcher, because I thought it was going to be mine. You watched me do it for months. You helped me pick out the *faucets*, for Gaia's sake. We had sex in the fucking *wine cellar*."

Fletcher glanced around furtively. "Keep your voice down, can't you?"

"No, I don't think I can. You could have been honest with me at any time. But you weren't."

"I should have been. I know that now." He lowered his chin to peer up at Rusty from beneath his brows. *That doesn't look nearly as alluring as when Cas does the same thing.* "You've always put the good of the clan first, Rusty, just like I have. So forgive me? Please? We can still have what we had before. It won't be any different."

"That's what I'm afraid of. Always second best. Always the afterthought. Always in the dark." Gaia strike him blind, even if he spent the rest of his life with Cas, their relationship would see more daylight than he'd ever had with Fletcher.

The light bulb in Rusty's brain that had been flickering since the engagement announcement finally switched to full power. "You don't give a shit about the good of the clan. The good of the clan is way down on your list of priorities. The good of Fletcher Dawson is at the top. The good of Rusty Johnson? I didn't make the top twenty. I'm probably not even *on* the list."

Fletcher's eyebrows bunched together, and he took another step forward. If Rusty's arms weren't in the way, they'd be chest to chest. "This isn't you. You've never acted this way before. It's that vampire, isn't it? He can't have you. I won't stand for it."

"Really? You have no say in my marriage. And since you've been married for less than three hours, shouldn't you pretend to be faithful through the wedding night at the very least?"

"I'm warning you," Fletcher growled. "We're watching. And at the first sign of instability, we're tagging you faster than you can blink."

"Won't that ruin your little plan to get some on the side? Don't forget, Fletcher. If I'm tagged, then they'll track my movements and interactions. All of them."

"I don't care. Once you see reason, I can get the order rescinded just as easily."

Rusty cracked a laugh. "But for my own good, right?"

"Of course." Confusion warred with rage on Fletcher's face. "I'll always have your interests at heart, Rusty. You know that."

"You have a piss-poor way of showing it. Secret engagement. Passive-aggressive posturing. Threats—and at your own wedding, no less. Can't you see how ridiculous that is?"

"Did somebody say ridiculous?" Cas snaked an arm around Rusty's waist, and suddenly Rusty could breathe again. "I am *so* there. Ridiculous is my favorite flavor." He tilted his head to glance sidelong at Rusty. "Well, aside from you, darling."

"I don't believe we've met." Cas held out his hand, but didn't release Rusty's arm. "Casimir Moreau. Congratulations . . . Felcher, isn't it?"

"Fletcher," he replied through clenched teeth.

My, my, my. If looks could kill, I'd be a flaming torch. "Lovely ceremony. I'm sorry we weren't able to make it to the rehearsal dinner last night, but, well, something *came up.*" Cas snuggled closer to Rusty, who flushed beautifully.

"Cas, not *now.*" Rusty's voice was the perfect blend of agonized, embarrassed, and amused. *Really, he couldn't have done it better if we'd rehearsed for a week.*

A vein throbbed in Fletcher's temple. "You missed the receiving line."

"Oh, did we? What a shame." He nudged Rusty's ribs. "I guess we shouldn't have dawdled so long in the park, darling."

He turned back to Fletcher. "But it was so romantic. The stars. The moon. The balmy night breeze."

"It's No*vem*ber!"

Cas widened his eyes. "*Oh.* I hadn't noticed. I guess it's because Rusty keeps me so warm."

Rusty started coughing into the crook his other elbow. "Sorry. We'd like to meet Sylvie. Offer our best wishes. Do you mind if we go inside now?"

"We won't be staying for dinner, for *obvious* reasons." Cas smiled, allowing his fangs to run out part way. "So disappointing, since that means we'll miss the dancing too, and I'd love nothing better than to dance the night away with my husband." He cast another sly glance at Rusty. "Well, *almost* nothing."

Rusty made an odd sound, as if he was trying to clear his throat and choked in the middle. "Yes. Dinner. Disappointed. Uh . . . dancing. Right."

"We're still on our honeymoon." Cas fluttered his eyelashes at Rusty, whose lips twitched with what was clearly a suppressed smile. "I'm sure you understand, Felch— Fletcher, being a newlywed yourself."

Fletcher folded his arms, which wrinkled his tux jacket in an unfortunate way. *Really, his tailor should be shot.* "I don't know what the fuck you think you're doing, Rusty, but I refuse to let you embarrass Sylvie and make a bigger fool out of yourself than you already have. Drop your gift on the table inside and then get out."

"Gift? *Gift?*" Cas's skin was hot with rage. "He built you a *house,* Felcher."

"*Fletcher.*"

"Did you tell your wife that? Or does she think it's a present from you?"

"My father bought that lot for me years ago. We paid for the materials. And the materials alone—"

"Yes, the materials alone. That's all you shelled out for and damn *straight* you paid for them. Or do you seriously think Rusty owes you for that as well as for design and labor?"

The way Fletcher's neck bulged over his too-tight shirt collar made him look more like a puffer fish shifter than a beaver. "Rusty. Are you going to stand there like a block and let him talk to me that way?"

"No. I'm not." Rusty put his hand over Cas's. Cas's belly fluttered. Was Rusty about to fling him off and go slinking back to his asshole ex? But instead of prying Cas's fingers off his arm as Cas half expected, he laced his fingers on top and turned them both around.

"Rusty!" Fletcher called as they marched toward the elevator. "Don't you walk away from me!"

Rusty didn't respond, but his arm muscles were hard as stone. Cas was afraid he'd crossed the line—he'd be gone after tomorrow, but Rusty had to put up with these assholes for the rest of his life. But as soon as the elevator doors closed behind them, instead of punching the button for their floor, Rusty grabbed Cas and practically devoured him in a searing kiss.

When he pulled back, he was breathing heavily. "Felcher? *Felcher*? Gaia strike me blind, Cas, I thought I'd die."

Cas patted his chest. "That was not my intent, darling. However—" he narrowed his eyes and glared at the elevator doors as if he could laser through them "—I wouldn't mind dealing a few telling blows on Fletcher the Fuckhead. Seriously, Elmer, what did you ever see in him?"

"He was different when we were kids."

"Was he? Was he really? Or were you simply more innocent than you are now?"

Rusty snorted, releasing Cas to lean against the elevator wall. "I'm not innocent. I've done plenty of stuff I'm ashamed of."

"But I'll wager you never did it out of spite or selfishness. You don't have that in you. And believe me, I'd know—I've had years dealing with vampires who are *experts* in both, which is why we're such sticklers for social courtesy. Otherwise, we'd be so unbearable that nobody, even other vampires, would want to speak to us."

Rusty stroked Cas's cheek, running his thumb across Cas's lower lip. "I don't believe you have it in you to be unbearable."

"That's not what you thought the night we met."

"Yeah, well, I'm not the best judge of character, as you've just pointed out." He rested his forehead against Cas's. "Nobody's ever defended me like that before. Nobody's ever shown Fletcher that someone other than him might find me attractive, that I have other choices. Even if you were just pretending, I appreciate it."

"Pretending? Really, Elmer, you ought to know me better by now." Cas hit the button for the third floor. "We've been married for over two weeks now. I find you insanely hot, and not just because your skin practically scorches me when we touch. You deserve better than Fletcher the Fuckhead." He stroked Rusty's face from smooth skin to springy beard. "Actually, you deserve better than me."

"I don't. But I hope that maybe someday I'll be worthy of someone like you."

Fuck someday. You're worthy of anyone today. Maybe it made Cas a worse person than he knew himself to be, but tonight was their last chance before they had to give in to the demands of their clans and councils. The doors slid open, and he took Rusty by the hand and hauled him down the corridor to their room. "You know what, Elmer? I refuse to give Fletcher an opportunity to gloat." He keyed open the room. "Now get in there and let's spend the next few hours fucking like weasel shifters."

Rusty didn't laugh as Cas had hoped. Instead he shut the door and leaned against it. "I shouldn't. We shouldn't. It's too dangerous for you."

Cas advanced on Rusty. *My turn to be the lion and your turn at gazelle.* "If you really believed *that*, darling . . ." He reached up and loosened Rusty's tie, then unbuttoned his collar. "You wouldn't have bought those condoms."

"What if I—" Rusty gulped, his Adam's apple nudging Cas's fingers. "What if I told you I left them at home?"

"I wouldn't believe you, of course. What if I told you I didn't want to use them anyway?"

Rusty's jaw tightened. "Cas—"

"Please, Rusty. You gave Felcher a whole *house*. Can't you give me this?" Cas focused his entire *being* on Rusty, wanting this, craving this. *Why can't mesmer work on supes, just a little bit?* "Can't you give me one night? Unless . . ." Cas remembered Bryce's theory about vampire origins. "You *are* freaked out by the alien thing, aren't you? I disgust you now."

Rusty caught him around the waist. "No. Gaia, no. Hey." He smoothed Cas's hair away from his face. "Remember making out with me in the park an hour ago? And again in the elevator? Did that seem like disgust to you?"

"No?" Cas hated that uncertainty made his voice wobble.

"You're beautiful and brave and crazy as fuck, but I like that about you." He pulled Cas closer, their hips aligning so perfectly Cas's eyes nearly crossed. "I like the way I feel with you. You don't treat me like I'm less than."

Cas captured Rusty's face between his hands. "That's because you're not. That idiot downstairs? He's the lesser man." He kissed Rusty gently, and at least Rusty didn't resist. "Let's take this time, as many hours as we can before we have to race the sunrise home. Tomorrow we're due back at Supernatural Selection to meet our real matches—"

Rusty's hands tightened on Cas's waist. "What we have feels pretty damn real to me."

Cas smoothed an errant lock of hair off Rusty's forehead. "It is. I'm closer to you than I've been to anyone ever, in my First Life or my Second. But you're a shifter. I'm a vampire. There are too many . . . complications, not the least of which is that Henryk will take our relationship as an excuse to escalate." The last thing Cas needed was for Henryk to get *more* leverage over him. If the bastard discovered just how much Rusty meant to Cas, he'd target Rusty just as he'd targeted Archie. *Not if I can help it.* He ran his hands down Rusty's lapels. "You look so handsome in your new suit."

Rusty blushed adorably. "It was supposed to be for your reception, but they screwed up the sleeves and the pants."

"Well, the pants fit *very* well now." He rose on his toes to whisper into Rusty's ear. "Take them off."

"Oookay."

Rusty's pulse beat in a seductive rhythm in his throat. So he could see it better, Cas removed Rusty's tie. "And darling. I'm serious. Forget the condoms. Bryce told me that I wasn't in any danger."

Rusty frowned, catching Cas's wrist. "That's not what he told me. He said prolonged exposure—"

"Although I want to expose as much of me to as much of you as possible, it will hardly be *prolonged*. It's our *last night*." Cas's throat tightened, his voice breaking on the final word. "Besides, don't you think deciding what risk is acceptable for me is a little paternalistic, Elmer? It's *my* risk to take—and remember, I'm older than you are."

"Not by that much. I may be inactive, but I'm just as long-lived as any normal shifter."

Cas growled deep in his throat. "If it wouldn't cast a definite pall on the wedding party, I'd go downstairs and eviscerate Fletcher the Fuckhead right now." He unbuckled Rusty's belt. "'Normal' can be a temperature. It can be a grade curve. It can be the name of a city in Illinois. But when the word is used to exclude people who are outside of the speaker's comfort zone? To boost their own self-esteem?" He whipped the belt off and tossed it across the room. "It's beyond revolting."

"I, uh, guess you have some feelings about that."

"I do. *Own* your uniqueness, Rusty. *Own* your strengths, your weaknesses, your abilities, your shortcomings because they make you *you*. And *you* are extraordinary. Now." He backed Rusty toward the bed until his legs hit the mattress and he plopped down. Cas straddled his lap. "All those self-righteous beavers are downstairs getting drunk on second-rate champagne. It's only fair that we have our own celebration up here."

"But—"

"The night in the boathouse?" Cas pushed Rusty's jacket off his shoulders and started unbuttoning his shirt. "That high was better than gin from Bakersfield's finest bathtubs. Better than real champagne smuggled in from France. Better than the last bottle of bourbon from Fatty Arbuckle's illegal cellar. I want to get drunk on *you*, Rusty, the way I can't get drunk on alcohol anymore."

Rusty groaned as Cas scraped his fingernails across that incredible chest. "Cas, you're killing me here."

Cas grinned and popped the button on Rusty's trousers. "Not me, darling. Remember, I'm a no-kill vampire." He stood up and stripped off his own clothes, the heat in Rusty's gaze warming him like the sun he hadn't seen in nearly a century. "Playfulness and fun are all well and good. But I'm completely serious when I say that I want this. I want to know how hot you'll be inside me without the latex. I want us to have tonight, *no matter what*." He stepped forward, nudging Rusty's knees apart, and took that dear, dear face in his hands. "Don't you?"

Rusty clenched his eyes shut, throat working, and nodded. "More than you'll ever know."

"Well, then." Cas tugged Rusty's beard. "Lose the pants and show me."

Cas turned away and sashayed over to the nightstand where he'd stashed the lube before they'd left for the wedding. He bent over (completely unnecessarily) to open the drawer and was rewarded with Rusty choking on a groan behind him. *Oh, my sweet man, if you think* that *was hitting below the belt . . .*

Staying in the same position, Cas *snicked* open the lube and squirted a good-sized dollop onto his fingers. He couldn't hold back the moan as he worked it into himself. Not because it felt good—although it most certainly did—but because of Rusty's tortured growl.

Cas glanced over his shoulder. Rusty was standing next to the bed, his pants and briefs tangled around his ankles, impressive shaft at full, mouthwatering extension, his gaze riveted on Cas's ass. "See something you like, darling?"

Rusty grimaced, grabbing the base of his cock. "You really *will* kill me if you keep doing that."

"We mustn't have that." Cas drew his fingers out, slowly and with maximum sound effects. He squeezed another handful of lube and advanced on Rusty. He nudged Rusty's shoulder with one glistening finger. "Sit." Rusty plopped down gracelessly, his feet still trapped in his clothing. "Stay."

"I'm not a fucking werew— *Oh!*" Rusty's gasp as Cas slicked him up sent a *zing* to Cas's balls. *Must move faster before . . .*

Cas straddled Rusty's hips and lowered himself onto Rusty's cock, the stretch and burn as heavenly as he remembered. But then Rusty grabbed Cas's waist, stopping him before he was fully seated. "Damn it, Elmer, I really *will* kill you if you don't —"

"Easy, sweetheart." Rusty's voice was rough, strained. *Good. At least I'm not the only one suffering here.* "Slower. I don't want you to hurt yourself."

"I'm a vampire, remember? I'm virtually indestructible as long as we stay away from toothpicks and tanning beds."

"Don't joke, Cas. I couldn't—"

"Rusty." Cas cradled Rusty's face, managing to slide down another inch as he caught Rusty's protest in a kiss. "The only thing that can hurt me now is if we stop. So if you really don't want to hurt me—" Cas leaned forward to nuzzle under Rusty's ear, the scent of earth and water and spice nearly dizzying "—you'll move. Now."

And Rusty, bless him, did. With a throaty growl, he tensed those impeccable abs, rolled his hips, and brought Cas *down*.

Yes! Right there! Cas buried his face in Rusty's neck, muffling his cries as Rusty hit his gland again and again and again.

"Cas. Gaia, Cas . . ."

That reverent whisper sent Cas over the edge. He sucked in air through his open mouth, his lips grazing Rusty's skin . . . right . . . over . . . his . . . carotid.

And bit.

Chapter
Seventeen

Rusty's orgasm went on. And on. And on. *Gaia, it's never been like this. How can it be like this?* In between one thrust and the next, he felt it. The exquisite pain in his neck, the pull, the blinding euphoria.

He bit me. He's drinking my blood. Oh, Gaia. It feels so good, but it's bad. Dangerous. Oh help.

"Cas." He could barely grind the words out. "You have to stop."

Cas let go and reared back, gasping, still impaled on Rusty's cock. "Gods, Rusty, I'm so sorry." He leaned forward, but Rusty held him off.

The fireworks in his nerves started to flicker out, and his brain came back online. *Sort of.* "Don't. You're already compromised. Are you about to latch on again?"

Cas's expression turned from horrified to stormy. "No, you idiot. I need to seal the wound. Now let go."

"Not if it means you poison yourself." He lifted Cas off his lap and set him on the mattress.

"I refuse to let you bleed out on me." Cas set his jaw and grabbed Rusty's nape in a steel-clamp grip. He pulled Rusty forward and licked a stripe up his neck. "There."

Trying to reason was like swimming through honey. "We've got to fix this."

"No need. You're set. Vampire saliva has a coagulant and certain healing properties that—"

"Not *me*. You!" Rusty scrambled out of bed, fighting the urge to curl up in bed with Cas and never leave. *But this is important.* "I'll get the neutralizer. After you take it, we'll call Bryce. Take you to the VER. *Shit.* The nearest one's in Portland. We'll—"

"No." Cas grabbed Rusty's hand. His gray eyes were sparkling and his cheeks were tinged with pink. With his rumpled caramel-colored hair and skin like silk, he was more beautiful than anybody or anything Rusty had ever seen. "I'm not taking the damn neutralizer."

"You're— But, Cas. Sweetheart." He dropped to his knees, capturing Cas's hand between both of his. "You have to. You'll die, and then I don't know—" His breath caught in a half sob. "I don't know if I can handle it."

Cas smiled, and even though he stroked Rusty's hair gently, that smile still held a hint of the same crazy-wild-reckless that Rusty found so exciting. "You can, darling. You can handle anything. But I can't. I'm not as strong as you. This life—" He gestured to himself, his voice almost dreamy. "This wasn't what I expected when I agreed to the Turn. I didn't mind so much. Not until Archie." He cupped Rusty's cheek. "Not until you."

"Cas—"

"Shhh." He placed his finger over Rusty's lips. "Archie made me think about what I've given up to extend my life. But you? You made me realize what I want. If I can't have this with you, if we can't make love, if I can't feel your vitality coursing through me when I—" He closed his eyes. "Gods, just thinking about it . . ." He took a deep breath—*he actually took a deep breath!* "Your blood didn't kill me before. The broken condom didn't kill me. Going bareback tonight didn't kill me. And feeding from you just now won't kill me either."

"How do you know? The greater volume could do it. It could trigger the allergic reaction." Rusty spoke against Cas's finger, and Gaia blast it, the brush of his lips against Cas's skin was getting him hard again.

"You made me feel more alive than I have since 1926. You make me fly."

"I knew it. You're high again. I need to—"

"I am *not* high—merely floating, a *most* pleasurable experience, I might add. Bryce said I might develop a certain resistance to the effects."

"Cas—"

"If making love with you means I'm facing my own mortality? Then it's a risk I'm willing to take."

"But you could live forever," Rusty whispered.

"Why would I want to live forever the way I was before? I know exactly how Archie feels. It wasn't until we started spending time together, and you had to make so many concessions for me, handling me like I was made of glass, that I realized I hate this life because it's *not* a life. I know why the vampire population has decreased so sharply. Because eventually there's no point. Wealth and luxury don't mean anything if there's no *reason* for them. Living for its own sake is the same as being rich for its own sake. It's empty, Rusty. Empty and lonely and so boring you're ready do anything, risk anything, just to feel that spark again, the spark that made you think eternal life would be worth the sacrifice."

"Spark?"

"Mm-hmm. I lost that spark a long time ago and I never knew. Not until I met you and found it again. Without you . . ." Cas stared at the wall for a long moment, then finally shrugged. "The spark will die again. And maybe it's time for me to let it all go."

"Don't say that. Please don't say that."

"Then do me the courtesy of letting me choose how I decide to go on. I want to hold on to this feeling. I don't want to neutralize it. This is our last night, Rusty, and I want to pretend that I'm a man again. A living man. And that means holding you. Kissing you. Loving you at least one more time—without the damn condom." He touched Rusty's throat, featherlight, yet it went straight to Rusty's dick.

Rusty clenched his eyes shut. "Gaia, Cas." *Resist. Do it for him.* But where did he cross the line into arrogance and paternalistic bullshit? This was Cas's choice. *But I want it too. So badly. Isn't that selfish?* Damn it, where did he draw the line between being responsible and being condescending?

"Do you suppose," Cas murmured, a breath away from Rusty's ear, "you'd let me taste you again?"

"F-feed from me, you mean?" The memory of Cas's bite, the way it had extended Rusty's orgasm, made his cock perk up. *Hello, refraction time.*

"Yes."

At what point did Rusty's resistance slide from protective to paternalistic? *And when does desire outweigh risk?* But Cas was an adult. Had been for decades. Shouldn't he be allowed to make his own decisions? Set the terms for his existence? *It's what I would want. It's what I* do *want.*

So Rusty nodded, although he couldn't claim completely unselfish motives. He wanted Cas too much. Wanted that rush of closeness again. "You sure you're not feeling—"

"Poisoned? Far from it. I feel more clearheaded than I've felt in decades, and rather as if I could bench-press this hotel."

He took a huge breath. "Okay then. One more time." *One last time. For him. For both of us.* He stumbled to the bathroom.

"Elmer!" Cas called. "Your dick is impressive but even you can't reach me from in there."

"Hold on. Just want to clean us up a bit before the next round." Rusty soaked a washcloth with warm water and grabbed a towel. When he glanced in the mirror, he saw two tiny red marks on his neck below his beard line. He touched them with a shaking finger. *How can something that felt so huge look so trivial?*

"Elmer? Did you get lost in there?"

"Coming." He switched off the light and hurried into the bedroom, nearly tripping over his own tongue when he saw Cas lying back on the sheets, cock already hard. He shook himself, and sat down on the edge of the mattress so he could gently wipe Cas's spunk off his chest and belly, and his own—*gulp!*—from between Cas's cheeks when Cas helpfully raised his knees and (not so helpfully for Rusty's self-control) exposed his hole.

He swiped the cloth haphazardly across his own midsection, then tossed everything aside to crawl onto the bed next to Cas. *My lover. My husband.* His breath caught in the back of his throat. *At least for one more day.*

Rusty nuzzled Cas's chest, savoring the dark, seductive scent of his skin. "Have I ever told you how beautiful you are?"

"I don't recall." Cas inhaled sharply when Rusty teased his nipple with his teeth. "But feel free to expand on the subject. Especially—" he moaned "—if you do it like that. *Gods*, Elmer!"

Rusty nibbled his way across Cas's chest to the other nipple. "When it comes to teeth—" *nip* "—vampires got nothin' on beavers."

Cas giggled—he flat-out giggled, one arm flailing to the side until he grabbed the bottle of lube and smacked Rusty in the ribs with it. "Save the jokes for when your johnson's inside me, Mr. *Johnson.* Gods above and below, is your last name ever appropriate."

"Shut up." But Rusty couldn't fight a grin as he slicked himself up again. "Or I really will tell you jokes, and then you'll be sorry."

"Why will I—*ungh*—be sorry?" Cas's voice turned breathless as Rusty draped Cas's legs over his shoulders, lined his cock up with Cas's hole, and pushed inside.

Rusty lost his own breath when Cas's cool, tight channel hugged his cock. "Because—" he rolled his pelvis, sliding in farther with each little thrust "—I'm terrible at it."

"Mmm." Cas closed his eyes. "I can't believe you'd be terrible at anyth— *There!*"

"How many vampires"—*thrust*—"does it take"—*thrust*—"to screw in"—*thrust*—"a light bulb?"

Cas shuddered underneath him. "That's a—gods, Rusty, please touch my dick—trick question."

"Trick?" Rusty somehow found room in his brain to pump Cas's cock in time with his own rhythm.

"Yeeesss." Cas arched his back, his chest brushing Rusty's. "Because everyone knows vampires only screw in the dark."

Rusty faltered as he choked on a laugh, then sped up as if he had no control over his hips. "Now, Cas." He thrust again, aiming for Cas's gland. "I'm about to— Bite me. Now."

Cas did, and it hurt—of course it hurt, he was sinking his fangs into Rusty's neck. But twined with the pain was a pleasure so enormous that it pushed Rusty off the cliff and into a free-fall that lasted almost forever. Cas moaned, his mouth latched on to Rusty's neck with that erotic pull, and his spunk fountained between them.

Then Cas let go, humming as he licked long, slow stripes up Rusty's throat. "Mmm. You're yummier than anyone I've tasted in the last nine decades. Delicious."

Rusty laughed. "I'm flattered, I guess."

Cas looked up at him, his cheeks pinker than Rusty had ever seen them. *He looks alive.* "You should be. Darling, I hooked up with Cary Grant. James Dean. Paul Lynde."

Rusty's heart made an odd sideways lurch. "Did you— I mean, was there—"

"Fucking?" Cas peaked his eyebrows. "Not always. And like I said, I never bottomed. Something about feeding makes our hosts want to *receive* for some reason. It's really quite annoying." He grinned. "I can't tell you how thrilled I am that it doesn't have that effect on you."

"I imagine." He disengaged as gently as he could, then padded to the bathroom to get a washcloth to clean them both up. But then he remembered the ridiculous amount of jizz he'd released into Cas, and eyed the massive bathtub in the marble-tiled bathroom. "Hey, Cas?"

"Yes?"

"How do you feel about a slightly warmer swim?"

Cas appeared in the doorway as if he'd teleported. "Are you suggesting what I think you are?"

Rusty grinned and turned on the tap. "Not quite as roomy as the lake, but I think it'll accommodate both of us. As long as you don't mind getting a little cozy."

"With you, darling? Never."

So they soaked in the bath—not too hot, because beaver shifters were built for cool water, not hot, and Rusty didn't want Cas to overheat either. Cas rested between Rusty's legs, which allowed Rusty to stroke all that smooth alabaster skin. Skin that now held decidedly pink undertones, although Rusty wasn't sure whether that was due to the bath or . . . other things.

"Cas?"

"Mmm?" Cas drew his fingers up Rusty's thighs, making them both shiver.

"You sure you're not feeling poisoned?"

Cas leaned back against Rusty's shoulder and glared up at him. "Seriously, Elmer? Do I *look* poisoned?"

"No. But it might be a, you know, slow-acting one."

"Don't be ridiculous. Now." He leaned forward, wriggling his ass against Rusty's crotch with the expected results. "Wash my back and stop worrying. I'm so far beyond fine that I may be orbiting the moon." He grinned over his shoulder. "Appropriate, since I might be a spaceman, don't you think?"

"You're crazy."

"Yes, and you are too, or you wouldn't be taking a bath with a vampire." He splashed water over his shoulder. "Now get to work. Because after you've done me, I'll do you, and with all the real estate I have to cover on your most magnificent body, it may take some time."

It did—although it would have taken much less time if they hadn't gotten distracted by mutual blowjobs.

After drying each other off with the hotel's high-end towels—although as Cas said, they were only big relative to him; on Rusty they were practically hand towels—they returned to bed and spooned together under the down comforter.

And nestled here, Cas tucked up against his chest while snatches of music drifted up from the party downstairs, Rusty felt safe. *Safe while sleeping with a vampire.* He chuckled, kissing the top of Cas's head, and was rewarded by a sleepy murmur as Cas wriggled closer.

They didn't have to leave until four or so to get back to Rusty's place before dawn. Then they could hang out in the house, maybe go for another round or two before dark when they'd have to leave for Portland.

Rusty yawned, his thirty-six hours without sleep finally catching up with him now that he was relaxed. *I'll close my eyes. Nap for just a bit. We've got time.*

Cas drifted up from the most peaceful sleep he'd had in decades to the feel of Rusty's prodigious cock poking his backside. He chuckled, his eyes still closed. "Planning to impale me with your morning wood?"

"Hmmm?" Rusty sounded just as sleepy as Cas. "Is that how vampires meet their— Shit!"

Suddenly Cas was being smothered by a down comforter.

"What the—" He batted at the covers, trying to get them off his face. He hated having his face covered. *Flashbacks to that blasted coffin.* Panic swelled in his chest as he wrestled the blanket off himself, only to have it thrown over him again.

"Cas. Stop it. You have to stay under there."

"Why? I have to tell you, Elmer, that Hide and Seek has *never* been my favorite game."

"It's morning."

Cas stilled, the comforter floating down onto his face. "What?"

"It's morning. Almost ten o'clock."

"It can't be."

"It is. And there's sun *pouring into this room*. Fuck, why didn't I close the damn blinds?" The mattress dipped and Rusty tucked the comforter more firmly around Cas's body.

"Will you cut that out? I haven't fried yet and I'm not Imhotep, for pity's sake."

"Who?"

"*The Mummy*, of course. Now—"

"Cas." Rusty's tone was rough. "Your foot."

"What about it?" Cas wiggled his toes. "Both of them seem fully functional, not that I need them while I'm in bed and being swaddled like some kind of infant."

Rusty's hand closed on Cas's right ankle. *Wait. How can he touch me when I'm cocooned in this— Oh.*

Rusty pushed Cas's foot under the blanket, and Cas let him. "The room is sunny, you say? Where exactly is the sun?"

"It's, ah, shining on the floor."

"Not the bed?"

"No."

Well, that's something. Cas had no idea how much sun exposure was required to reduce a vampire to dust. Nobody did, because nobody had ever conducted any experiments with indirect light, and given the elder vampires' paranoia about sunproofing their houses and office buildings, nobody ever would. *The Great War made cowards of us all, indeed.*

Fuck this. My foot is fine and I need to know.

He rolled on his side, away from the sound of Rusty muttering as he fumbled with the window shades, and slowly lowered the edge of the comforter until he could peek out with one eye.

Sunlight. A bright spot on the pale-blue wall dimmed as Rusty succeeded in lowering the blinds, but didn't vanish altogether. The wash of light across the sheets, the walls, the door, was so soft and *natural* that Cas sucked in an unneeded breath. *I'd forgotten how beautiful it is.*

"Damn it, these aren't room-darkening."

Good. Cas lowered the comforter until his whole face was exposed. Yes, he had to blink a little in the unaccustomed brightness, but it didn't hurt. It didn't hurt *at all*.

"Maybe if I wrap you in the— Casimir! What the fuck are you doing?"

Cas sat up, the covers falling away from his bare chest. *So this is what I look like in daylight.* He held out his hands, turning them palm up and palm down, over and over. Natural light cast different shadows. *Softer.*

Then Rusty tackled him to the mattress, covering him with his body.

"What the fuck, Elmer?"

"That's exactly what I should ask you. Are you insane? You're sitting here naked in a gods-bedamned *sunny room*."

"Don't be a drama queen. It's not *that* sunny. And as much as I appreciate the skin-on-skin contact—get *off*!"

"No."

"Elmer. If I have to, I will demonstrate the true power of vampire strength and heave you across the room. Cooperate."

Rusty pushed to his hands and knees, peering down at Cas with worry practically oozing from his pores. *Oh. The sunlight makes his beard even redder.* And although the light wasn't direct, it still brought out unexpected copper highlights in Rusty's hair.

Rusty felt Cas's forehead, throat, chest. "We need to get you back to Portland. To Bryce's."

Cas forced himself to stop admiring Rusty in the sunlight to meet his worried gaze. "If you're freaking out about me being in a sunny room, how are you going to behave with me in your truck for a two-hour drive in the middle of the day?"

"I don't know. I—" He pushed himself off the bed. "Stay here. Get in the bathroom and close the door."

"Really, your repeated insistence on forcing me into bathrooms is starting to look like some kind of plumbing kink."

"Cas, please. Don't joke. I'm going out to get some stuff."

"Some stuff. Care to be more specific?"

"How can I be more specific when I don't know what the fuck I'm doing? Just—don't test the boundaries, Cas. Please." Rusty leaned down and kissed him then, hard and hot. "I'll be back as soon as I can." He let go and strode toward the door.

"Elmer? You might want to put on some clothes."

Rusty looked down at his naked body. "Oh. Good point." He hunkered down by his overnight bag and pulled out jeans and one of his ubiquitous flannel shirts. As he yanked his jeans on— *commando. Yum.*—he kept sneaking worried glances at Cas. "If you won't get in the bathroom, could you *please* get under the covers? I really, really, *really* don't want to watch you get fried by a stray sunbeam."

Despite the delight burbling like champagne in his veins at his forbidden desire to bask in this unexpected indirect *heavenly* light, it was obvious Rusty was truly distressed, and Cas didn't want that. Not at all. He made himself a little blanket fort and peered out at Rusty from the shadows. "Will this do?"

"Yes. *Thank* you." He finished dressing, shoved his feet into his boots, and took two giant steps to the bed to grip Cas's ankle through the comforter. "I'll be back as soon as I can. I promise."

"I'll be here."

Once Rusty closed the door, Cas emerged from under the comforter—slowly, because he might be a risk-taker, but he wasn't *stupid*—and sat on the edge of the bed. The blinds didn't cover the windows entirely—slivers of sunlight spilled out from either side, gilding the carpet with narrow stripes of gold. He flinched away, clenching his eyes shut, but when he didn't suddenly flail around the room, screaming, *"My eyes! My eyes!"* he cracked them open again.

It doesn't hurt. I can look at the sun on the carpet and it doesn't hurt.

Mesmerized, he crept across the room toward the seductive glow. *If I can look at it, can I feel it too?*

He extended a tentative finger and swiped it through the sunbeam at vampire speed. *Nothing.* He tried it again at half speed. *Still nothing.* Human speed—also nothing.

His whole body trembling, he held his finger under the sunbeam, unmoving. *Nothing! Gods above, below, and everywhere in between, nothing!* Well, not entirely nothing. But how to catalog the sensation? If he—

His phone shrilled from across the room where his suit jacket was hung on the back of the desk chair. He snatched his hand out of the light as if the phone could see what he was doing. *Stupid.*

Thinking it might be Rusty with a question, he hurried over to dig the phone of his pocket. *Not Rusty. Kristof.* "Hello?"

"Casimir. I have received a very troubling call this morning, just as I was about to retire for the day."

"I'm sorry to hear that, Kristof. Perhaps you should mute your phone when you're ready for bed."

"Don't be impertinent, Casimir. Earl Dawson called me to complain that you crashed his son's wedding."

Cas rolled his eyes, although nobody could see him but the sunbeam. "I didn't *crash* the wedding. I was my husband's plus-one. Furthermore, we only attended the ceremony, not the reception, so no crashing there either." *Although I'd have liked to crash Felcher into the nearest wall.*

"You alarmed the bride and offended the other guests."

"By existing? Because all we did was sit in our pew, civilized as you please, during the entire service."

"He said you threatened the bridegroom."

"Threatened?" Cas scoffed. "The only threat to Fletcher the Fu—Fletcher Dawson was that I'm married to the man he wants to continue to fuck despite his oh-so-conventional wedding vows. He propositioned Rusty *right outside the reception hall,* for pity's sake, with his bride of less than three hours on the other side of the doors not twenty feet away. I fail to see how my behavior is the more egregious here."

"Nevertheless, from the perspective of the council, your willingness, indeed, your insistence on provoking conflict is one more nail in your coffin."

Another fucking joke. Damn it, why can he get away with it and I can't? Cas sidled toward the window, as if the sunbeam were beckoning to him. "I merely accompanied my husband to an event which he was expected to attend. Surely my duty as an attentive spouse demands no less."

Kristof didn't respond right away. Cas could swear he heard an irritated huff, but that had to be his imagination. Display such a gross lack of control? Not Kristof. He'd been the perfect vampire for centuries. *If you didn't count the blood aversion.* "The vampire council isn't the only body concerned with your transgressions, Casimir. The full supe council is reviewing the evidence as well."

"What evidence?" A frisson streaked down Cas's spine. Surely they hadn't learned about him feeding on Rusty, or the effects of his—Cas's neck heated—other bodily fluids.

"Your antics have been a matter for public record since your Turn. You've made very little effort to conceal them. Your ill-considered marriage is the last in a long line, none of which you've bothered to justify in any reasonable way. Or in most cases, at all."

"I didn't see any point." Cas sounded sulky even to himself. "You were always ready to believe Henryk's testimony first." *The damned blackmailing tattlemonger.*

"Your antipathy toward Mr. Skalding, when he's demonstrated nothing but concern for you, is yet one more reason the council doubts your stability."

"He's not the angel you imagine, Kristof."

"Indeed? Would you care to expand on that? Perhaps offer testimony of your own?"

"No." *Not if I don't want your stake in my chest for cursing you.* Cas held his hand in the sunbeam, letting it play across his fingers. *Warmth. A tingle. Nothing more.* "But if I were you, I'd take a good look at his statements. The way he frames his case as if he's so concerned about me. If he was that sincere about helping—"

"He'd keep his mouth shut?" Kristof's tone was as dry as graveyard dust.

"No. But he could try not to sound so freaking smug and obsequious."

"I hope you know, Casimir, that the council always welcomes knowledge that either promotes our species or threatens it. If you have such information, coming forward with it voluntarily would go a long way toward mending your tarnished reputation."

Cas turned his hand over and caught the sunbeam in his palm. "I've got nothing."

"Very well. But be aware that if we discover that you've concealed anything—whether critical or slight—the council will take it very poorly indeed. I bid you good day."

Well, that *wasn't ominous at all.* Cas tossed his phone on the table and turned his attention back to the sunbeam. *I'd say this was pretty fucking critical. A vampire who could tolerate sun? Oh yeah. Definitely critical.*

But it's my secret. Mine and Rusty's. Would he be able to tolerate more than just this little sliver? Could he actually go out in broad daylight? Lift his face to the sun and feel its warmth again after almost a century? Experimenting with that little activity could be catastrophic if the effects of Rusty's blood—and that had to be the cause—weren't as far-reaching as Cas hoped.

His gaze snagged on his phone. *Bryce MacLeod.* He'd given Cas his number during that embarrassing boathouse exam. He already knew the effects a taste of Rusty's blood had had, as well as the effect of his semen. Maybe Bryce would have an idea about this.

He grabbed his phone again and dialed Bryce's number. After five rings he was about to hang up, but Bryce answered.

"Hello?"

"Dr. MacLeod. Bryce. This is Casimir Moreau." Cas winced, glancing at the clock, but it was nearly eleven. "I hope I'm not interrupting anything."

"Not at all. I was just collecting some samples from the wetlands and couldn't get to my phone immediately. How can I help you?"

A druid who actually wants to help. So weird. "I have a question for you. Or a statement. Maybe. A thing anyway."

"Very well." Bryce's tone held amusement and surprisingly little impatience. "Could you describe this thing?"

"Well, the thing is me, more or less. I'm standing in a hotel room in Corvallis."

"I see."

This time, Cas angled himself so the sunbeam lay all the way along his arm. "With my arm in the sun."

The clatter on the other end of the line hinted that Bryce had dropped his phone. "Sorry. Sorry! *What*?"

"You heard me. The hotel blinds aren't the greatest, and the room is full of diffuse light, which doesn't seem to bother me at all. In addition, they let in a stripe of sun and my skin can handle it with no trouble whatsoever."

"Did— May I ask whether you and Rusty—"

"Yep. We did. Several times. From, er, both ends. No condom."

Bryce made a choking sound. "Several times?"

"Uh-huh. Also, I fed from him. Twice. And not just a little smidge. A full-on feeding. I may be replete for a month."

"Oookay, that is verging on TMI even for me." Cas could hear the thump of footsteps over the phone. Bryce must be pacing. "From a discovery perspective, it's too bad your parameters aren't a bit more defined. We don't know what exactly might have effected this change. Was it the sex? The blood? A combination of both? For that matter, the quantity may or may not be a factor. You might have had the same reaction that first time, if we'd had any sun to test, or the other night at the boathouse."

"Sorry, Doc. I wasn't really thinking along chem lab lines."

"Yes, of course. Occupational hazard, what can I say?" He hummed under his breath for a moment. "Listen, Cas. I'm sure you're aware that supe power structures are precariously balanced. Vampires have significant power because of their enhanced strength, speed, and longevity. Their heliosensitivity is one of the only things that levels the playing field for humans and other supes. If we remove that limitation, do we, well, introduce an apex predator with no weaknesses? Upset the natural balance?"

"If you're right and vampires are from outer space, then balance is already about as unnatural as you can get."

"Point taken." Bryce was silent, although a faint tapping echoed in the background. "As a scientist, I object to the suppression of knowledge, of progress. But as a druid, I'm not sure there aren't some things that should never come to light, er, so to speak. If I were you, I'd keep this quiet. For Rusty's sake as well as your own. As soon as you're back in Portland though? Come to see me immediately. We have a *lot* to discuss."

Cas closed his fist over the sunbeam, although of course it simply jumped to gild his knuckles. "Of course."

"And whatever you do—*no experimentation.*"

"Naturally. You can count on me."

Chapter Eighteen

Rusty pulled back into the hotel's underground garage, mentally inventorying everything he'd picked up. *Firefighter's turnout.* Check. *Welding helmet.* Check. *Zinc oxide.* Check. *Gaia, please let it be enough.* On the other hand, maybe he should stop freaking out and just extend their hotel stay for another night. They could wait until dark and then drive to Portland to be ready for their Supernatural Selection appointment. Although nobody had told him when that was supposed to be.

Screw it. I've got the stuff now. He parked as close to the elevator as he could and started pulling everything out of the truck cab and stuffing it into a second-hand oversized duffel. As he was shoving the welding helmet on top of the boots, though, he heard a faint repetitive click.

He straightened up and whirled, arms out as if he could shield the truck from view. Fletcher was standing by the rear bumper, snapping pictures with his phone, a nasty smile on his face.

"What the fuck, Fletcher?"

Fletcher tucked his phone into his pocket. "Just gathering evidence of exactly how far you've gone around the bend. The beaver council will be *very* interested in this."

Rusty scowled and shouldered the duffel, even though it wasn't zipped. "It's none of their business what I buy."

"No? Mind telling me what your plans are for all this fireproof equipment in the hotel where your lover just married somebody else?"

"*Ex*-lover."

Fletcher ignored him, peering into the truck bed. "I know for a fact you carry extra gas in that lockbox."

"Because my jobs can be out of range of the nearest filling station."

"Maybe." Fletcher stepped closer, his jaw tight. "But you could use it for something else, couldn't you? You already destroyed my house once. Are you planning to escalate?"

Rusty grabbed the other backpack from the cab. "Fuck you. I repaired that damage at no cost to you, plus repainted the whole damn interior."

Fletcher bared his rather protuberant teeth. "Covering your tracks. Obviously."

Gaia, had Fletcher always been this much of a fuckhead? "Get out of my way, Fletcher. It's the morning after your wedding. Why are you chasing me? Shouldn't you be on the way to the airport with Sylvie to start on your honeymoon? Where was it again? Branson?"

Fletcher flushed, but didn't move. "It's my duty to my clan and *my wife* to protect them. You're clearly a threat. I'm reporting this to the council. That tagging order will be on the books before you can blink."

"Do your worst." Rusty pushed by him, knocking Fletcher off-balance with the giant duffel. "I've got things to do."

"Rusty!" Fletcher shouted as Rusty stalked toward the elevator. "Don't you *dare* walk away from me again!"

"Get used to it, Fletcher." Rusty punched the elevator call button, and the doors opened immediately. "It's the new normal."

All the way up to the third floor, he tapped his foot, urging the car to go faster. *Stupid hydraulic elevators. Too damn slow.* He rushed out into the thankfully empty hall and keyed open his room. When he stepped inside, though, his jaw sagged.

Cas was standing in the middle of the room, his pants on but bare-chested.

"What— You— Didn't I tell you— You can't—"

"Elmer, what have I told you about using your words?"

"Get in the fucking bathroom!" Rusty roared.

Cas folded his arms and met Rusty's gaze calmly. "No."

"Cas—"

"It's not necessary. Look." He strode to the window and, before Rusty could tackle him, thrust his hand in the beam of sunlight leaked by the lousy blinds.

Rusty's knees buckled, and he ass-planted on the floor, his head spinning.

"Gods, Rusty!" Cas hurried over and knelt down next to him, smoothing his hair and petting his beard. "Are you okay? I should have made you eat something at that wretched reception last night. You're probably starving."

"No. I—" He swallowed, trying to reconcile the disconnect. *Casimir. Sunlight. It does not compute.* "Picked up a couple of bagels while I was out."

"That's not enough. You need protein. After all—" Cas's sly smile held a hint of fang. "I depleted your reserves last night."

Rusty lowered his head to his knees and tried not to hyperventilate. "What are you doing? Why aren't you safely in the dark?"

"I'm not in the dark because I don't have to be." Cas's voice was soft, a little singsongy, as if he were talking to a roomful of kindergartners. "Don't you understand how fabulous this is? I haven't seen the sun in ninety-two years, Rusty. I never realized how much I missed it."

"But why—"

"It's you."

Rusty lifted his head and met Cas's shining gaze. "Me?"

"Your blood. Or maybe your spunk. Or both. Bryce wasn't sure." Cas wrinkled his nose. "Apparently we didn't conduct a very controlled experiment. But whatever it was, it's blocking some of my vampire symptoms. Isn't that great?"

"Great," Rusty said faintly. "How long will it last?"

"I don't know, but that doesn't matter. Every minute, every second, is a gift I can never repay." He leaned forward and kissed Rusty gently. "Thank you."

The kiss helped Rusty focus. A little. "You're welcome?"

Cas laughed then, a true joyous laugh, not the snide chuckle of their first acquaintance, but as if he were happy and maybe even carefree. "Oh my darling. You are so—" He shook his head and sat down on the carpet, taking one of Rusty's hands between both of his. "After you left, I called Bryce and described my experience. He wants to see us when we get back to Portland, but he said something else too."

"That you shouldn't be waltzing around in the sun?" Rusty couldn't help it. His words had a definite edge.

Cas looked down his nose at him. "He said nothing of the kind. But he suggested that we keep this little bit of information to ourselves, since he seems to think it may cause some kind of vampire revolution if the news gets out."

That cut through Rusty's fugue. "Gaia, he's right. Vampires who can withstand daylight? It's a game changer."

"Exactly."

Ice spilled into Rusty's belly when he remembered Fletcher lurking in the shadows with his camera. If he should photograph Cas, or make good on his threat to contact the council— "We've got to get out of here." He levered himself to his feet and held out a hand for Cas. "Now."

"I'm amenable." Cas took Rusty's hand and rose to his feet with a bounce. "But why the rush?"

"I ran into the fuckhead in the parking garage. He made some assumptions about the, uh, equipment I gathered and threatened to testify to the council that I'm a danger to myself and others. Well, mostly to him."

Cas snorted. "Figures. Everything is all about him. Let's go, then."

"First, I want you to put this gear on." Rusty heaved the duffel onto the bed and started unloading it.

Cas picked up the welding mask. "What is this? Heavy metal hazmat?"

"It's a welding mask. It's got good eye and face protection and if you wear it with this—" he tapped the fireman's helmet "—it'll protect your head and neck too."

"Seriously?" Cas tossed the mask onto the bed. "No."

"Cas, you have to. What if whatever this is wears off halfway to Portland? You could—" He swallowed. "I couldn't deal with that. I just couldn't."

Cas lifted the heavy jacket and slipped his arms into the sleeves, which hung down below his fingers. "If I wear this in your truck, I may seriously suffocate. And I don't even breathe."

"But it's *sunny*. Big sunny. Not hot sunny, but no clouds and way more intense than a little stray sunbeam." Panic swirled in Rusty's gut, threatening to crawl up his spine. "It might be too much."

"There is zero sun in the elevator or the parking garage. I'm in no danger."

"But it's a two-hour drive. If the effects wear off—"

"Elmer. Settle down." Cas shrugged out of the jacket and let it drop onto the duffel. "We'll take your"—he flicked his fingers— "equipment in the truck with us. If I start to feel warm around the edges, I'll put it on."

"But—"

"That's my final offer. Now can we go?"

"You are one stubborn vampire." *But I'm one stubborn beaver.* He scooped up the jacket and held it out. "We'll go when you're suited up. What if we run into Fletcher on the way to the truck?"

Cas squinched his nose. "I hope we *never* run into Fletcher."

"It's a possibility. He was lurking. And the hotel is full of hungover wedding guests who all know you're a vampire. If they see you out in the daytime—"

"Oh fine." Cas shoved his way into the turnout gear. "But this is all coming off once we're in the truck."

As it happened, their trip was uneventful except for Cas's muffled complaints and the *swush swush* of his oversized pants. They got everything down to the truck in one trip, even though Rusty looked more like a luggage rack than a person while carrying the equipment duffel, the backpack, his regular duffel, and both garment bags. Cas wrangled his suitcase, only a little impaired by the bulky gloves.

Nobody was in the garage, so Cas shucked off the turnout gear, although Rusty made him keep the jacket draped on the seat behind him. Within twenty minutes, they were loaded up and on I-5 heading north.

Cas hummed under his breath, peering out the windows with that same wide grin. "Look, Rusty! Sheep!"

"Yeah." Rusty wrestled the backpack onto the seat and dug around in it with one hand, keeping the other on the wheel, until he found what he was looking for. "Here."

Cas took the little packet, turning it over in his hands. "What are these?"

"Eclipse glasses. Put 'em on."

Cas slipped on the funky cardboard spectacles. "I can't see a thing."

"That's the point. They filter out enough light that humans can stare at an eclipse, so they should give you some protection against the daylight."

Cas ripped the things off and tossed them on the console. "I don't need these, Elmer. Your truck windows are tinted darker than the inside of a tomb."

"Cas, please." Rusty's hands were damp against the steering wheel. "For me?"

"I'll do a lot for you, but—" Cas opened the glove box and rummaged around until he found Rusty's extra pair of sunglasses. He popped them on. "Will this do?"

Not really, but since Rusty wore them on jobsites, they were at least top rated against UV rays. *But who knows what part of the spectrum affects vampires?* Gaia, he was going to have a heart attack, and Cas was over there humming like he'd had a three-mimosa brunch.

As they passed through Salem, Cas laughed out loud. "I just can't believe it. I'm out during the day. I'm seeing the sunlight glint off cars and the snow on Mount Hood. No vampire has *ever* done that. None of them would ever believe . . ."

"Believe what?" Rusty glanced at Cas. He was staring straight ahead, his hands clutching his knees. Rusty's panic spiked again. "Cas? Is it wearing off? There's a rest stop up ahead, we can pull over and get you into the gear. Just hold on for—"

"No, I'm fine. Don't fuss. But listen." He turned toward Rusty and fumbled the sunglasses off. "Don't take me to Supernatural Selection or to my house." He gripped Rusty's biceps. "Take me to the hospital. Take me to Archie."

Rusty jerked, swerving in his lane until he corrected his steering. "What the *fuck*? Why?"

"I—I want to . . . to apologize."

"Apologize." Rusty slanted a glance at Cas, but he was staring out the window, avoiding Rusty's gaze. *He's hiding something.* "Is that really necessary? His condition is not your fault."

Another sidelong glance revealed the determined set of Cas's jaw. "It might not be my fault, but it's my responsibility. This is important to me."

"They're not going to let you anywhere near him. How are you going to manage this apology?"

"I'll . . . write a note."

"Seriously? If that's all you want to do, you can send it through the fucking US mail. Be reasonable, Cas." Rusty smacked the steering wheel. "Shit. You're still high, aren't you?"

"*Au contraire*. I've reached a never-before-achieved level of clarity. This could be my last chance, Rusty. They'll never let me see him again. I'll never be able to—" Cas's voice caught on the last word. He cleared his throat, hands gripping his knees. "We can sneak into the VICU. No one will suspect that I'd visit during the day, and the regular guards aren't on duty."

Despite his simmering panic, Rusty was startled. "They're not? Kinda stupid and not very secure."

Cas shrugged. "What can I say? Vampires didn't get rich by wasting money on nonessentials. Although now that I think of it, they probably depend on those bespelled badges to do the work for them."

"Yeah, about those. How are you going to get around them?"

"Details. Besides, those keep us *in*, not out." He waved a hand, and Rusty winced when it passed through the sunlight slanting in through the tinted windows. "If I don't act like a vampire, they won't *see* a vampire."

"Unless they know you."

"Then I'll fake another bout of shifter blood poisoning. Sunstroke. Shingles. *Something*. Don't you see? This is a once-in-a-life-or-death-time opportunity."

Cas argued all the way from Keizer to Portland, and somehow, against his better judgment, Rusty found himself pulling into St. Stupid's parking garage at two in the afternoon. Talk about unstable behavior. *They'd tag me for sure if they knew.* "This is idiotic. It's never going to work."

"Then we'll be no worse off than we are now. We can at least try." Cas laid his hand on Rusty's thigh. "Okay?"

Rusty inhaled deeply and huffed out through pursed lips. "Right. Fine. But I should warn you—I suck at lying."

"That's all right, darling." Cas grinned toothily. "I'm an expert."

"Okay. But put on the protective gear. The atrium is really bright." Rusty opened his door and slid out of the truck. The parking garage was dim, but sunlight spilled in down the on-ramp. Would it be too much? He circled the truck and put his hand on the passenger door handle. *We can still bail. Cas doesn't have to risk the sun, and I don't have to risk being tagged as an unstable Inactive.*

Before he could screw his courage up enough, the door opened, banging his hip. "Ow!"

"Sorry," Cas said as he slipped out of the cab, clad only in his street clothes.

"What the fuck? You can't walk through the lobby like that. You need more protection."

"I am *not* walking in there, my first time in the sun in ninety-two years, dressed like an extra in a low-budget science-fiction flick from the fifties."

"But—"

Cas put his finger over Rusty's lips again. "No arguments. I need to be unremarkable, and I can't do that if I look like a metal-head Jawa. Remember?" He rose on his toes and kissed Rusty—mostly gentle but with a little prick of fang—which shouldn't have turned Rusty's crank the way it did. "This is me making my long un-life meaningful, or—"

"Don't say 'die trying.' Please."

"All right." He tugged the edge of his leather jacket. "Shall we?"

Rusty gulped, rubbing his palms along his jeans. "Um, sure." He offered his elbow to Cas, who tucked his hand around it, and they walked toward the elevator. "Maybe we should take the stairs."

"Any reason?"

"We can ease into the room. Reconnoiter."

Cas raised an eyebrow. "Retreat if I start to smoke around the edges?"

Rusty's knees threatened to buckle. "Don't joke about it."

"I'm sorry, darling, but if we're going to make this work, we can't half-ass it or we'll look suspicious. I'm going all in. Are you?"

"Sure. But I still think we should take the stairs. What if there's somebody in the lobby that we know?"

"Hmmm. A point. Very well. Lead on."

They clattered up the stairs, but the door at the top didn't have a window in it. "Wait here. I'll . . . investigate."

Cas patted Rusty's chest. "That's my big bad spy."

Well, big, anyway. And if they went through with this, he'd technically be bad—at least in the eyes of the beaver council. *Guess two out of three?*

He pushed the panic bar slowly, opening the door with barely a sound.

"Oh, *that's* not suspicious," Cas whispered.

"Shut up." But Cas had a point. Rusty had every right to be here—he was a regular outpatient, after all. He had no need to *skulk*. In fact, that would probably attract attention. He straightened his shoulders and gazed around the lobby. *I don't believe it. Our luck may actually be holding.* Because Alice wasn't at the admitting desk. In fact, the woman behind the desk was a complete stranger.

He glanced at the waiting area and through the atrium at the gift shop. There were a few people around, but not many, unusual for a Monday afternoon. He snapped his fingers, pretending that he'd forgotten something—even though nobody seemed to be looking at him.

He turned, blocking the door with his bulk before opening it, just in case Cas *did* start smoking around the edges. "All clear."

"Subtle, Elmer. Real subtle." Cas poked him in the chest. "Move please."

"Are you sure? It's sunny."

"We've been *over* this. Let's go, before we lose our window of opportunity."

Rusty gulped, but nodded, standing aside but staying within pounce range in case of . . . well . . . fire.

Cas sauntered over to the admissions desk and smiled at the woman behind the counter, whose name tag read *Trudy*, being careful not to expose any fang. When she returned his smile, his nose twitched as he caught her smell. *Shifter, damn it.* And from the overtones of wet dog, probably a werewolf. If she'd been human, he could have *mesmer*ized her and gotten past in a heartbeat—which was probably why the hospital didn't employ humans in the supe wards. *Guess I'll have to depend on charm alone.* He leaned closer, despite the stench.

"Hi. I hope you can help us. We're here to see Archie Ellis. He's down in the VICU."

Her smile faltered. "We're supposed to have advance notice for any visitors for Mr. Ellis." She glanced at her computer screen. "I don't see anything noted here."

"Trudy." He leaned closer, gazing deep into her eyes like he did when *mesmer*izing a host to forget an encounter. "May I call you Trudy?"

She glanced up at him. "Yes, of course." Her eyes glazed over and her smile turned vacant. *What the . . .* Mesmer *working on a supe? But how— Gah!*

He'd worry about *how* and *why* later. Instead, he gazed into her unblinking eyes. "Trudy, we need two passes to the VICU because we're on the list."

"Of course." She fumbled in a drawer and dreamily handed over two red badges.

"Thank you, Trudy. You have a lovely day."

Cas turned to hand Rusty his badge and found his mouth ajar. Any sharp noise or movement would jerk Trudy out of her *mesmer* trance before they made their escape, so he grabbed Rusty's elbow and hauled him across the lobby to the elevator bank. *Damn it, I didn't even get to enjoy the atrium.*

He slapped Rusty's badge on his chest. "Take this, Elmer, and close your mouth before someone deposits a sample in it."

"How did you do that?"

"Oh that little trick? Vampire *mesmer*. Although . . ." He peered through the fronds of a sheltering potted palm to check on Trudy in time to see her shake her head and look around as if she'd forgotten what she was doing. *Which she had.* "I engaged it out of habit, even though it should have been pointless since it's never worked on a supe before." He grinned at Rusty. "Guess you boost my mojo in other things besides sun invulnerability."

"You're not—"

"Invulnerable. Yes, I know. Just put on your badge and let's go."

Cas punched the down button, but when the doors opened, a security guard was already inside. *Ooohhh shit.*

The guard grinned and held the door for them. "Hey, Rusty. Long time no see."

"Clint. Nice to see you." Rusty sidled into the elevator like he was on the edge of a thousand-foot drop. *Subtle, Elmer. Real subtle.*

"You gents going down?" Clint glanced at their badges. "Ah. Of course you are. Vampire unit visitors." He chuckled. "Better you than me. They kinda give me the creeps."

Oh really? And you smell like a cat who lost a smack-down with a sewer rat. Cas attempted to keep his expression bland, however, as he punched the button for the first VU level.

Luckily, Clint didn't seem to be in the mood to chat with his long-lost friend Rusty, because said long-lost friend resembled an exhibit in the Paul Bunyan wax museum rather than a living person. Clint got out on his floor, the last one above the vampire unit.

"See ya around, Rusty."

Rusty raised one hand and waved, a sickly smile on his face. As soon as the door closed again, Cas selected the VICU floor.

"Gods almighty, Elmer, you truly *suck* at subterfuge."

"I can't help it. I know that guy. If anybody ever finds out what we're doing, my reputation is tanked."

The elevator dinged their arrival on the first VU level, and both of them stared ahead until the doors whispered shut again. "Trust me. If anybody finds out what we're doing, our reputations are the least of our worries," Cas muttered.

Rusty's eyes popped wide. "What do you mean by that?"

"Nothing, just—" The doors opened onto the tiny VICU lobby. "Act natural."

"Natural. Right. Got it."

Cas absolutely did not roll his eyes, but it was a near thing. *Brother. Good thing he's a contractor because if he were a spy, he'd be so unemployed.*

When Cas approached the reception desk this time, he tried for less casual and more concerned and businesslike. "Good afternoon"—he checked her name badge—"Debbie. May I call you Debbie?"

Her forehead wrinkled ,and she looked at him with a little more suspicion than Trudy upstairs. "Yeees."

Aaannnd gotcha.

"Thank you." He leaned forward and captured her gaze. "We're the men you were expecting to visit Archie Ellis today. Could you sign us in, please?"

"Of course."

"Thank you." He towed Rusty down the short hall to Archie's room.

"You're scarily good at that."

"What can I tell you? It's a gift." Cas put his hand on the glass, his throat constricting as he watched Archie's unmoving form. Were his burns a little less severe today? He couldn't tell. He hoped so.

"Cas." Rusty's voice was low and intense. "Are you gonna tell me why we're *really* here?"

He glanced sidelong at Rusty. "I don't know what you're talking abou—"

"Don't even try it. I know you by now. You're hiding something. Tell me what it is, or I'll drag you out of here right now."

When Cas glared up at him, he couldn't meet Rusty's eyes. A beard glare was as much as he could manage because, *damn it*, the man wasn't wrong. "Seriously, Elmer? You really think the caveman routine will work on me?"

"Stop trying to redirect." He stroked Cas's cheek. "Don't you trust me?"

Gods, why did he pull out the trust card? But as Cas glanced between the medical equipment and Rusty and the notable absence of nursing staff he'd need to make his plan work, he realized he'd been monumentally stupid. Again. *So much for clarity. Maybe I really am high.* "I thought— It's stupid, I see that now, but I thought we could let Archie feed from you. Let him see the sun again, even if it was the last time. At least he'd *know* it was the last time."

Rusty's brows pinched together, hurt flickering across his face. "But— Isn't that— What about the vampire revolution? The game changer? You said we had to keep the effects a secret."

"Yes. From most people. I thought we could sneak in and— But there are no windows, so he couldn't see outside anyway."

"Not to mention I'm not letting any vampire near my neck except you."

"I was thinking a transfusion, the way Kristof feeds, but we'd need a nurse for that and . . . well . . . like I said. Stupid."

Rusty's shoulders drooped, and his big hand settled at Cas's nape. "It's okay, sweetheart. You wanted to give him a chance to say goodbye. I get it." He kissed the top of Cas's head, and for a moment, both of them were silent, watching Archie not breathe. "Can he hear us in there?"

Cas shrugged. "Some people think coma patients can hear what's going on around them, but—"

"No, I mean in the room, with the door closed and this." Rusty tapped the glass with his knuckle. "Bespelled, isn't it?"

"Yes. It's supposed to prevent interference from other vampires."

"Does it work?"

Cas glanced sidelong at him. "Only if the other vampire doesn't go in through the door." He pressed down on the handle and eased the door open.

"Cas," Rusty hissed. "You can't go in there."

But Cas was already in. Maybe he couldn't execute his grand see-the-sun plan, but he could at least do this. *And maybe he'll hear.* He moved quietly to the end of Archie's bed and gazed down at him. "I'm sorry. I'm so sorry this happened to you." He rested one hand on Archie's foot, just as Rusty wrapped an arm around Cas's waist.

"Do you have any idea what happened that night? He'd already been Turned by the time you found him in that cave, right?"

"I suspect he was Turned in the cave, actually, but I don't think he went there voluntarily. We—" A lump formed in Cas's throat. "He was a Grindr hookup. He came to my house. I gave him a drink. He gave me a . . . um . . ."

"Let me guess." Rusty squeezed Cas's waist. "Blowjob?"

"Well, yes. And I fed from him." He glanced at Rusty. "That usually makes them come, if I do it right."

Rusty huffed a quiet breath. "I can vouch for that."

"But then, he left. I thought that would be the end of it. I don't know if Henryk lured him back to my place when I wasn't there, or whether the evidence of his earlier visit was enough for the council to assume my guilt. Maybe he came back. Maybe he didn't. But somehow Henryk zeroed in on him as the perfect way to get me to take the fall for creating an illegal fledgling." Cas pressed his trembling lips together. "Just to score off me, he ruined an innocent man's life." *But how am I any better? Just to score off the council, I screwed up Rusty's life, exposing him to more shit from his clan, embarrassing him, dragging him into risky adventures purely for my own benefit.*

Both their cell phones pinged simultaneously.

Rusty raised his eyebrows. "What do you reckon?" He pulled out his phone. "Ah." He seemed to deflate. "Reminder for our Supernatural Selection appointments. They don't want me to forget that I'll be getting divorced at 10:45 and married at 11:30."

Cas checked his screen. "Me too."

"I guess that makes sense. But Cas . . ." Rusty squeezed the back of his neck. "What if I don't want to do either of those things?"

Cas's heart tried to beat. "You mean—"

"You're wearing clothes." At those words, rough and reedy and uncertain, both their heads whipped toward the bed. Archie's eyes were open, and he was blinking blearily at Rusty. "I'm thirsty."

Thirsty? Excitement hopscotched up Cas's spine. *No—hungry! And he's sensed an irresistible food source: Rusty.* "Archie—"

A dozen different alarms started beeping.

Rusty grabbed Cas's elbow and hauled him out of the room.

"What are you doing?" Cas tried to break out of Rusty's iron grip. "He's awake! We can talk to him!"

"Shut up and run. You're not supposed to be here, and I'm guessing we're about to get invaded by every nurse and doctor in a three-mile radius." Rusty glanced around wildly. "Emergency exit. Let's hope there're stairs and that the thing doesn't have a siren attached." He dragged Cas over to the door and hit the big red paddle to open it just as footsteps pounded across the lobby.

"Stairs. The security in this place *sucks*, thank Gaia." Rusty took them two at a time. Cas couldn't quite manage the stride length, but he made up for it in speed.

They'd only climbed three flights before the stairwell dead-ended at another door.

"You're shitting me? Their emergency exit dumps us into the VER?"

Cas leaned against the cinder block wall. "I guess their security doesn't suck as much as you thought. At least anyone taking the stairs from the VICU has to pass through here."

"What are the odds nobody'll notice us walking through this door?"

"Realistically? Slim to none."

"As long as there's at least a chance." Rusty grasped the door handle. "Act casual."

"Wait." Cas put his hand on Rusty's arm. "Archie recognized me. Is that a good thing, do you think? Does it mean he's recovering?"

Rusty let go of the door and enveloped Cas in a hug. "I'm a contractor, not a doctor, sweetheart. I couldn't say."

"They put him in a healing trance on purpose before, you know. When he woke up and cried because he couldn't see the sun."

"Guess he's got some therapy in his future then, poor kid." He eased back and took Cas's face between his hands, and Cas wanted to burrow into his warmth. "I need to tell you something. Something I was trying to say back in Archie's room."

Cas placed his hands on Rusty's chest. "I'm listening."

"I—I don't want to marry Ted anymore." Rusty's voice was soft, but Cas could hear every word. They echoed to the bottom of his soul. "I don't want to divorce you. I know we went into this for completely bogus reasons, but it worked out pretty well, don't you think?"

So I didn't screw up his life? Cas nodded, tears prickling his eyes. *If anyone sees me crying, they'll revoke my vampire card.* "It did."

"Maybe we can talk to Supernatural Selection. Talk to Ted. Talk to your incubus. Let them know that we've changed our minds. The temporary contract will expire, sure, but that doesn't mean we can't think about another one. Or, you know, just date for a while until we decide what we want to do. One thing I know I *don't* want, though, and that's to be married to somebody else."

"Me either," Cas whispered.

"I want to give this a try. Give *us* a try."

Cas's heart expanded like a helium balloon. "You do? Really?"

"I do. Really. What do you say? Should we—"

Cas's phone shrilled, echoing in the stairwell. "Shit." He fumbled it out of his pocket before it could bring hospital security down on their asses. *Kristof.* Oh hell. "Hello?"

"Casimir." Kristof's tone was colder than a Frost Giant's dick. "I have just been informed that your alleged marriage to Mr. Johnson is only temporary."

"Um . . ." Cas glanced up at Rusty. "Where did you hear that?"

"Our treasurer received a final invoice from Supernatural Selection, since the council is the financially responsible party for their services. The invoice included a personal note from a Zeke Oz, apologizing that the fee for the original contract was due in full as of 11:30 p.m., although he very kindly didn't charge us for the secondary contract, which apparently expires tonight at 10:45."

Cas clenched his eyes shut so he wouldn't have to see the mingled hope and fear in Rusty's face. "That's correct. But—"

"In that case, I expect you to fulfill your original obligation and sign the permanent mating contract with Quentin Bertrand-Harrington tonight." Kristof sighed and Cas nearly dropped his phone. He'd *never* heard Kristof sigh. "Don't you understand what I'm offering you here? A husband who can meet any vampire on equal footing, who can grant you the prestige and influence of which your own sire robbed you. This is an opportunity, Casimir, possibly the last one I can broker for you.

Whatever you do . . ." Kristof's pause drew out five seconds. Ten. Twenty. "Don't fuck it up."

Chapter Nineteen

"Is everything okay?" Cas had gone pale—okay, pal*er*—after the phone call from Kristof, which was noticeable because he'd been looking so much pinker. Rusty squirmed a little in the corner of the stairwell. *That's from my blood. I did that to him.* Which, of course, had its predictable dick response. *Gaia, I am so gone.*

"Yes." Cas smiled at him, but it was a piss-poor attempt. "Just Kristof doing the usual council song and dance."

"Uh-huh." *In a pig shifter's eye.* "I know how that goes." Rusty eyed the door, trying to remember the layout of the main VER from his one previous trip. It wasn't easy. He'd been so freaked out about Cas ingesting his blood that the admitting clerk had had to ask him for his name three times.

But Rusty was a builder, and evaluating space was what he did. He closed his eyes and visualized the room. "Okay. The egress to the other stairs isn't far, but I think it'll look less suspicious if we head for the elevators."

"If you say so."

Rusty looked down at the defeated note in Cas's voice. "Hey. They haven't caught us yet. We can do this." He held out his hand. "Gimme your badge."

"Why?" But Cas unclipped his badge and passed it to Rusty. "Won't that get us kicked out?"

"Yeah. But that's what we want, right?" Rusty tucked both of them into the inside pocket of his jacket. "We'll slip out this door and head toward the reception desk. Since we came straight from the main desk upstairs on our way down, they won't have seen us before. We can just pretend to be lost. They give us directions, and boom, we're on our way."

"You're forgetting it's daytime and I'm a vampire."

Rusty ran a finger along Cas's cheek. "Trust me. I haven't forgotten. If they ask, we can say you were on one of the regular vampire floors. A follow-up visit. That's a thing that could happen, right?"

This time Cas's smile was more genuine. "It's so crazy, it just might work."

"Hiding in plain sight. It's tradition. It's how the supe communities have survived, after all."

Most of Rusty's confidence was bravado put on for Cas's benefit, but hey—*fake it till you make it.* He grabbed Cas's hand and opened the door.

When they walked out of the stairwell, the SMTs were just bringing in another gurney, so the admitting clerk and the nursing staff were focused on them, not the VICU exit. Rusty heaved a relieved sigh. *This really is going to work.*

But the SMT team was the same one who'd picked up Cas that night. *Shit. Ky and Pete. Can't let them see Cas.* Rusty took Cas's elbow and hauled him to the elevators and inside. They almost got away clean, except at the last minute, as the elevator doors were closing, Ky glanced up and spotted Rusty.

Rusty nodded a greeting as if visiting the vampire ER was something he did every day. Ky looked as if he were about to head toward them, but a nurse asked him a question and the doors slid shut.

Rusty exhaled shakily, wiping sweat off his forehead with the back of his hand. "I am *not* cut out for a life of espionage."

"You seem to be doing admirably, darling. You engineered two narrow escapes within ten minutes. I only wish—" Cas shook his head. "Never mind. Why the last-minute manhandling though? Not that I minded."

"The SMTs who collected you from Bryce's office the night of our reception were there, bringing in a patient. I didn't want them to see you and wonder what you were doing there during the day."

Cas's brow knotted. "Hmmm. For that matter, what kind of emergency would another vampire have before dark? None of us is stupid enough to go outside in the daytime." Rusty shot him a *Seriously, dude?* look. "All right. *Virtually* none of us. And other than sunlight and random wood issues, we're pretty much indestructible. Even malnourishment has a new treatment protocol now. Maybe they got a splinter."

"I don't care who it was. Hope they're okay, of course, but I'm just glad for the distraction."

They got off the elevator in the main lobby and walked to the parking garage stairs, nobody in the now-busy atrium paying the least attention to them. Cas didn't seem to be having any, er, crispy-around-the-edges reactions, but Rusty steered him away from patches of direct sunlight anyway.

They took the stairs to their parking level, and Rusty heaved a sigh of relief when the garage was deserted. "Okay. I think we're good. All we have to do—"

"Rusty? It is Rusty Johnson, isn't it?"

Oh shit. Rusty turned, trying to keep Cas hidden behind his bulk. Ky, the SMT, stood outside the service elevator. "Hey, Ky. How's it going?"

"Oh not so bad. You know how it is. Work." He shrugged. "What can I say?"

"I hear you."

"I saw you upstairs in the VER. Everything okay?"

"Me? I'm fine." Rusty forced a laugh, and Cas groaned behind him. *I know. Pathetic. But I am not spy material.* "Not like I'm a vampire. Or can donate blood for them. Or anything. Because that would be— I couldn't— Not that I—"

"Use your *words*, Elmer," Cas whispered.

Easy for you to say.

Luckily, Ky laughed as he headed toward one of the ambulances parked in the emergency bay. "No worries. I can imagine their faces if you volunteered. They'd probably accuse you of attempted murder!"

"Yeah. Heh heh heh." He backed up until Cas was smooshed between his body and a cement pillar. "Out in the daytime for a vampire call? That's gotta be unusual, right?"

Ky frowned, although he seemed more confused than angry. "Yeah. First one ever, far as I can remember. And the reason—" He grinned apologetically. "Sorry. Shouldn't be talking about patient stuff to civilians. Have to get back upstairs anyway. Forgot the patient's messenger bag in the rush." As he strode past, he murmured, "Don't worry. I won't tell anyone you're getting busy in the garage, but you might want to pick a less public place next time."

Rusty's face heated so fast he was surprised his beard didn't catch fire. His knee-jerk reaction was to deny the assumption that he'd be stupid enough to hook up at a hospital. *But he thinks I'm hiding Cas for another reason, so it's all good.* "Right. I'll, uh, take that under advisement."

As soon as Ky passed by and climbed into his ambulance, Rusty hustled Cas into the truck and shut the door. Then he tried to be casual and nonchalant as he circled the rear of the truck to the driver's side. *Epic fail there.* He probably looked as if a *Bean Sidhe* were on his tail.

Ky didn't seem to notice anything unusual though. *Why should he? I've behaved like a lunatic every other time he's met me.* He lifted a hand as he passed by with a fancy monogrammed leather bag over his shoulder. *No wonder the patient was freaking out about the bag.* Vampires sure liked the finer things.

A burst of adrenaline-fueled relief had him grinning when he climbed into the cab. If he expected Cas to be similarly thrilled, though, he was disappointed.

Cas's eyes were blazing red, his teeth bared in a full-fanged snarl. Rusty nearly jumped out of the truck again.

"Cas? What the fuck, man?"

"That bag. The one Ky had. Do you know who his fucking patient is?"

"Of course not. That's privileged information."

"It's Henryk fucking Skalding, that's who." Cas glared at the elevator doors. *Good thing vampires can't actually set things on fire with their eyes, because... damn.* "I've seen that bag way too many times to mistake it. He uses it to deliver the council's lovely missives to me, the smug bastard."

Rusty started the truck. "Buckle in, Cas. I really don't want you to turn into a bat and fly out the window."

"We don't turn into bats. We're not fucking *shifters*."

Rusty's hand froze on the gear shift. "Ah. Right."

"Shit, Rusty. I'm sorry. I didn't— You know I don't think of you that way. You're different."

"You don't have to tell me that. It's been drilled into me practically my whole life."

"That's not what I mean and you know it."

"Okay."

"You're the most—"

"I said *okay*, Cas." Rusty clipped each word off like taking a chop saw to his voice. "So Skalding was the patient in the VER. So what?"

"There's absolutely zero chance that there's anything wrong with him. He *never* takes risks with his person. There's only one reason for him to be here." Cas glowered at Rusty from beneath lowered brows. "Archie."

"So? No vampires are allowed in his room."

"*I* got into his room. And if you say he won't be allowed into the VICU, may I remind you how I originally got in? That asshole couldn't even come up with his own fucking *plan*. He had to steal *mine*."

"Cas—"

"Henryk is Archie's sire, and Archie is so new that he has no power to resist anything Henryk says. You saw me convince two different people to violate their own security protocols with *mesmer*. That's *nothing* compared to what a sire can do to his fledgling. Henryk can tell Archie to testify that I'm the one who Turned him—and furthermore, he'll *believe* it himself, which means Henryk can set himself up as the benevolent mentor of the traumatized new fledgling and nobody will bat a fucking *eye*." Cas threw himself back against the seat. "Gods, I *hate* this mind-control shit."

"Kinda hypocritical, considering you did it yourself."

"Yes, but I used it for good, not evil."

Rusty barked a laugh at Cas's sulky tone. "Even if they let Henryk out of the VER, there's no way anybody other than hospital personnel will get close to Archie, not given all the alarms that were blaring when we left. If it makes you feel better, call Kristof and warn him."

Cas's gaze flickered to Rusty's for an instant before he returned to staring at the concrete wall in front of the bumper. "I —I can't."

"Why not? I still can't figure out why you didn't tell them Henryk was Archie's sire in the first place."

"Because *reasons*, Elmer." Cas still wouldn't meet Rusty's eyes. "Can we leave it at that?"

Rusty wanted to argue, but swallowed his frustration and backed out of the parking space. "Then let's go ho— get over to your house and relax. Because I don't know about you, but my nerves have been shorting out since I saw you playing chicken with a sunbeam this morning."

"Fine." Cas folded his arms and stared out the window for the rest of the drive. He didn't show any of his earlier delight over being out in the daytime, and Rusty was afraid to push on the subject of eclipse glasses.

Now I know why people are afraid of vampires. Because Cas in a temper was pretty freaking scary.

When they got to Cas's house, though, Rusty sat in the driveway, staring at the expanse of yard between his truck and the front door. Sure, the yard was dotted with trees, but they were all leafless at the moment and so didn't afford a lot of shade.

"Uh . . . Cas? How are you going to get into the house?"

"I'll just walk." He reached for the handle, but Rusty flung his arm across Cas's chest.

"Don't be an idiot. It's been hours since you fed. We don't know what your light tolerance is. And you're not exactly thinking clearly."

Cas heaved a huge sigh, and since it wasn't necessary for survival, Rusty knew it was strictly for the drama. He pulled a set of keys out of his pocket. "Go inside. You can get to the garage through the kitchen. If you pull the Jag out, you can jam enough of your monster truck inside for me to get out under a roof. Happy?"

"It'll do in a pinch."

Rusty got out, but before he shut the door, he pointed at Cas. "Stay."

Cas glared at him. "Woof."

As soon as Rusty got indoors, he heard the beep of a security system. *Great. Thanks for the warning, Cas.* On a whim, he entered the same code as the gate: three-two-six-four. The alert light flashed green. *Talk about sucky security.*

Rusty played musical cars without the benefit of music, shifting Cas's *really* nice Jag and his truck, making sure Cas got indoors safely, then swapped everything back before going inside and laying the keys on the breakfast bar. Cas was standing at his dining room table, facing away from the door, head bowed.

Rusty swallowed his nerves and approached until he was close enough to touch. He stroked Cas's nape. "Cas. I know things kind of blew up there at the end, but I meant what I said in Archie's room. I—I don't want to marry someone else. I want to be with you."

Cas hunched his shoulders and flinched away from Rusty's touch. "You can't."

"Why not?" Rusty chuckled, but he didn't try to touch again. "We've already hashed out the whole me-shifter-you-vampire thing."

"That doesn't matter. The call I got in the stairwell? Kristof found out about the temporary nature of our contract. He's ordered me to fulfill the original agreement with the incubus or else."

The skin between Rusty's shoulder blades prickled. "Or else what?"

Cas looked up at him, and the expression on his face . . . *Gaia.* "You don't want to know." He looked away. "I'm not sure I do either."

The prickles burst into full-blown heat and Rusty grabbed Cas's shoulders, turning him so they faced each other. "Fight them, Cas. We'll fight them together. They want you to get married. Why does it matter to them who it is as long as you're happy?"

Cas laughed mirthlessly, his face bleak. "My happiness is not their primary goal. My *rehabilitation* takes precedence there. Making me a perfect functioning drone in the high-society vampire hive. They're trying to *fix* me, Rusty. Do you seriously imagine a shifter—a blue collar, *inactive* shifter at that—will ever be acceptable to the council?"

"I don't give a shit whether I'm acceptable to the council." Rusty smoothed his thumbs over Cas's collarbones, causing Cas to shiver. "Am I acceptable to you?" Cas stared resolutely at Rusty's chest. "Cas? I love you." Cas flinched. *Not a good sign.* "Don't you— I mean I thought you felt the same about me."

Finally, Cas met Rusty's eyes, his own bright with tears. "I do. You know I do."

"Then isn't that enough reason to fight for what we've got?"

"It's not just about me. There are . . . other factors."

"Factors like Archie? Henryk and his vendetta? Then *tell* them, Cas. Tell them the truth and then tell them to fuck off."

"I *can't*. I *told* you."

"Yeah, but you didn't tell me why."

Cas pulled away, crossing his arms over his chest. "It would be easier to overcome millennia of vampire-shifter bias than it would be to convince the council they've been wrong about Henryk and me from the beginning."

"You'll never know until you try."

"Yes, I do know. And it's a risk I'm not willing to take. For your sake as well as mine."

Rusty hadn't missed that Cas hadn't answered the question. "You won't tell them the truth about Archie, even though you're freaking out about him every five minutes. You won't stand up to them for us, even though you claim to love me. What the fuck, Cas? What exactly are you playing at?"

"I'm not playing. I'm trying to do the right thing."

"It sure doesn't feel like the right thing for me. And I don't believe it feels that way to you either." Rusty shoved his hands into his pockets. "Funny how trying to do the right thing can be so wrong for so many." He turned and strode to the door. "Goodbye, Casimir. See you at the divorce."

"Rusty—"

Rusty closed the door, not wanting to hear any more excuses, each one another clue of how little Cas thought of him and their relationship.

Relationship. Ha! It was a temporary contract, with a little *I'm going to Disneyland!* thrown in at the end when Cas got his daylight tour.

He tromped to his truck, and when he got behind the wheel, he pulled up the Supernatural Selection app on his phone. His connection to Ted was live again, so he dashed off a quick text.

Hey. Looking forward to tonight. New life FTW, am I right?

When Ted responded with, *You bet. Can't wait.* Rusty put his truck in gear and headed into town.

Because, damn it, I really need a drink.

Cas *hated* that he'd hurt Rusty, making him believe their love wasn't the most important thing in Cas's world. He'd come *this* close to confessing the truth, the decades of leverage Henryk held over him, culminating in Kristof's curse. But he couldn't trust Rusty, with his fine, upstanding moral center, not to rush right off and lay it all out for the council—which might have gotten Cas staked, depending on Kristof's mood. The big noble doofus would probably have spilled about his magical blood effects too, and *that* was a risk Cas couldn't allow. Who knew what the vampire council would do with that juicy bit of information.

A clean break is better. Well, maybe not better, judging by the hole in Cas's chest, but definitely safer for them both. *At least I'll get to see him again when we dissolve the contract.* Maybe Cas could get him to smile one last time.

But as it happened, he didn't get the opportunity. Zeke, the same curly-haired demon from before, greeted him at the front desk.

"Ah, Mr. Moreau. Welcome." He beamed while the AI pulsed sullenly behind him. "Mr. Johnson has already signed off on the dissolution decree and is awaiting his new spouse upstairs. If you could just sign here?" He passed over a one-page statement that declared the temporary mating between Elmer (aka Rusty) Johnson, beaver shifter, and Casimir Moreau, vampire, to be expired. Rusty's spiky signature stared at Cas from the bottom of the page. Cas added his own with an extra vicious swipe at the end.

Zeke blinked behind his bespelled glasses at Cas's obvious irritation. "Ah. Yes. Well. If you'll follow me, I'll take you up to the altar chamber. It's all prepared for your wedding to Mr. Bertrand-Harrington." Zeke glanced at him nervously as they climbed the stairs to the third floor. "It's, ah, a blood contract, you know. Are you—"

"Sufficiently fed that I won't attack everyone in the room in a blood-crazed frenzy? Yes, thank you for asking."

"I'm sorry," Zeke said humbly. "I didn't mean to offend."

Cas carded his fingers through his hair. The poor guy was just doing his job, after all. "Don't mind me. I've had one hell of a day."

Zeke perked up. "Of course. Perfectly understandable. I'm sure your mood will improve immensely once you and Mr. Bertrand-Harrington embark on your new lives together."

"Whatever," Cas muttered.

Zeke stopped several yards down a curved hallway and gestured to an open door. "Here you are. Please make yourself comfortable. Mr. Bertrand-Harrington will be along as soon as his escape ritual— I mean, he'll be along shortly, along with our celebrant. Congratulations!"

Cas walked through the door, and he could have sworn he heard a mean cackle emanating from inside the AI pillar. *Angels. So judgmental.* He flipped it the finger as he passed, and for an instant, it pulsed red. *So you can dish it out but can't take it, can you, buddy?*

Zeke closed the door, leaving Cas alone with his thoughts, and seriously? Was that really . . . Cas looked closer, and sure enough, the sideboard held a small, white-frosted cake, its topper obviously meant to be a vampire and an incubus, judging by the clichéd black cape on one and the bat-like wings on the other.

Cake. I'm a vampire, for fuck's sake. I can't eat cake. They'd have done better to have stretched his future husband out on the table for a postceremony snack. *Not that I'd have an appetite for him.*

What would Quentin Bertrand-Harrington be like? Would he be tall? Broad? Bearded? Would he smell like the lake and the forest? Would he taste like— *Stop it.*

Just my luck to be married to a sex demon when I don't want to have sex with anyone except another guy's husband.

Although after their fight, Rusty wouldn't want to have sex with Cas anyway. *How could I have been so stupid?* The first time the idea of giving Rusty's blood to Archie had occurred to him, he'd *known* it was a lousy idea, that it would expose Rusty to needless danger. Now Rusty thought his safety meant less to Cas than Cas's own.

How many times over the last few days—practically since they'd met, if Cas wanted to be honest—had Rusty put his own needs below Cas's? Cas wasn't sure he could count that high. Math had never been his strong suit.

How could I have made him think he didn't matter? That for some reason Archie was more important?

Fear? Yes, he could admit that. Fear of what the council would do if he refused their edict. Anger? Gods, yes. That Henryk had the means—practically blessed by the council itself—to victimize not only Cas and Archie, but any number of other hapless fledglings in the future. Even the best vampire sires—assuming there was such a thing—didn't exactly choose their intended fledglings for their strength of character and staunch moral centers. The mental image of a vampire community run by Henryk Skalding and his minions made Cas want to flay his own skin off.

It doesn't matter anyway. It's over. We're divorced. I'm about to marry the fucking sex demon. He eyed the cake and shuddered.

Maybe if I send Rusty a note. A text. Some kind of apology so he knows how much he meant to me. Would he think Cas only liked him because of his super-blood benefits? Ewww. That made him no better than Fletcher the Fuckhead. But Rusty deserved something. Something better than Felcher. Better than Cas. *Better than anybody.*

About to pull out his phone to compose an appropriately abject message, he was distracted by footsteps pounding in the hall, coming closer, although they had a soft, indistinct sound, as if the building were encompassed by a sound-deadening spell. Otherwise the runner would have to be—

The door burst open and Bryce MacLeod rushed in.

Barefoot.

Cas leaped to his feet. Bryce was barefoot, yes, but bare everywhere else as well, his modesty only preserved by a rather skimpy linen cloth clutched around his hips. *Why is it that half the time I see this man, he's naked?* Maybe it was a druid thing. Sky-clad rituals and all that.

But then Rusty loomed behind Bryce, and Cas took an unexpected breath. *Gods, he's so gorgeous.*

Bryce glared at Cas. "Come with me. Both of you. Now."

Cas gaped at him, but when Rusty growled, "Casimir," he shook off his daze and left that fucking cake behind with no regrets.

Bryce led them down the curved hallway and up another flight of stairs to a door next to a soda machine. "This is a translocation door. It'll dump you out in Faerie near a portal that leads to the wetlands behind my house."

Rusty's warm, solid presence behind him steadied Cas's nerves, despite the adrenaline rush of pelting through a building owned by witches in pursuit of a mostly naked druid. *Just another day in the life of a vampire.*

Rusty put a hand on Cas's shoulder. "Aren't you coming with us?"

Bryce smiled crookedly. "I can't. I'm already there."

Cas blinked. "What?"

But Rusty seemed to understand. "Got it."

"Heilyn—the bauchan who brought me to the lake—is waiting for you in Faerie. They'll lead you safely through to the wetlands behind my house where I'm waiting."

"Got it."

Cas's gaze bounced between them. "Got what?"

Bryce pointed a finger at them, almost causing him to lose his mini-kilt. "Don't step off the path."

"Why?" Cas asked. "Because we'll be trapped in Hades forever?"

"No," Bryce growled. "Because if you damage the wetlands ecosystem, I will *end* you." A flicker of alarm passed over his face. "Well not that. But please. Be careful. And hurry. You don't have much time."

Chapter Twenty

The whole time Heilyn led them through Faerie and into Bryce's precious wetlands, Rusty could tell Cas was about to explode with curiosity. It was like a roiling cloud over his head, complete with lightning strikes.

But every time Cas started to ask a question, Rusty shushed him.

"If you tell me to hush *one more time*, Elmer, I swear, I'll—"

"This isn't the time or place, Cas. Just wait. When we get to Bryce's, I'll explain."

"You'd better," he muttered. "Or else."

Despite everything—the pitiful trappings of a wedding he didn't want, the shock of Bryce's time-surf warning, the urgency of the flight through Faerie—Rusty couldn't help the joy that burbled in his chest. *Cas is here. Cas is with me again.*

And yeah, Rusty had been truly pissed at Cas the last time they'd seen one another, but so what? Lovers had quarrels all the time, and they worked through them. Maybe this togetherness wouldn't last forever, but damn it, Rusty would enjoy it while it did.

Heilyn pointed the way up a gentle slope, where a neat one-story house sat, windows glowing in welcome. Before they'd made it to the patio, Bryce opened a set of French doors that, judging from the heavy round table behind him, led to his dining room.

"I'm glad you made it. Please come in."

Rusty shared a glance with Cas. Bryce was fully clothed this time, in a plaid shirt paired with his pants and vest of many pockets. They followed him inside.

"Have a seat."

They sat next to each other, across from Bryce, who had two half-full glasses of murky liquid at his elbow. Rusty cleared his throat. "Why did you do it? Come for us, I mean?"

Bryce laced his fingers together and stared at them for a moment before lifting his chin. "Because tonight, not half an hour ago, the combined supe council issued an order to tag Rusty as an unstable Inactive."

"What?" Cas wasn't using his inside voice. "They can't do that!"

Rusty placed his hand over Cas's clenched fist. "Calm down. Fletcher threatened as much. But don't worry. He can't make it stick. He doesn't have any grounds, since the only evidence he's got is me hauling some protective gear up to our hotel room."

"I'm afraid that's not accurate." Bryce's tone held regret and maybe a hint of anger. "The hospital has footage of the two of you using *mesmer* to break into Archie Ellis's room in the VICU, forcing his consciousness—"

"We didn't. Hells, I'm a building contractor. I wouldn't know how."

"Forcing him to consciousness, and escaping before the authorities arrived."

"Shit," Rusty muttered.

"Two weeks from now, the edicts will be returned by unanimous vote of the tribunal. Rusty will be tagged, his business forfeit, and sentenced to ten years of forced labor at Govannon's forge."

Rusty felt the blood drain out of his head. Black spots danced in front of his eyes. "But I'm not fae," he croaked. "They can't —"

"The council has found Govannon a very convenient warden for its prisoners lately. I'm afraid they can and they do."

Cas stirred for the first time. "Wait. *Two weeks* from now? But that means—"

"What can I tell you?" Bryce shrugged. "I time-surfed. The paradox can be confusing."

"Time-surfing is real?" Cas whispered. "How does it—

"Not the point right now, Cas. But that's why Bryce was naked. You can't take anything with you." Rusty uncurled Cas's fist and laced their fingers together. "What about Cas? Did they punish him too?"

"They . . . ah . . ." Bryce rubbed the back of his neck, his gaze shifting to a spot behind Rusty's shoulder.

"They what?" Cas straightened his shoulders. "Tell me. I can take it."

"They staked—*will* stake you in the sun the same day."

"No," Rusty groaned.

"Wait," Cas said. "When they stake me, do I disintegrate, or am I still light-tolerant from Rusty's blood?"

"You disintegrate." He winced. "Sorry."

Cas glanced at Rusty with a wry smile. "Well at least we know the effects last less than two weeks."

Rusty's breath sawed in his throat, his chest. "Don't *joke* about this, Casimir. I can't—"

Bryce pushed one of the glasses across the table. "Drink this."

"What—"

"It'll calm you down and let you think."

Rusty grabbed the glass and chugged it, the astringent taste zinging his salivary glands. His breathing eased immediately, helped along by Cas stroking his hair. "Thanks, Doc. But how did you—future you—tell now-you that I'd need this? Or that we'd be here now at all?"

Bryce patted a pocket of his vest that sported a book-shaped bulge. "I've started recording every trip in Gran's old journal. I've had it near me ever since she died, so it's present in my personal time stream, and I always know where it is. So when I take a trip, I make sure to record the details of the jump while

I'm there. Then when I get back, I just look up the old entry—well, the *new* old entry—and add notes on the outcome."

Cas leaned forward. "Do you know the outcome of our escape?"

He shook his head. "It hasn't happened yet then." He pinched the bridge of his nose. "You know what I mean."

"Do you know what happens to Archie?" Cas's voice held a note of desperate hope, yet it turned Rusty's insides to lead. And the way Cas's shoulders slumped when Bryce shook his head? *Ugh.*

Archie again. Always Archie. Maybe Cas never really wanted Rusty at all. *Of course he didn't. I was the revenge husband.* He let go of Cas's hand and sat back in his chair.

Cas cut a glare at him. "I know what you're thinking, Elmer, and you can stop it right now." He grabbed Rusty's hand and kissed his knuckles. "Archie is a responsibility. Not my soul mate."

"Do . . . do you think I'm that?" The words got tangled up on Rusty's tongue. "Your soul mate?"

"Do you even need to ask?" Cas kissed him, his fangs nicking Rusty's lip. "You're my perfect match. Fuck all those people who see us as too different."

"And Archie?"

"I told you. Didn't I? He was a Grindr hookup. A one-time feed, but he was a nice boy, and something horrible happened to him because Henryk Skalding has a personal vendetta against me." Cas dropped his gaze to Rusty's chest. "I hate being a vampire, Rusty. Nobody should be Turned against their will."

If Rusty hadn't already been head over drill press in love with Cas, that little hitch in his voice when he said *hate* would have done it. "I get it. Thank you. And I really don't care if you got naked with anybody, including Archie, once upon a time—"

"But I didn't. Dicks were bared, of course—"

"Naturally," Bryce murmured.

Cas glared at him. "I have *some* consideration for clothing, thank you." He turned back to Rusty. "But that's it. I swear."

Rusty frowned, bouncing his knee under the table with the need to punch something. *What I wouldn't give for a hammer and a handful of nails to drive.* "That can't be right."

"You question my word? Granted, my moral center may not be as strong as your own, but I assure you I'm far more upstanding than your average fundamentalist Republican congressman."

"That's not what I mean. I mean he had to have seen you naked sometime. Otherwise why was your *not* being naked the first thing he noticed?"

"He's been in a coma for months. Don't you think it's likely he was a little disoriented? After all, his eyes weren't even tracking properly. I'm surprised he could focus on me at all because he was . . ." Cas's eyes widened. "Gods, Rusty. He wasn't looking at me. He was looking at you."

"Me?" Rusty blinked. "But I've never seen him before."

"No." A manic grin spread over Cas's face. "You've never seen him *yet.*"

"Cas." Rusty drew the name out for about ten extra syllables. "What are you thinking?"

"He recognized you, but remarked that you weren't naked. Therefore, you must have time-surfed in your birthday suit to somewhere he could ogle you."

"But so what? Obviously it didn't do any good, because he was still in the hospital. Still undead." He glanced at Bryce. "Or still alien, depending."

Bryce waggled one hand in the air. "It's a gray area. Once you introduce time-surfing, chronology becomes rather . . . shall we say . . . fluid?"

Cas tugged on his arm. "Come on, Rusty. Don't you see? You can keep Archie from meeting me. And if he doesn't meet me, he's in no danger of Henryk Turning him. He won't be in the hospital. We won't have violated the security regulations. I won't be under interdiction by the vampire council, and the beavers won't be after your blood."

"Not so fast, please," Bryce said. "I've found very few other first-person accounts, but most of them refer to observing, not altering."

Cas faced him, eyes glowing. "But if the stream was altered, how would you know? It would have always been that way from your perspective."

"They're rather cagey about that, as a matter of fact—as if they're pretending they were strictly hands-off while at the same time subtly bragging about their success. From what I can determine, though, it seems the surfers themselves, because they're present in both continua, are immune from the effect."

"Wait a minute." Rusty frowned, trying to get his head around this timey-wimey shit. "Do you mean that if we *do* change something . . . if Archie is never—was never— Hell, what verb tense do I use? If he's not Turned, then the vampire council won't have ordered Cas to get married. I won't have ever met him. He won't know that my blood can reduce his symptoms. We won't— I won't—" *Be in love.*

"Without data supporting time alteration, it's difficult to tell." Bryce shrugged apologetically. "But it's definitely possible. In fact, it's the most likely outcome."

"Then I'll go too." Cas nestled against Rusty's side. "We'll go together."

"You can't," Bryce said. "You're already there, and you can't be twice in the same place and time. I do know that much."

"Oh." Cas drooped, and his defeated tone burrowed past Rusty's apprehension.

"But there's no choice really, is there? If we don't fix this, I'm in a chain gang for ten years and Cas *dies*. For good. I'm not down with that. At all." He raised his chin, forcing a smile despite the constriction in his throat "I'll do it. The sooner the better."

"*Elmer.*" Cas caught Rusty's face between his hands. "You know what? I say screw chronology and time paradoxes and the horse they rode in on. I *refuse* to forget you. Furthermore, I can't imagine meeting you and not falling in love with you." He grinned, although his eyes glinted with tears. "Eventually." He threaded his fingers in Rusty's beard the way that Rusty loved. "After all, you're in my blood. And nothing and nobody—not even Father Time himself—can ever change that."

When Rusty declared his willingness to *holy shit* time travel, Cas's heart swelled to twice its size. He wanted to dance, sing, fuck Rusty into next week, *all of the above*, but they had a job to do, and who knew how long they could hide out in Bryce's house from the various supe posses out for their blood?

Cas grabbed Rusty's hand and faced Bryce. "How does it work? I mean do you just sit in a chair and push the launch button and then you're wherever and whenever you want to be?"

Bryce smiled crookedly. "Hardly. In order for you to surf time, you have to be in the same spatial point *now* as you need to be *then*. When I came to get you out of the Supernatural Selection building, I snuck in through the translocation gate and made the jump from beside that soda machine because it hasn't moved in years. That gave me my fixed spatial point. Since I knew when the tagging order went down, I used the stars to target the correct time."

"When you went to see your grandmother," Rusty said slowly, as if working through something in his head, "why did you pick *that* particular time?"

Bryce pulled the journal out of his pocket and turned to a page marked with a narrow brown ribbon. "Because it was here. She wrote that I visited her, as an adult. That I was well and happy. So she knew she—" He rubbed his eyes under his glasses. "She knew she could die and I would still be all right.

She described the weather, the room, the position of the furniture, everything in minute detail, which wasn't like her at all."

Cas nodded. "She was giving you landmarks. Breadcrumbs. So you'd know where to go when the time came."

"But wait." Rusty leaned forward, tapping the table with his forefinger. "You made that jump from your office. I thought you couldn't switch places as well as times."

"That's the thing," Bryce said. "My grandmother taught at the college. I have the same office she did." He lifted one eyebrow. "The facilities director thought she was being very clever to do so. Little did she know, eh?" He turned to another page. "The actual jump is accomplished via a druid potion which has a very short life. When it wears off, you come back. Simple as that."

Rusty shared a glance with Cas. "Sounds easy enough."

Bryce held up his hands, palms out. "Don't take it lightly. It can seriously warp your biosystem on a cellular level. It takes some time to reset, and it's possible that too much exposure could cause permanent damage."

Rusty shrugged. "I'm already damaged. What's a little more?"

"Rusty." Bryce gripped his arm. "Please don't be flip. I'm serious. It's possible that prolonged use might rob you of the shifter abilities you *do* possess. Or it might alter them in such a way that they're no longer beneficial or even benign to Cas."

"Believe me, I get it. But we're not talking about prolonged, right? One and done. I've got no desire to be Doctor Who, trust me, so let's do this."

Bryce slapped the table. "All right, then. I'll mix the potion for your body mass. The only thing we need is the time to target. Cas?"

Cas blinked at them, his stomach doing a barrel roll. "Time?"

"If we're going to keep Archie from meeting you, we need to know when to send Rusty to stop him. It needs to be somewhere that he can be naked without comment too."

Cas glanced at Rusty. *If he's naked, trust me, it'll provoke comments. Or possibly wolf whistles.*

"If we don't know *when* to go," Bryce said, "there's nothing we can do."

"I know, I know. Let me think." Cas closed his eyes and leaned back in his chair. "It was the weekend before the national swim meet, because he'd gotten special leave to attend his sister's wedding before he reported for pre-meet training. April. The day after his sister's wedding, so we can find that easily enough."

"Good. What time?"

Gods, what time? He usually didn't get desperate enough for a Grindr hookup unless the bars had been a washout. "Maybe nine? Ten?"

Bryce heaved an exasperated sigh. "That's not precise enough. The potion only lasts a few minutes."

"A few *minutes*?" Cas flung his hands in the air. "It was over seven months ago. How am I supposed to figure out minutes?"

"Hey." Rusty gripped Cas's nape and nuzzled behind his ear. "Just get as close as you can. If I need to, I'll take an extra trip or two. No big."

"It might be very big." Bryce scrubbed a hand through his hair, although considering its usual disarray, it didn't make much difference. "The more I research it, the more I believe the reason time-surfing is nearly mythological is because nobody can do it for very long without damaging their genetic makeup. Time-surfing is a very short-term career, and that's a good thing, since tampering with the time stream shouldn't be done lightly. We don't know what kind of ripples it could cause."

Rusty kissed Cas's temple. "Then I guess we'll just have to be careful. But one way or another, we're doing this. As often as it takes. So let's get started."

Chapter
Twenty-One

The three of them lurked in Cas's yard, Bryce and Cas tucked along the side of the house and Rusty next to the Zen bridge, which was his "fixed spatial point." Using a process of elimination, they'd narrowed down the time window for Archie's visit to Cas's house, and Bryce had done his star hustler thing and mixed the potion to zap Rusty to the right day and time.

That wasn't all it took, though. Apparently Rusty had to build what Bryce called a "definitive mind picture" of where he was headed. So Rusty had studied Cas's notes about what his place looked like in the spring, including the pictures he had on his phone. They couldn't grab any more detailed pictures off Cas's laptop because they didn't want to risk getting trapped inside if the council showed up with blood in their eye. So to speak.

Every creak of a branch, every skitter of a dead leaf, every distant car engine sent another jolt along Rusty's jittery nerves. *The sooner I get this done, the safer he'll be.*

He sat on the end of the little bridge and unlaced his boots, setting them underneath a slatted bench on the bank of the stone "river." He took off his jacket, shirt, pants, and T-shirt, folding them on top of the bench, and stuffed his socks in his boots. He shivered in the chilly breeze, not because he was cold, with his shifter temperature tolerance, but because he was about to *time travel*, for Gaia's sake. Surely that was enough of a reason to be nervous, and on top of that, they could get raided by the vampire police at any moment.

Oh. And don't forget—the beavers are after you too.

Whatever.

Bryce strode over to him and handed him the vial with the potion. "Here it is. Don't take it until you have—"

"My definitive mind picture. Got it." Rusty had picked the Zen part of Cas's yard because it didn't change seasonally, so he didn't have to imagine quite so much. He glanced at Cas, whose eyes gleamed in the shadows. When Cas made the sign of a heart with his hands, Rusty smiled, warmed from the inside out. But he didn't get closer, despite how desperate he was to feel Cas in his arms because hello, naked? Not a good time to cuddle one's boyfriend. *Because we're not husbands anymore. But we will be again. I won't stand for anything less.*

"Okay. Here goes." He stared hard at the bridge, then closed his eyes and built the Zen garden in his mind's eye, just like he'd envision a new house. Once it didn't wobble anymore, he tossed back the potion.

As soon as it hit his belly, his body jerked as if he'd caught himself on the edge of falling. He opened his eyes, but closed them immediately because the garden was spinning around him, making him dizzy. He thought he heard Cas call his name, but it was faint, distant, so he might have imagined it.

He hunched over, grabbing his knees as his stomach threatened to empty itself. Taking several deep breaths, eyes clenched tight, he held as still as possible until the sensation of falling had passed. *Motion sickness. Bryce didn't mention that.*

When he straightened up, though, he wanted to punch the air in victory. He was standing in Cas's Zen garden still, the stones of the "river" rough under his bare feet, with the little ornamental bridge right next to him just as it had been before he'd taken the potion. But the trees weren't bare anymore. Instead, the yellow light of the streetlamps filtered through the new leaves of early spring, and dappled the tulips that edged the flower beds.

Music wafted from inside the house. Jazz? Instrumental anyway. *Cas's "let's get it on" soundtrack?* Good. They'd gotten close enough that Cas was home from the clubs, so Grindr was on the agenda now.

But then the murmur of voices cut through the music. *Shit. We're too late. He's already here.*

Sure enough, the door opened and Archie stepped out, tugging the collar of his denim jacket straight. Archie turned toward the house, and there was Cas.

Rusty's breath stopped in his chest. *Gaia, he's so beautiful.* And had also clearly had some kind of sexual encounter because he had that postcoital look on his face, one that Rusty recognized from personal experience.

Don't be jealous. He didn't even know you then.

Cas smiled up at Archie and kissed him briefly. "Good night."

"Can I see you again?"

"I don't think that would be wise, darling. But thank you for a lovely evening."

Archie's hand came up, but he let it fall when Cas closed the door. His shoulders rose in a sigh, and as he turned toward the gate, a breeze kicked up, rustling the branches and shifting the shadows in the garden.

The light must have hit Rusty's body because Archie's head snapped to the side and he met Rusty's eyes full-on.

"Who are—"

And suddenly the time whirlpool hit, and Rusty was gasping next to the bridge, Cas rubbing the base of his spine.

"Are you all right, darling?"

Rusty gulped in air until Bryce handed him a bottle of water. He downed half of it before he could say, "Fine. But I got there too late. He was already leaving."

Cas's eyes glowed, and he dropped a kiss on Rusty's shoulder. "Did he see you?"

He capped the water. "Definitely. So hospital mystery solved, I guess. Better try again."

"This time will work. I just know it. He was at the house for about an hour, so adjust the Wayback Machine accordingly, Professor."

Bryce rubbed his eyes under his glasses. "We can calibrate for earlier in the evening and a longer stay, yes, but that means a larger dose. A larger dose means a greater risk." His lenses glinted in the yellow light as he shook his head. "It's too dangerous."

"I don't care. We're this close. We can do it. We can save all three of us."

Cas leaned against Rusty's side. "You don't have to."

"Yeah, I do. Because it's the right thing." He forced a grin. "Gotta use my powers for good, not evil. Right?"

"Elmer . . ." Cas's voice broke, and Rusty's heart broke with it.

"Hey. It's all good." He kissed Cas's forehead and then his lips—soft and quick, because he was already having his usual Cas-proximity reaction. "Go back to your hiding place. I don't trust those vampires. They're sneaky."

Cas's laugh was a little watery. "You have no idea, darling." But he returned to hunker down next to the house.

Bryce handed him two vials. "You'll have to toss them back simultaneously or you'll start the jump before you ingest the second dose." His eyebrows were bunched over his nose. "I should have brought a bigger receptacle, damn it."

"No worries. I've got this."

Rusty centered himself and closed his eyes again, imagining the Zen garden as it was in the spring, then emptied both potions into his mouth at once.

Falling. Dizzy. Nauseous.

In other words, time-surfing business as usual.

He opened his eyes to spring again, but he could already tell it was earlier than before. From inside, a TV program cut off mid-explosion to be replaced a few seconds later by a familiar jazz soundtrack. *We did it! Just the right time!* Now as long as the potion didn't wear off and send him back too soon—

The gate swung open and Archie stepped inside. *Bingo.*

It's a damn good thing I don't want anyone but Cas, because a hard-on right now would be really *awkward.*

Rusty stepped out from under the trees into the full light of the streetlamp. "Archie Ellis."

Archie whirled and his mouth opened, but nothing emerged except a gulp as if he'd just swallowed half a swimming pool. His eyes widened and he scanned Rusty from head to bare toes —and everything in between. Then he crouched in some kind of martial arts stance. "I know Krav Maga."

"I don't care what you know, just get out of here."

Archie got that self-righteous belligerent thrust of his jaw that belonged to the very young and very naive. "I have a right to be here. I was invited. Were you?"

"I don't have to be invited." Rusty flashed his wedding ring. "I live here." *I'll be forgiven for lying. It's a good cause.* "You really want to get called out for fucking a married man? How would your coach feel about that? What about the Olympic committee?"

Terror flashed across Archie's face. "You wouldn't. I didn't. Not yet. I won't."

"Use your words, Archie."

"How— How do you know who I am?"

"How?" Rusty bared his teeth in a grin. "I'm a Beaver too, just like you were once. Now take my advice. Save your career." *Save your life.* "Get out of here and never come back."

Rusty did his best to look imposing, folding his arms across his chest and planting his feet wide—only to jerk his foot up when he landed on a sharp stone. *Ow, damn it. So much for impersonating the Colossus of Rhodes.*

Archie didn't seem to notice. He hurried out the gate with only a single nervous glance over his shoulder.

Mission accomplished. I hope. Now what? His heftier dose of time-surfing potion wouldn't wear off for a while. He gazed longingly at Cas's windows. *I could go in and see him now. Warn him. Give him my number.*

Yeah right. *Ding dong. Big naked man calling.* The cops would probably be on his ass before he could blink.

Still, he didn't want to leave without some kind of gesture. But what? Re-rake the Zen river rocks into a heart with *Cas + Rusty*? It wouldn't be legible even if Cas looked, and Rusty didn't get the impression that he spent a lot of Zen time.

He padded around the edge of the yard, hoping that by keeping his distance from the windows, if Cas *should* look outside, Rusty wouldn't seem like a Peeping Tom. The garage door was open, Cas's Jag gleaming silver in the dim light. Maybe—

Rusty hurried over, stroking the smooth side of the car as he passed. Cas obviously didn't spend a lot of time in the garage because it was far too neat for any normal person. *Normal is just a city in Illinois.* After minimal digging, though, Rusty found what he wanted and set the scene. *There. That should do it.*

He raced back to the bridge as fast as his bare feet would carry him and arrived just as his ears popped and his stomach roiled. When the dizziness receded, he was back in November, his clothes folded neatly on the bench.

He could hear the faint sounds of a television from inside Cas's house, but of Cas himself, and of Bryce, there was no sign.

I guess it worked? Something had changed anyway. As Rusty, shivering, climbed into his clothes, he hoped like hell he hadn't just made everything worse.

Chapter Twenty-Two

Barely able to lift his feet, Rusty made his way to his truck. Gaia, that second time-surf had really taken it out of him. Of course, it was four in the morning, so maybe his bone-deep weariness was justified.

He crawled into the cab where the alert light was blinking on his cell phone. *Huh. A text* and *an email from Supernatural Selection.* The text was timestamped earliest—a rather tart request from the AI regarding his failure to appear at his own wedding. The email was sent two hours later, an abject apology from Zeke informing him that his perfect match, Ted Farnsworth, was no longer available. At least Rusty didn't have to feel guilty about jilting Ted—Ted had taken care of the jilting himself. *I'm two for two, I guess.*

He was under strict orders to report to Bryce, but not until nearly dinnertime. Rather than drive back to Eugene, he checked into a hotel, arranged for late checkout, and slept until almost two. When he woke up, he found several voice mails from Fletcher, each one pissier than the last, all assuming that Rusty would be meeting him at "the usual place," whatever that was. Apparently, Rusty wasn't about to be tagged, which was a relief. But without Cas, it seemed he'd continued to be Fletcher's doormat.

No more.

After he showered and dressed, he hit the road for Bryce's house. He had no trouble finding it—after all, his company had helped build this subdivision when Bryce was still immersed in the wetlands reclamation project. When he pulled into the driveway, though, his heart was beating fast, and his hands were clammy on the steering wheel. *Why am I so nervous? It's not like he'll refuse to talk to me.* They were colleagues, for Gaia's sake. Bryce had said so himself.

Yeah, but he said it in a different time stream. However, Bryce would know the results of Rusty's time tampering. Whether it had worked. *Whether it was worth it.*

Rusty blew out a breath. "Suck it up, Johnson," he muttered. "Don't be chickenshit."

He climbed out of the truck, walked up to the door, and after a moment's hesitation, forced himself to knock.

Bryce answered the door. His eyebrows rose, his eyes widening in obvious surprise. "Rusty. To what do I owe the pleasure?"

"Hi. Am I too early? You, um, asked me to come over at around dinnertime."

He frowned, tilting his head. "I did?"

"Yeah. And I'm supposed to tell you to check your grandmother's journal."

"My— Oh!" His eyes lit up and he stood aside, motioning Rusty into the house. "Come in, come in." He led the way to the familiar round table in the dining room. "Can I offer you something to drink? A beer? We're fond of Double Mountain IRA in this house."

"A beer would be great. Thanks."

Bryce collected the bottles and popped the tops with an opener mounted under the counter. He flashed a grin. "So, did I surf or did you?"

"Both of us, actually." Rusty accepted the bottle. "Thanks."

Bryce settled in the chair across from him. "Both, eh? Must have been serious."

"Life or death."

"Yup. That's serious." He took a swig of his beer, then pulled the journal out of his pocket, opening it to the brown ribbon mark again. He read for a moment, his brows climbing higher until they snapped down into a frown. "Good lord." He closed the journal, folding his hands atop it. "First, I happen to know that Archie Ellis is alive and well. Although he didn't qualify for the Olympics, he's still swimming for Stanford this year." He lifted one shoulder in a half shrug. "What can I say? I'm a swim fan."

Rusty slumped in his chair. "Thank Gaia. I wasn't sure— When we had to try a second time— I'm so fucking *relieved*."

"I haven't heard a hint of any sanction against either you or Cas. That may not be completely definitive, though. The druids aren't always privy to supe council politics, especially anything related to vampires, who tend to be a secretive and self-sufficient bunch."

"That's probably a good thing."

"Perhaps. Let me ask you, were you and Cas . . . attached?"

Rusty blinked, his beer halfway to his mouth. "You don't remember anything?"

"If your surf was successful—as apparently it was—then the events set in motion by Archie's Turn never occurred. Although . . ." He grinned, then took another sip of beer. "Cas *did* try to hit on Mal a couple of weeks ago, despite the werewolf twenty-oner party taking place behind us.

Rusty's chuckle snagged in his chest. *Gaia, I miss him. And it's been less than a day.* In one time stream anyway. In the other, it had been forever.

Bryce leaned forward, his bottle cradled between both palms. "Tell me something. What's it like? The two conflicting sets of memories? I've never done anything other than observe."

"Not always. You intervened on our behalf, remember?"

"I don't. Remember, that is." His gaze grew unfocused. "Or do I? There's something at the edge of my consciousness, like a half-remembered dream or the vague recollection of a party where I consumed too many mind-altering substances."

"Heh." Rusty downed a quarter of his beer to ease the burn in his throat. "I remember them both. The time without him, sure, but that's the misty part. The time with him is much clearer."

"Maybe because that's where you were happiest."

Rusty shrugged. "That's over now." *I've got to accept it.* "I've learned some things about myself, about people I thought were my friends, about my clan, and that's all thanks to him. My life will be different now, that's for sure." *If only it didn't stretch out like an empty road.*

"Better? Or just different?"

"I don't know. That depends, I guess."

"Well, regardless, don't try to go it alone."

"I won't. I've got my clan, after all. They weren't big fans of me taking a vampire for a mate, so they should be happy." He grimaced. "Not that they'll ever know they had a reason to be *un*happy."

Bryce studied him, his head tilted to one side. "Is your clan's happiness more important than your own?"

"Not more important. But they're still my clan. Who else will put up with me? I'm not a guy who's good with being alone, Bryce. I need friends. I need my clan."

"Do you really want to surround yourself with people who are only willing to 'put up' with you? How much better would it be to find those who are with you because they see your strengths rather than your flaws? You don't need your clan, per se. You need your tribe. And a tribe can consist of anyone, not just those who share your particular supe profile."

Rusty laughed mirthlessly. "Not sure who'd be willing to be in my tribe."

"Your construction crews for one. Yes, they're human and so can't participate in any supe activities, but they're devoted to you. And there's me."

"Really? You're in my tribe?"

Bryce smiled wryly. "We're the only two successful time-surfers that I'm aware of. That makes us brothers under the skin regardless of our heritage. But even without that shared experience, I'd still volunteer. Hell, I'd beg, I'd *demand* to be in your tribe. And so would Alun, and, I have no doubt, his husband, and my . . . my fiancé." His smile turned a little goofy. "Man, I still can't get used to that."

Now I need to get used to not having a husband or a fiancé. Because Ted was married to somebody else, and Rusty wasn't about to hurry into another rushed match. There was no reason, after all. Fletcher's wedding was in the past, and Rusty had no intention of being his piece on the side. Cas had at least given him that.

He'll forever be either Fletcher the Fuckhead or Felcher to me now.

"Do you plan to contact Cas?"

Rusty flinched and covered it with a long swallow of beer. "I don't— There's no reason— He wouldn't—" He sighed, hearing Cas in his mind. *Use your words, Elmer.* "He was only registered for Supernatural Selection at the order of the council. He's probably perfectly happy with his Grindr or random bar hookups. Besides, he'd never consider a shifter for a mate. We were only together because we both had scores to settle."

"I wouldn't be too quick to dismiss the possibility. The time stream is more resilient than you think."

"Yeah, you told us that."

He raised his brows. "I did? I'm remarkably repetitive, aren't I? It must come from teaching the same courses year after year. Anyway, other time-surfers, the few who actually admitted attempting a change, speak of 'impressions' that don't fade, even if the stream is rewritten. They'd strike most people as remembrances of faded dreams, but the more intense the feeling or meaningful the event, the more likely it is to leave footprints in time."

"Footprints in time, huh?"

"Exactly." He raised his bottle in an air toast. "Don't give up yet. From what I've seen, you're a rather unforgettable man."

When the knock came at his door, Cas stopped his restless pacing, his heart attempting to crawl up his throat. This was it. The verdict. The one he'd been awaiting since the day he'd finally decided Henryk Skalding was too dangerous to be at large. The day Cas had gone to the council and come clean about the way Henryk had used their mutual animosity to his advantage, discrediting Cas while forwarding his own agenda for seizing power. The day Cas had confessed the truth about the necromancer to eliminate Henryk's blackmail leverage.

It had been a risk—and not particularly well-thought-out, Cas had to admit to himself. He wasn't entirely sure why he'd done it, except that he'd awoken one day with the absolute certainty that it was time.

He'd half expected Kristof to decapitate him in the council chamber when he'd testified about the redirected blood-aversion curse. Kristof's rage had been terrifying, but Cas had counted on his innate sense of justice, and luckily that had held.

Both Henryk and Cas had been on house arrest while the council conducted their investigations. And now, it was about to be over.

Cas licked his dry lips. *I'll either be free. Or dead.* Either one was preferable to being perpetually under Henryk's thumb.

He opened the door to find Kristof standing on the doorstep alone. "Welcome, Kristof. Won't you come in?" Cas attempted an inconspicuous scan of his yard. Where were the enforcers?

"If you're looking for Lars and Waldemar, they're not here."

Cas swallowed, holding the door for Kristof to enter. *Is that good or bad?* "May I offer you anything?"

Kristof gave a wintry smile. "Thank you, but I've already dined."

At Kristof's dry tone, Cas took a closer look. Kristof's cheeks were no longer hollow—in fact, they were tinged with pink. "The curse. You were able to get it lifted?"

He inclined his head. "Yes. It wasn't easy, but thanks to the information you provided about the necromancer, a task force of witches, fae, and druids were able to reverse-engineer the curse. I no longer experience the aversion."

Heat suffused Cas's chest, although ice was still lodged in his belly. "I—I'm glad." But what did that mean?

"While I could wish you had come forward before—"

"I know. I'm sorry."

Kristof tilted his head a fraction. "Yes. I believe you are. I understand why you did not. I believe you will be pleased to know that the council has chosen to tag Henryk Skalding indefinitely, and we will be closely monitoring his actions. While many on the council would have preferred to tag you as well, if only for a limited time, I have convinced them that a looser probationary period is acceptable."

"Probation?" Cas's voice was faint because he couldn't take in enough air.

Kristof's eyebrow twitched. "You think you should get off scot-free? Regardless of your relative innocence in Henryk's ploys, you still have not behaved very well. Do you disagree?"

"No!" Cas held up his hands, palms out. "I'm just surprised the punishment wasn't more severe."

"I hope we know better than to blame the victim." He turned to the door. "You will meet with your probation officer weekly for the next year, as well as perform community service."

"Community service?"

"Yes. The druid council, in particular Dr. MacLeod, have a number of initiatives you would be suited for." He paused, his hand on the doorknob. "Do you have a problem with that?"

Druids. Cas's eyebrows drew together when his usual instant druid revulsion didn't materialize. "Dr. MacLeod?" For some reason, the name called up feelings of gratitude and . . . safety?

How can that be? I've never heard of the man. "That is, no. Of course not."

"Excellent. Would you care to join me at the club? Some of the other council members will be there. It would be a good opportunity for you to begin forging new relationships with them."

"I'd like to, but I can't. I've, ah, got an appointment this evening."

"That seems rather precipitous considering you were confined to quarters until this evening."

Kristof didn't have to tell Cas that. Cas couldn't really believe it himself. "What can I say? Optimism?"

"Very well. Have a pleasant evening, Casimir." Kristof placed a hand on Cas's shoulder. "And thank you. Truly." Then he was gone in the flicker of an eyelash.

Cas closed the door, trudged across room, and dropped onto his sofa, letting himself sink into the cushions. An *appointment.* More like an insanity. For the last weeks of his house arrest, he'd been plagued with recurring dreams—highly unusual dreams for him. Yes, they were sexy, which he expected. After all, he'd been celibate since April. But they weren't only erotic—and any dream where Cas got to bottom was *epic*—they were *romantic,* and all of them featured the same large man, although Cas could never make out his face.

Out of frustration, and in the hope that the council's verdict would go his way, he'd lost his mind and filled out an online application with a matchmaking agency, for pity's sake. Supernatural Selection guaranteed a perfect match, and though Cas told them he'd be, er, tied up for a while, they'd almost set him up with an incubus, which he supposed was reasonable. It wasn't like sex demons could look down on the undead. Although maybe they could—because the agency had sent an apologetic email yesterday that the incubus had married somebody else. A bear shifter, of all things.

Better him than me. But then, maybe shifters didn't reek to demons.

He ought to withdraw himself from the agency's candidate pool. Why let a witches' collective dictate who he should hook up with? He was free now, no threats from Henryk hanging over him. Surely he could find his own partner with the club scene, or in a pinch, with Grindr or another hookup app.

And although he'd been isolated for six long months, he couldn't muster the energy. Why did hookups seem so fucking *pointless* now? They never had before.

It's the fault of those damn romantic dreams. Sometimes they seemed so real that he'd turn around, expecting somebody to be there, somebody that he desperately missed, although he couldn't for the life—*heh*—of him figure out who it might be.

So he'd let the demon at Supernatural Selection talk him into another appointment, and since Cas was all about tempting fate, he'd scheduled it for the night of the verdict. *One more. Then I'm over it.*

He heaved himself to his feet and made a cursory pass at grooming—he didn't hold out a lot of hope for his alleged perfect match, but that didn't mean he needed to be slovenly—then trudged out to his Jag, raised the garage door, and started the car. But when he gripped the gear shift, suddenly it seemed worthless. He stared out the windshield at the garage shelves illuminated by his headlights. *I should just bag the whole thing.* How likely was it that a matchmaking agency, regardless of their guarantee, could find a perfect match for *him*?

But as he was about to switch off the ignition, he glimpsed something white protruding from beneath the green metal fishing tackle box that contained his meager collection of tools. He climbed out, leaving the car running as he approached the tool kit and its teasing white triangle. When he got close enough, he could see it was a piece of paper. He tugged it out from beneath the tool kit—which he had never used, and had frankly forgotten he owned.

It was blank.

Talk about anticlimactic. A lot like his life—great anticipation followed by crashing disappointment.

He was about to crumple it and throw it in the recycling when he caught a flash of something on the reverse side. He turned it over.

I love you. Can't wait to meet you for the first time again.

"What the fuck?"

Since when did vandals break in to rearrange his toolbox and leave him love notes? For that matter, since when did vandals break in at all? He was a fucking vampire, for pity's sake. Not exactly an easy mark. *Maybe I should change my security code.*

He stared at the idling car. *Ah what the hell. It's not like I have anything else to do.* He climbed back in, drove down to the Pearl, and parked a couple of blocks away from Supernatural Selection.

When he walked in, the lobby was empty except for one man, a bearded mountain of a guy reading a magazine in the corner. He looked up when Cas entered, and the smile that bloomed on his face was bright enough to make Cas's skin sizzle. Figuratively, of course.

He studied the guy, eyes narrowed, trying to scope out his nature. In this place, he had to be a supe. But what? *And why do I want to thread my fingers through that beard? Why do I remember threading my fingers through that beard?*

Bearded Guy's smile didn't dim. "May I help you?"

"You can't be a shifter. You don't—"

"Stink?"

"Uh . . ."

"Beaver shifter, as it happens. Inactive status."

Cas cocked an eyebrow. "Thanks for that." He was hit with an odd wave of déjà vu, but shook it off. After ninety-two years as a vampire, there wasn't a lot that he hadn't experienced at least once. "But perhaps TMI?"

"I don't know. You *were* wondering, weren't you?"

"I suppose."

Bearded Guy chuckled and nodded in the direction of the unoccupied reception desk. "They'll be back in a few minutes." He held out his hand. "Rusty Johnson."

"Rusty?" Cas hesitated. *Why does that seem wrong?* Nevertheless, he shook hands, Rusty's grip strong and firm, yet somehow intimate.

He held on to Cas's hand for a moment too long, and oddly Cas didn't want him to let go. "What's the matter?"

"I don't know. I'm sure it's nothing, but for some reason, I was suddenly certain your name was something entirely different." Cas shook his head. "But it couldn't be. You don't look anything like— Never mind."

"Come on. Don't leave me hanging. Like what?"

"Like, well, an Elmer?" Cas inhaled. "And you smell . . . familiar." *Earth and spice. The sough of pines. Cool water and hot skin.* "Do I . . . know you?"

"Not yet. But you will." Rusty grinned—a groin-tighteningly attractive flash of teeth inside his red-brown beard—and held up his phone, where the Supernatural Selection app displayed Cas's picture. "I'm your perfect match."

E.J.'s
Free Stories

Follow E.J. on Ream (https://reamstories.com/ejr) or subscribe to her newsletter (https://ejr.pub/news-from-ej) to get these stories for free!

The following QR codes will get you there with your smartphone camera or other code reader.

Second First Date

Rusty has a plan to win Cas again…

A Mythmatched companion story that takes place immediately following the last chapter of Vampire with Benefits.

Rusty's Really Bad Day

Something is terribly wrong—and it's up to Rusty to put things right.

A Mythmatched companion story that takes place after Howling on Hold.

A Very Quest Solstice

It's our first holiday together, and I'm determined to make it special for Lachlan. Only problem? I know zip about how selkies celebrate, so I don't even know which winter holiday to pick.

With Lachlan out on a fishing charter, I try to tease some suggestions from my friends, but they're surprisingly unhelpful. And when we get a tip about a Disappeared sighting, my opportunity for more research evaporates.

I guess I'll just have to improvise. Again.

Dammit.

A holiday coda which builds on characters and situations from the first four Quest Investigations books. It takes place the month following Death on Denial *and is not intended to stand alone.*

First Flight

Will Seb overcome his fear of heights and take to the air with Nevan and Lulu?

A Mythmatched companion story that takes place between Chapter 33 and the Epilogue of Assassin by Accident.

Possession in Session

When an outcast demon is thrust into a medical technician training program, are death and destruction sure to follow?

After centuries of being bound to one greedy magician after another, Auni-jel-Chandu broke free and retreated to Sheol, outcast even among other demons. But then the Realm Accords passed, and suddenly he's thrust into the Sheol Retraining Initiative as the newest supernatural medical technician student at United Memorial Hospital (aka St. Stupid's).

Uh oh.

Wash Hernández might be a dud witch—he'd never been able to attract a familiar, so he's as magic-null as any human—but as a St. Stupid's orderly, he's still able to assist supernatural beings who need medical care. But when he meets a bewildered naked demon wandering the hospital corridors and forms an instant connection, he's not certain who needs help the most.

Poor Zeke has one last chance to save his job at Supernatural Selection and stay out of Sheol. But how can he succeed when his client, the kangaroo shifter drummer for Hunter's Moon, simply *will not engage*. A desperate Zeke resorts to a more hands-on approach in *Demon on the Down-Low*, the last book in the Supernatural Selection trilogy.

About Demon on the Down-Low

After decades of unrequited love, this kangaroo will jump at the chance for a date. Any date.

Lovelorn kangaroo shifter Hamish Mulherne, drummer for the mega-hit rock band Hunter's Moon, waited years for the band's jaguar shifter bassist to notice him. Instead, she's just gotten married and is in a thriving poly relationship. How is Hamish supposed to compete with that? But with everyone else in the band mated and revoltingly happy, he needs somebody. Since he can't expect true love to strike twice, he signs up with Supernatural Selection. Because what the hell.

When Zeke Oz was placed at Supernatural Selection through the Sheol work-release program, he thought he was the luckiest demon alive. But when he seems responsible for several massive matchmaking errors, he's put on notice: find the perfect match for Hamish, or get booted back to Sheol for good. The only catch? He has to do it without the agency's matchmaking spells, and Hamish simply will not engage.

But Zeke starts to believe that the reason all of Hamish's dates fizzle is because nobody in the database is good enough for him. And Hamish realizes that his perfect match might be the cute demon who's trying so hard to make him happy.

a message from
ej

Dear Reader,

Thank you so much for reading *Vampire With Benefits*. Cas and Rusty are one of my favorite couples ever (which is probably why I've written two short stories about them!).

I'm so happy you've taken this journey with me. I'd be immensely grateful if you'd take a moment to leave a review at the retailer and any other site you use for reviews. Believe me, reviews make an *enormous* difference to the health and well-being of books (and not incidentally, to their associated authors!).

If this is your first taste of my Mythmatched story world, you might want to travel back to the Fae Out of Water trilogy, where it all began. *Cutie and the Beast* is the first in that series, but Bryce makes his debut (and earns his HEA) in the second book, *The Druid Next Door*. His enemies-to-lovers journey with Mal Kendrick (with bonus forced proximity and only-one-bed) approaches, dare I say, mythic proportions?

Pop on over to my website, https://ejrussell.com, for all the deets on my books—the rest of my Mythmatched tales, my other paranormal rom-coms and mysteries, my contemporary romances, and my one lone historical. If you're an audio fan, you can find the audio scoop there too. The Supernatural Selection trilogy, for instance, is narrated by the wonderful Greg Boudreaux. (The QR code on the next page will get you there with your smartphone camera or other code reader.)

My newsletter is the place to get the latest dish on new releases, sales, and more. I promise I only send one out when

I've got…well…news. You can subscribe here: https://ejr.pub/news-from-ej.

All my best,
—E

Also by ℓj

Paranormal Romance
Mythmatched Universe
Fae Out of Water Trilogy
Cutie and the Beast
The Druid Next Door
Bad Boy's Bard

Supernatural Selection Trilogy
Single White Incubus
Vampire With Benefits
Demon on the Down-Low

Other Mythmatched Romances
Howling on Hold
Possession in Session
Witch Under Wraps
Cursed is the Worst
The Skinny on Djinni
Assassin by Accident (part of Carnival of Mysteries)

Mythmatched Companion Stories
Rusty's Really Bad Day (free to newsletter subscribers)
Second First Date (free to newsletter subscribers)
First Flight (free to newsletter subscribers)

Quest Investigations Mysteries
Five Dead Herrings

The Hound of the Burgervilles
The Lady Under the Lake
Death on Denial

At Odds with the Gods (A Mythmatched / Purgatory Playhouse
crossover)

Art Medium Series
The Artist's Touch
Tested in Fire
Art Medium: The Complete Collection (omnibus edition)

Legend Tripping Series
Stumptown Spirits
Wolf's Clothing

Enchanted Occasions Series
Best Beast
Nudging Fate
Devouring Flame

Royal Powers Series (shared world)
Duking It Out
Duke the Hall
King's Ex

Magic Emporium Series (shared world)
Purgatory Playhouse

Science Fiction
Sun, Moon, and Stars Series
Partnership
Principles

Interdimensional Time Bureau

Monster Till Midnight

Historical Romance
Silent Sin

Contemporary Romance
Camera Shy
Summer Kitchen
The Thomas Flair
Mystic Man
For a Good Time, Call… (A Bluewater Bay novel, with Anne Tenino)

Christmas Kisses (holiday shorts)
The Probability of Mistletoe
An Everyday Hero
A Swants Soiree

Geeklandia Series
The Boyfriend Algorithm (M/F)
Clickbait

Writing as Nelle Heran
(traditional cozy mystery)

Crafty Sleuth Series (with C.K. Eastland)
Die Cut
Mixed Media
Found Objects (*coming soon)*